# Chapter One

Leena

I never knew the woods could be silent.

Teeming with life and the movements of nature, it was impossible for there to be no sound in a place like this. But right now, in these woods, I heard nothing. Even the wind had stopped whistling. One moment, my boot was breaking a twig, my hunting pack dragging empty across brittle leaves, and then it stopped. As if every sound had been ripped away.

An odd sensation rippled through me, like mismatched piano keys playing in the back of my mind. I took my time steadying myself, holding my stomach to fight back the nausea threatening to send bile up my throat. When the feeling passed, I slid my hunting pack under my cloak and focused on the path back home.

Each quiet step unnerved me to the core. All I could think about were the legends that had taken over the village as of late. Of something being in these woods. Something not human.

The leaves were already turning, falling like butterfly wings from the weathered branches of sky-reaching trees. There was something about this place that gave it a haunting glow, no matter the season. A sudden autumn had fallen upon us, turning the forest around our traveling town from a lush green sea to a flash of crisp ruby and burnt orange. Though awe-inspiring, the sudden change was eerie. It shouldn't have happened in a matter of weeks, and I shouldn't be able to see my breath in what should have been late summer.

I kept my eyes on the path, occasionally watching the wildlife around me, hoping a threat wouldn't pounce at me before I returned to Woodsmeadow.

And then it was back.

Every sound all at once, a raucous symphony that almost sent me toppling to my knees. I closed my eyes to stop the world from spinning, but the moment I heard the crunch of a leaf beneath my boot, I choked out a relieved sob. The sounds of the world had sprung back to life. I could even hear the distant chatter of the townsfolk ahead and the chirps and scurries of animals behind me. Letting out a long, thoughtful exhale, I found my bearings and walked into town.

As usual, no one paid me any mind, which didn't bother me in the slightest. The last thing I wanted was to be noticed, especially right now. I was too focused on ridding myself of the thoughts gnawing at the back of my skull—of ignoring the cause of the strange experience I'd just left behind. Of what could have caused it.

A chill slithered down my spine.

# A WHISPER IN THE WOODS

## FATED FOLKTALES: BOOK 1

### ELISE NELSON

SHATTERED GLASS PRESS

# CONTENTS

*To everyone who helped make this happen.*

Pulling my cloak's thick scarlet hood over my head, I let it drape over my face, keeping my head down so all that poked out was the straw-colored braid that snaked nearly to my waist. I wished the old cloak wasn't such a bold red. It only drew unwanted attention, but it was all I had left of my mother. I wouldn't give it up for anything. Still, I might as well be wearing a sign for the one person in the village I actively tried to avoid.

"Ah, Leena." As if on cue, the man's voice sent something cold bolting through my blood. I cringed before peering up at him. As thin as he was tall, the redhead stared me down in the lecherous way he always did, dragging his gaze from my boots to my hood, taking his time doing so, particularly around my bodice. "How long have you been going into the woods alone?" The words came out dark and playful, like a cat toying with a mouse.

Fear wriggled beneath my skin like a cluster of worms.

"Leave me alone," I said, my voice clipped.

I tried pushing past him, but he stepped in front of me and continued. "Why were you out there? It's awfully dangerous for a young maiden to go in there alone, especially with everything that's been happening."

"I had an errand to run. It's not usual for me to go on my own, and I likely won't do it again." I didn't dare tell him the truth—that this was something my uncle had forced upon me due to his supposed injury and our lack of food. I'd been around Casimir long enough to know what to look out for and how to protect myself.

He flashed me an impish grin and circled me.

"Your grandmother and Vasska are keeping you busy, as always, I see." He stopped just long enough to trail a finger down my jawline to the tip of my chin. I slapped his hand away.

"Don't touch me!" I hissed, successfully pushing past him this time. He shouted something at me with a chuckle, but I didn't hear it, nor did I look back. I kept moving, ignoring the heavy thumping in my chest and the frenzied pulsing in my ears. I didn't stop until I made it safely to the hut.

Before my hand reached the wooden door, my uncle came bursting out. His eyes were fierce as they fixed on mine, his six-foot-two frame looming over me. Vasska was so wide he nearly broke the doorframe every time he came bounding out. I'd been hoping he was in a good mood today, but from the way his pale face was crimson, and his wisps of yellow mustache hairs twitched, it was clear that my wish was a foolish one. His gray eyes fell to my empty arms and limp hunting sack.

"Where is it, girl?" he barked. I tried keeping my gaze on his, but I'd never been able to stand strong against him. Not when I was a child, and not now.

Vasska hated it when I stared at my feet, so I spoke before he could continue. "Th-the rabbit was too difficult to catch—"

"There are plenty of animals in the woods!" he bellowed. "You couldn't catch *one*?" Even with passersby staring, he didn't hold back. I was surprised anyone stared at this point. Our village was small, and he stopped hiding his personality when he realized he could get away with it—that he could get away with pretty much anything. This display wasn't new. They knew him. They knew what he was like, even if they turned their heads to avoid my gaze and never intervened, even and especially when things escalated.

"I know, but—"

"But nothing," he growled, grabbing me by the arm so tightly I let out a high-pitched squeal. "Get in here." He threw me into the hut, slamming the door behind him and limping to me in an angry hobble. His uneven footsteps shook the small, makeshift cabin. I couldn't hide the tremor in my legs, especially as he grabbed me by the shoulders and forced me to look straight into his soulless eyes. "You were too soft again, weren't you?"

My mouth went dry. I couldn't bring myself to kill, and I'd never had hunting duty before the past week. Not until the food started going missing or spoiling at an unnatural rate. Not until Vasska supposedly had a branch fall onto his leg when he was squeezing the life out of some woodland creature. He never even brought back half the creatures he killed.

"I..." I couldn't grasp any words. There weren't any that could save me from the inevitable. When enough time passed, I winced, bracing myself for the worst. I felt him move closer, leaning in and then slapping me across the face.

Dishes clinked at the table. My grandmother tried not to move as I steadied myself, but I saw her flinch. If Vasska saw her reach for me, she'd be the next one on the ground. My eyes darted to Karina, who was knitting on our one good, upholstered chair by the small fire, ever the dutiful wife Vasska had trained to turn a blind eye.

This life was so different from the one I'd had with my parents. After all this time, I still wasn't used to it. Fourteen years had passed since they'd died, but sometimes it still felt like I was the same twelve-year-old girl waiting for them to come home.

I tried picking up a saucer that had fallen from the table, but Grandmother took it with shaking hands, whispering low. "I've got this, dear. Please get up. You know what he's like."

"Leena! Why are you standing there?" he barked. "Make yourself useful." He nodded toward the scant kitchen where a pot was situated over a crude fire, burbling with days-old porridge. "Wash up and help your grandmother with supper. Then you can at least try to make up for the fact that we won't have any game for our stew."

I peered up at him, weighing my options. I so badly wanted to snap at him, but I could still feel the sting on my cheek from his strike.

"Fine."

"What was that?"

"I said 'fine,'" I hissed. His jaw set. His eyes widened. Fuming, he grabbed me by the arm and threw me at the pot. Boiling muck and old food splattered across my chest, my fingertips nearly brushing the flames. I had to bite my lip to stave off the pain of hot fluid as I wiped it off.

Grandmother quickly brought over a cloth to help me before returning to set the table. But she didn't say anything. She never did. Her late husband left her with a lasting injury that clearly ran deeper than the scars along her spine. Whenever Vasska's hand was raised, she'd flinch and either freeze or panic. It used to bother me that she didn't speak up, but I understood her better now, and I was more afraid of her frail body crumpling at the hand of the brute than her trying and failing to speak.

Vasska had never laid a hand on his mother until food became scarce. Before now, I'd been the only one he took things out on, and I desperately wished it could go back to that, no matter how twisted that was. But at least if I were the punching bag, Grandmother would be safe.

Everyone sat at the table while I doled out the porridge. I tried not to cringe as it fell like balls of green mud into each bowl. We'd never eaten like royalty, but it had never been like this. Vasska was the only one who wrinkled his nose.

"Is this the best you could do?" He shot me a cutting glare, and again, I tried not to react.

"We'll eat better when I get better ingredients," I said, setting the pot back in the kitchen.

"We'll eat better when you do your damn job and bring us meat."

I scooted close to the table, nodding in reply, though I knew I didn't possess the skill or stomach to kill anything. But as I saw my grandmother pick up her spoon with a weak hand and getting thinner by the day, I had the motivation to at least try.

"Did you hear any news at the pub today, dear?" Karina looked at her husband, doe-like.

He slurped a large spoonful of porridge and grunted. "Something's out there. A wolf or something." My eyes instantly met my grandmother's. Vasska didn't miss it. "What? Don't tell me you believe the nonsense being spouted about some ghost or demon."

"Grandmother and I think it's—"

She grabbed my hand a little too hard.

"Not now, Leena," she hissed.

"What? What do you think it is, Mother?" Vasska growled, then shoveled in more porridge. It dribbled off his chin. I tried not to gag.

"Nothing," she said quickly.

His fist tightened on the table, and he turned to me. "What do you think it is, Leena?"

I stared into my bowl. "We believe it's something malicious. Not a common beast. Something supernatural." I looked at her, but she kept her head down. At Vasska's narrowing eyes, I realized my mistake. "She was going off of what I'd told her," I lied. "I overheard some women talking about it near the creek outside town. The best news comes on laundry day."

Vasska snorted, "Don't believe anything you hear from those wenches. They're likely bored housewives looking for gossip." My fingers tightened around the neck of my spoon. "I'm looking into it, though," he continued. "Me and a couple other men in town. We'll figure it out."

I shot him a look. "*You* will figure it out?"

"Leena!" Grandmother gasped. Vasska slammed his spoon against the table. The surface shook, rattling our broken, mismatched silverware as his eyes went wild.

"Yes, *me*."

"You and who? Casimir?" I snorted. I knew I would get it, but I couldn't let him be this arrogant and vile. He made his inexperienced niece hunt because he claimed to have injured himself, even though his limp from his alleged accident switched from leg to leg. "Such brave men. I'm sure you two diligent huntsmen will find the root of our town's troubles."

He jumped to his feet and slapped me so hard across the face I fell out of the chair and hit the floor with a pop to my shoulder.

"Leena!" Grandmother cried as she helped me up. I winced, trying my best to stand. I bit my lip to stop the tears and ignore the pain. Vasska kept eating like nothing happened.

"We'll find out what's going on, and then we'll stop it," he said. His empty words must have been for him alone because he had to know none of us believed him. He couldn't be that dense. Or maybe he could. I didn't care either way. I just turned away to head to bed, hoping something—anything—would happen to change things.

I would do anything to live a life better than this one. To give Grandmother a life better than this one. If it were up to me, I'd run so far away that the people I'd meet wouldn't know the name of this cursed village. But it was a pipe dream. As long as food was scarce and Grandmother was here, where Vasska's fist was an ever-present threat, I was stuck. I could survive his fury, but she couldn't.

Until things changed, we were walking a tightrope, praying we wouldn't fall.

# Chapter Two

## Leena

M Y SHOULDER WAS SURPRISINGLY better in the morning. Grandmother had come in before bed and wrapped it with a poultice and ointment she'd made after Vasska left for the Meade Room. I could even stir the pot of porridge without hearing popping sounds. The liquid burbled, and my gut churned at the thought of what was happening to the food that had been in it from the beginning. We'd added scraps of everything we could each day for almost two weeks. It was a miracle none of us vomited more than once a week.

Fortunately, today, we'd get tiny slivers of bread to go with it. Karina had sold scarves she'd knitted, and though she didn't get much for them, she was able to get the baker's oldest loaf, so we didn't have to dine on porridge alone. The bread would be stale, but it was still bread.

Vasska had already left the house before I woke up, and Karina and Grandmother left soon after, likely to join the other ladies in town for their daily sewing circle. Having the house to myself was always a welcome surprise, but the peace didn't last long. A ruckus quickly formed outside, intensifying by the minute. All I heard was shouting, but it was clear as day that at least half, if not more, of the village had gathered. Our hut, like most of the others in the village, was flimsy and thin. We'd settled here mere weeks ago because we'd been driven out of our last location due to lack of food and contention with another nearby town. Something about them overcharging for something. I wasn't sure. I figured it was probably more to do with the competition for food and resources.

Our houses were made from the bones of older homes we'd found upon our trek, fixed up with the aid of everyone in town. The flimsy boards did nothing but shield us from the wind, but at least we managed to create crude rooms and roofs before any beasts or storms came along. Until whatever had been lurking around showed up. No one had seen it, though, and no one knew what it was.

I set the spoon on the counter and left, following the voices of the crowd, trying to make out at least one conversation. When I couldn't, I leaned close to a man and woman talking in hushed voices. "Excuse me, but can you tell me what's going on?" I asked. The woman turned to look at me, and from the fear on her face, my stomach dropped.

"Another child has gone missing."

My blood turned cold.

"Two children," the man beside her corrected.

"What? Who?"

"The Wenzell twins. Bogdan and Vesna."

The crowd was a hiss of whispers and cries until a man I knew as the town baker, Mr. Morrison, shouted from atop a crate by the general store. "This will not end until we do something!"

Someone in the crowd yelled, "Like what?"

"That's what we need to figure out," he said.

The noise of the crowd amplified as he got off the crate. My head spun from the countless conversations and suggestions flooding the makeshift street. My mind was reeling from yet another misfortune occurring in such a short span of time. Things like this never happened before we moved into these woods.

"It's the Leshy, isn't it?" a teenage boy cried. All at once, the crowd was silent.

"It is." The whispered answer came from behind me, and I was pretty sure only I heard. I turned to face my grandmother, whose grave expression was enough to convince me that the legends could be true.

"Of course not! He's a myth!" someone replied, but their voice was small, as if unconvinced.

"We don't know that," Mr. Morrison said.

"The boy is right." An old man's voice tore through the crowd, and all eyes landed on one of the elders of the village. The weathered man staggered forward, crooked crane in hand, his form just as bent with age. "Everyone needs to go home.

Ms. Tomlin and I will come up with a solution to this. Go about your business."

"How can we go about our business when a monster is out there?" the teenage boy cried out. His mother hushed him, but his sister spoke too.

"We could be next!"

The murmurs of the crowd resumed, only silencing when the village elder smacked his cane against the hard crate and spoke louder than I thought he could. "Do not speak such things. Go home or about your business at once." His command was enough to finally break up the gathered group.

I turned to Grandmother, tucking my cloak around me as if that offered any semblance of protection. It gave me comfort, at least. "Do you really think it's him? The Leshy?"

She nodded. "I'm afraid so, dear. I really do think so."

"I thought he was a legend, a folktale to scare the children into obeying and not wandering into the woods."

Grandmother looked around before taking my hand and leading me back to the hut. She was silent until we got inside. "Leena." She placed her hands on my shoulders. "I've seen more horrible things in this life than you can imagine. Your mother..." She shifted her weight uncomfortably. "I think she saw things too. It's why she was so adamant about hunting. That curiosity got the better of her in the end."

"She had to hunt. Our village needed it."

"They had more than enough hunters at the time. She wouldn't listen. She..." her voice broke, and her chin quivered.

When the color drained from her face, I decided it was best to change the topic back to the issue at hand.

"What can we do?" I asked. "There has to be something."

"I don't know, Leena, but please stay out of this. I can't bear to lose you too." Her eyes bore into mine. The intensity was stifling. "You don't need to get to the bottom of this. Go into the woods only when you must hunt. Then come home. And *please*...if you ever hear or witness anything unnatural or threatening, come straight home. No matter what."

A hiss from the pot made me jump. I rushed over and covered it, thankful something broke the tension and allowed me to escape without giving her a reply or a promise. When I took the pot off the fire, I noticed my fingers were shivering.

"I don't know what I can do," I whispered, still staring at the pot. My fingers curled over the handles.

"You're just like your mother." She let out a long sigh, and I wondered if she'd heard me. "Leena, please promise me you won't get involved. I have lived long enough and heard enough stories to know what might happen if you do."

My hands slid from the pot as I turned to face her. "Is there something I can do then?"

She threw her hands up. "You are so stubborn! And I wouldn't tell you if there *was* something. Please don't be like this, Leena. This problem will be solved in time. Let the town matriarch worry about it and leave it be. Please." Her voice cracked. I couldn't bear to look at her.

"What if you get hurt? What if we run out of food?"

"I'm done talking about this." Her voice was firm, and when she shoved my hunting sack into my arms, she added, "Now go fetch some game. If you come back empty-handed again, Vasska won't be as generous as he was last night. But remember: come back if anything doesn't feel right."

We stared at each other for a long time. I contemplated whether or not I should argue about the fact that Vasska could get off his lazy ass and help us hunt, but I knew it would be no use. She always reprimanded me for standing up to him, even if it was to protect her.

Begrudgingly, I did as I was told and went into the woods, knowing it would go as it always did and I would pay for it.

Despite the unseasonably cold weather, I stayed there as long as I could. Each day in this strange place was like a race through time. It was even colder than it was yesterday. The wind's bite was sharp against my fingers as I plucked whatever edible fruit I could find. A lot of it had already gone bad from the premature frost and whatever the monster of these woods was doing to it. What hadn't gone bad had either been nibbled at or stripped from the bushes.

When I got home, my fingers were numb, but I had a sack full of berries. Vasska would take the substitute with scorn, but he'd take it all the same. When Grandmother saw my bloodless arrow, the bow strapped to my back, and the sack full of berries in my arms, fear twisted her features. Anxious dread remained splashed across her face as she returned to setting the table. It seemed like that was all she did. Set the table, sew, and clean.

"Where's Vasska?" I asked, looking around the cabin. Karina was in her usual spot, knitting by the tiny fire.

"Right here," he said behind me. I jumped, swiveling around so fast that a good chunk of my spoils rolled onto the floor.

"Oh, I, Vasska, I wasn't able to get any game, but I—"

"It doesn't matter," he said, closing the door and shrugging off his coat.

My eyebrows shot up. Even Grandmother and Karina turned to stare at him, Karina's expression more uneasy than Grandmother's.

"What?" I blinked. He nodded, chewing on something before spitting it out in the sink.

"I've secured a new job for you," he said, pouring water into the basin he'd just spat in.

"New job?" I kept my voice steady. The wrong intonation could set him off, and I was curious. I needed to know about this. New opportunities were hard to come by.

He poured the basin out the open window above the pot of stomach-churning supper. Grandmother made sure he wasn't looking before turning to me with wide eyes and a quick shake of her head. She mouthed the word "no" just before he turned back around.

"Ms. Tomlin is looking for ladies around your age for a special task. Everyone else has declined so far, or their families have on their behalf. I wanted to secure your spot before they changed their minds."

"The village matriarch? What for?" My stomach instantly dropped. A job that no other woman in the village would take? Food was getting scarcer by the day, money even scantier than that. No one was passing up opportunities, and they certainly wouldn't pass up a good one by the town's wealthy matriarch.

His lips peeled back, revealing his broken yellow teeth, thick with film and the stench from whatever he'd been chewing. "You'll learn the details soon enough, but it's about our town's predicament."

Run. Every ounce of common sense, every bone in my body, screamed at me to run. But I couldn't. Not when Grandmother was here. Not when I could do something that could save more children from getting hurt. Whatever it was, I had to do it.

He stared me down with that wicked grin and grabbed me roughly by the arm. "The deal is done. It was either you or Karina. I obviously wouldn't give up my wife, and you're not as scrawny. He might like you more."

My blood chilled, my stomach as tight and small as the gravel beneath my feet.

"He?"

Vasska didn't respond, which made everything worse.

"Leena, no!" Grandmother gasped.

"If you want to help our people and feed Grandmother, you'll do as you're told and take this job."

"Leena, what did I tell you?" Her voice was almost a cry. Vasska growled and shook the table on his way over to her.

I jumped between them. "Stop! I'll do it! Don't hurt her. Please. I'll do it, whatever it is."

"Good," he said, "I'll take you there in the morning. Now let's eat." He clearly wasn't surprised. As far as he was concerned, I didn't have a choice. And he was right.

Everyone but Vasska was solemn at supper, even Karina. The only interactions I had were the looks of disapproval occasionally shot at me by my grandmother. She dealt them to me all evening until I was getting ready for bed. With a knock at the board I used as my door, she let herself in.

"Leena, don't do this." She closed the door softly. Vasska was snoring so loud from the other room that it shook the shoddy walls.

"I don't even know what it is. It could be safe. It could be nothing."

"It will be dangerous."

"Grandmother, I can't say no to this. Vasska is getting more violent by the day without food coming in, and he could kill you. If we get a job from the matriarch, we could get enough food to buy us time until this problem is under control."

"Don't be stupid, Leena! This is about the Leshy. Do you really think any other task would be turned down by every woman in town? Vasska even said 'he' and that he would like you more. What do you think that means?"

"I don't know! But it doesn't matter! I have to do this." The room went quiet. Grandmother straightened with another shake of her head.

"You're going to leave me with nothing, and you'll be ending your own precious life, as your mother did." Tears glistened in her eyes, which only made them brim in mine, too.

"I won't be as reckless as she was. We don't have another choice. I told you this morning. Anything I can do, I'll do it."

"Taking on a monster is the most reckless thing you could possibly do."

"If I can help you and the children of our village, then it isn't reckless curiosity or anything that I will regret." I took her hands in mine and tried giving her a reassuring smile, but she turned away. "I'm twenty-six years old and don't have a family of my own. The other women my age already have a brood of children. It makes sense that a job requiring a woman would be turned down by everyone but me."

"Your life is worth just as much as theirs, Leena."

"That's not what I meant, and you know it."

"I think you do believe that, and you're breaking my heart offering yourself up to whatever so-called job this is."

"I'm not going to change my mind." My voice was firm, resolute. Contention filled the space between us like a thick brick wall, but a pang of guilt shot through my chest. She gave me one last look, somehow both an icy glare and a look so somber I thought my heart might shatter.

"I need to rest. I'll see you in the morning." The moment she turned around, I knew I wouldn't see her in the morning.

# CHAPTER THREE

LEENA

As I suspected, Grandmother was already gone before I got up. She never came to the room she and I shared; I wasn't sure if she'd slept in the parlor or if she'd slept at all. When Karina sauntered out of her and Vasska's room, I asked where she was.

She shrugged. "I haven't seen her since last night."

"Wh—"

"Come on, Leena, it's time to go." Vasska grabbed my arm and roughly led me out the door.

"I haven't had breakfast yet."

"I'm sure Ms. Tomlin will have something for you there."

I couldn't squeak out a word as he led me by the elbow and muttered directions for me to be amiable when Ms. Tomlin spoke to me.

When he threw me in front of the matriarch's cabin, he pounded on the door. "Drop the food off at my place, Agatha. She's all yours." He turned to me with one last sneer. "If you don't want your grandmother to die of starvation, you'll do as you're told." Fear rippled through me, and before I could respond, he was gone. I stared at the grooves in Ms. Tomlin's polished door. I'd never felt so cold and confused, but all I could do was wait. And think.

My nails dug into my cloak as I held it tight against my chest. I looked around at the small cottages in the middle of the woods and at the enormous trees draped overhead. Trees surrounded us like a storm, each one reaching out like they were trying to grab us. My eyes fell toward the heart of it, where sound came to a stop.

The doorknob rattled before the large entrance creaked open.

"Leena, I take it?" The elderly woman stared at me, white hair hanging in thick braids from either side of her skull. Her back was rigid and adorned with small turquoise beads of different shapes and sizes, strung from layered necklaces over an intricate robe. Her skin was thin and crinkled, resembling wet rice paper, and her eyes were somehow paler than Vasska's. They were so white that it appeared she only had pupils, which widened before turning to pinpricks as she stared me down, examining every inch of me. "Hm." She crossed her arms. "You should do just fine. Come." She nodded, gesturing inside, and walked into the house.

Was she pretending not to know me, or did she truly not remember me? I had met Ms. Tomlin plenty of times. Our village wasn't that big.

I followed her inside, instantly hit with the warmth of a fire most of us only dreamed of. Chopping down trees had proven difficult lately. We'd all been living on two or three slats of wood a day to make it last, but the town matriarch must have gotten the first claim on whatever anyone chopped. Just as she'd had first claim on the structures we'd turned into homes.

Her cabin had been in one piece, and most of the town helped with any repairs or renovations needed. It must have been nice to hold such a position, though I wouldn't want the only reason people treated me nicely to be because they either feared me or wanted special treatment, though she didn't seem to mind.

"Um, Ms. Tomlin?"

"Don't say, 'um' like that, dear. Be confident. You won't stand a chance if you lack confidence. Besides, it's improper, and you should know that at your age." She emphasized the last two words and looked me up and down with an unimpressed grimace. I resisted the urge to roll my eyes.

I ignored the slant and focused on the concerning words that came before it. "That's just it. I won't stand a chance against what? I don't understand what I'm being sent to do."

The woman's thin brows shot up. "Your uncle didn't tell you? Didn't he ask if you'd be willing to do it?"

"Do what?" My voice was hoarse, or else I'd be screaming. "Please," I said, my throat suddenly dry. "Tell me."

A look of pity washed across the woman's face as she chewed on her lip, pausing before speaking. "You can still turn back if you'd like. Your family doesn't own you."

"They do."

"No, they—"

"Please," I whispered. My hands were cold; I could barely move my fingers as I fumbled to clutch my cloak tighter against my chest.

The woman studied me. The mighty grandfather clock across her finely decorated sitting room ticked the seconds away. Finally, she let out another sigh. "We need someone to help end this issue plaguing our village. I'm sure you know how dire the situation is, and surely you know things will only get worse." I nodded. "We need someone..." The woman's mouth hung open for a moment and then clamped shut. The grandfather clock ticked as she chose her next words.

"I have been in search of answers since this began," she said. Her bony fingers fiddled with a string loosely hanging from the seam of her robes. "I'm sure you've heard that towns around this forest warned us not to settle here. I suppose we should have heeded those warnings."

"Why? What's out there?" My heart pounded.

□The woman's fingers stilled, then slid off the end of the thread. "The rumors around town are true. The attacks on our village—the broken carts that have made it near-impossible to travel for food and supplies, the missing villagers, the spoiled food—I have it on good authority that it's the guardian of these woods. A creature called the Leshy." A weight plunged deep into my gut, and the blood drained from my face. "We need someone to look for him," she said. "To *appeal* to him."

My whole body frosted over. The chill in the room was so palpable I could feel it seeping beneath my cloak, coating my skin.

"And do what exactly?" I looked down at the polished, intricately designed table the woman was standing next to. Her whole cottage was lavish despite none of her villagers having enough food. Most didn't even have straw for beds.

"I spoke with many experts and a reliable source, and I learned that the Leshy needs a companion."

"No..." Bile threatened to heave from my gut, but I choked it down, along with the tears that stung my eyes.

"Before you get too worried, this doesn't mean you must be his companion to solve our plight, but we need to prepare for the worst." She paused, avoiding my gaze as she added, "But we need someone to appeal to him, and sending an unmarried, vulnerable woman is our best bet to do that. Just in case."

A laugh erupted from my throat, both from disgust and disbelief. "You're joking. You must be."

"I'm afraid I'm not. This is the task."

The bleakness and harsh reality of the mission hit me like a punch to the stomach. I had to bite my lip hard to fight back the tears, but I couldn't stop my voice from wobbling. "You're sending me to die."

"I'm sending you to stop him from stealing children and from leaving our people starving and without resources. This may be our only chance at putting an end to all this."

"What makes you think he'll even speak to me or that he's even attracted to human women?"

"I was told that these deities are attracted to human women, though they don't accept them often. It may not work, but it's our best shot. Our only shot, really."

"One woman has already gone missing, but things are only getting worse. If she wasn't good enough, what makes you think I will be?"

"We don't know what happened to her. She may have been killed while trying to protect her child. Besides, she was far older than you and was married with a child of her own. These leshy creatures are finicky, but if we dress you up and you do as I tell you, you may have a shot."

I sat on the sofa, letting myself sink deep into the cushions. This little talk was only making things worse. "I'm not so sure."

"Are you not going then?" she asked.

"No, I am. I..." A lump formed in my throat as a myriad of possible horrors flipped through my mind. "What about my family? If I do this, my grandmother will never go hungry, right? And neither will the rest of them?" Vasska needed to be fed or Grandmother still wouldn't be safe.

"That's right," the matriarch said. "Even if you don't secure a solution, we will do what we can to feed your family. But the main issue is that our food is either going rotten or is too hard to obtain. That's why we need you."

"Promise me," I snapped. "Promise me they'll be taken care of or I don't go."

"I can't guarantee there will be enough food if you don't resolve our plight. There may not—"

"Promise me or I'm not going."

The woman placed a thin hand on the table's waxed surface. She looked down at her tapping finger as she let out a long sigh. "Very well."

My shoulders relaxed a bit, but my limbs were still cold. I couldn't stop from shaking. My uncle was far from perfect, but this? How could anyone be okay sentencing someone to this, let alone family? No matter how loose the term may be.

At least Grandmother would be safe. She might think this sacrifice was reckless, but it wouldn't be in vain.

Ms. Tomlin looked up, hope sparking in those white eyes. "Go into the forest and summon him. And put an end to it. I'll give you the means to attract him if my sources are to be believed. In addition to dressing you up, there's a song I will teach you to summon him. I know your father taught you how to play the fiddle. Any instrument will do. As long as you play this song in his woods, he should come."

"We don't know if he's behind any of this or if he's even real." I shook my head in disbelief.

"Oh, child. He is very real." The words hung in the air, thickening the tension like flour in a pot of water.

My throat was like sandpaper, and another tear skated down my face. "He'll kill me."

Ms. Tomlin kept her eyes on the table as she tapped that one gnarled finger against its surface. "Let's hope he won't."

I sucked in a sudden sob, my head falling into my hands. I couldn't stop the shaking from taking over my limbs. My whole body trembled violently, worse so when the woman took me by the wrist and led me into the back room of her cabin.

"Let's get you ready. You need your best chance at survival. We all do." She glanced over her shoulder before guiding me to a chair in front of a vanity set. "If you choose to do this, you cannot fail. We're all counting on you."

I couldn't speak anymore. There was nothing left to say. My fate was being written right before me, and I couldn't so much as pick up the quill. The woman sorted through a chest of clothes, rattling off who knows what while I tried gaining my bearings again.

"I don't understand what he'd want with me."

The matriarch closed the trunk, bringing a pile of red silk and tulle along with her. She tossed it at me, and it fell limply into my lap.

"Let's hope he wants you at all. That's the first step." She walked out of the room without so much as a glance my way, and panic set in. I ran after her.

"He won't—"

"Hush!" She moved like a shadow to my side, pushing me in front of a floor-length mirror and hissed, "Let's be honest, shall we? There's no time for false pleasantries. Other than your aging grandmother, no one will miss you if you fail." The words sent a distant ringing to my ears. "But you have a pretty face and decent form, so let's hope you're worth something to him." The words splintered a part of me, sending a thin crack scaling through my chest. But she was right. And I could no longer deny this strange new reality.

The forest spirit and monster known as the Leshy was real, and if I wanted to save my grandmother, if I wanted to save the children and innocents of Woodsmeadow, I was to be a sacrifice to him. "And who knows?" the woman said, smiling at me from the reflection in the mirror. "He may even like you." I stared at my pallid face next to hers. All color had drained from it, and the life had been sucked from my eyes. Ms. Tomlin unraveled the messy braid hanging down my back and brushed through the tangled knots. "And if he does, you might make it to the end of winter."

# CHAPTER FOUR

THE CROWD PARTED AS I walked toward the forest. Most of the village had gathered at the edge of town to see me off. Just yesterday, half the village didn't believe the legends of the Leshy were true, but now, everyone seemed convinced. One word from Ms. Tomlin, and the myth was revealed as fact. I wouldn't have believed in him myself if I didn't trust my grandmother so much. I knew that whatever lay out there—whoever I was being sent to—wasn't mortal and was nothing but a monster.

Children peeked through the crowd, yelling questions at their mothers, wondering what I was wondering most: where I was going and what was going to happen to me. Almost everyone in the crowd was speaking to each other in intrigued horror, maybe even excitement.

A trail of murmured whispers followed me, colder than the new autumn chill against my exposed skin. The wind whipped against my hair and made it even harder to breathe. The too-tight dress was impractical. A strong enough breeze might blow me over if I let it. I kept my spine stiff, my chin high, and stepped closer to that dark line where the trees welcomed me like an old nightmare. Where the first part of my life ended and the end of my life began.

I could be dead by nightfall. This would likely be the last I saw of any of them, but leaving the village in such a state without a single person stepping in to help made it a whole lot easier. Before sending me out the door, Ms. Tomlin told me not to come back until I fulfilled my mission. She hadn't spoken of much else while she got me ready, other than humming the song I had to play and instructing me to use any womanly wiles I could to appeal to him. I couldn't help feeling like there was something she wasn't saying.

The cold air bit at my shoulders and back, skating across the exposed portion of my chest. The silk dress draped across my bodice like red froth over a tightly laced corset; it pushed everything up in a way that made the display all the more humiliating. I especially wanted to sink into the ground when I spotted Casimir, whose eyes were latched onto my body like I was a piece of gourmet meat.

The skirts swished along the forest floor, a long train falling behind me like a trail of fresh blood. It matched the lip paint Ms. Tomlin had brushed onto my mouth not two hours earlier, complete with rouge and thick kohl along my lashes.

I was being served up like a truffle on a crimson platter.

Just this morning, the only thing I was worried about was the decision between killing an innocent creature for food or suffering my uncle's wrath. I never would have suspected that my failure would lead to me swishing through town in a gaudy, blood-colored gown made of silk, tulle, and an overabundance of lace.

Rationally, I shouldn't have been upset that this all happened so fast—that there was no ceremony or anything of the sort—but I couldn't help feeling that this rushed, last-minute display was just further proof that I meant nothing to these people. That I was disposable.

A piece of meat.

A tool.

A sacrifice.

If it wasn't for my grandmother and those who were either voiceless victims like me or children with no one else to protect them, nothing would stop me from running.

Whispers buzzed around me like flies on a carcass. I'd never done anything to these people, but here they were, gladly sacrificing me to the creature who'd likely been terrorizing us for weeks. Selfishness and pride seemed to be my village's biggest vice. A common trait of humanity, I supposed. An unfortunate trait that was hard to escape. I wasn't sure if I'd met many selfless people, but it was clear that few resided here.

My eyes flickered to the town's exit. The place I was so eager to escape from was now a dark maw, ready to devour me whole. To "speak" to the monster of the woods. To appeal to him by any means necessary.

I'd never heard of the Leshy until the disappearances started, but every villager outside of ours had apparently spat at Ms. Tomlin that we were fools to settle here. Of course, that piece of information had been hidden until everything started happening. Then, whoever must have witnessed it let it spill that there'd been warnings. Now here we were with no resources or strength to settle anywhere else and with sacrifice as our only option for survival.

"Don't forget this, love." Ms. Tomlin pushed the wooden instrument into my hand. The fiddle was crafted of fine wood—much better than the one my father had made for me when I was a child. I'd never exchange the two, but Ms. Tomlin insisted I use this one. So, I whipped my cloak over my shoulders to properly hold onto the instrument, and then Ms. Tomlin handed me the bow. It had taken some convincing and tears to get the matriarch to allow me to bring my cloak. It was the one semblance of peace I had—a piece of my mother to keep me safe, or at least comforted, as I walked to my death. "Don't forget what I showed you." The old woman pointed to the fiddle.

My fingers curled around the instrument and bow, the strings snagging on the elaborate gloves covering my skin in thin, black lace. For what felt like the hundredth time today, my mouth went dry. There was no point replying, so I nodded. "Good girl," Ms. Tomlin croaked. "Don't let us down." Giving me one last push toward the woods, she was gone.

I tried not to do it, but I couldn't help scanning the crowd. When I spotted my grandmother, my stomach turned to stone. Her eyes were red and swollen and locked on mine. Slowly, her head shook, and she mouthed, "Don't go." My eyes burned, but I couldn't look away. Not when I knew it might be the last time I ever saw her. Her head bowed, and after wiping her cheeks with a handkerchief, she gave me a single wave and disappeared into the crowd. My stomach coiled. I could hardly breathe, and it took everything in me not to burst into tears.

She shuffled behind a gleaming Vasska. Karina must have stayed behind. We'd never had a good relationship, but I was disappointed that she couldn't be bothered to say goodbye to the only person who'd ever stood up for her.

I ignored my uncle and tried to forget the pain on my grandmother's face. A lump formed in my throat. I had to focus on why I was doing this. With my sacrifice, the famine would end, and things would be different. With my sacrifice, the Leshy would stop stealing from us and stop rotting our crops and making it impossible to travel. Grandmother would be fed and hopefully no longer hurt by her only son. The children and innocents of the village would be safe, and the misfortunes would come to an end. I had to stay strong.

The temperature dropped the closer I got to the edge of town, but I didn't stop. I refused to look back as I staggered to the end of the path, and once I got there, I stared at the dark mouth of the forest. Had it always been that dark?

A cold gust of wind prickled my skin, whisking around me and sending leaves skating over my feet. If I didn't know any better, I would have thought it was alive. That it was beckoning me forward. Even the elements knew this was what I had to do.

Sucking in a breath, I took that first fatal step into the woods, and as the shadows welcomed me, I held onto the hope that one day I'd make it back here and see my grandmother at least one more time.

*** 

After about half an hour of walking, I realized I had no clue where I was going. Ms. Tomlin had instructed me to go into the middle of the woods, but it all looked the same. I twisted my hands along the neck of the fiddle, steadying myself as best I could, reining in the uncontrollable shaking of my arms and fingers. When a crow fluttered by, I shrieked and staggered back.

The moment I hit the ground, everything went still.

My eyes shot to the sky above, my body unmoving against the cold, rocky earth. The orange treetops scraped against the gray sky and spun the longer I looked at them. As soon as I wasn't seeing double, I got to my feet and whipped around, searching every direction for a sign of life. A sign of the Leshy.

Birds hopped on branches, leaves rustled in the wind, but nothing made a sound. Just like before, I could feel and see everything, but nothing made a peep.

Then I heard it.

It was a whisper. A whistle through the trees. A haunting melody. It was just as they'd said. I got to my feet, entranced by the off-kilter tune and the sudden unnatural stillness outside of it. My boots crunched against the leaves with every footstep, and beads of sweat formed along my hairline despite the frigid air.

I clutched the fiddle tighter, dragging the bow along the frozen ground beside me. I walked at first, and then I chased it, running toward the only sound among the trees. But no matter how deep into the woods I ventured, the song was still far away. No louder, no quieter. The same eerie tune. From some unknown source, it called to me.

A chill skittered up my spine as I thought of my next move. It was now or never, and the latter wasn't an option.

I placed the fiddle on my shoulder.

The time between when my chin hit the rest and my bow touched the strings was a lifetime of bated breaths. My fingers trembled in my useless gloves, and then I began.

It only took one shaky note before the beast's song came to a halt. Fear coated my skin and made my palms sweat. Even the wind ceased to breathe. Every stroke of sound had been sucked from the space around me. There were no indications of shimmying leaves or screeching crows.

Nothing.

The silence was suffocating.

Before I could attempt another note, a monstrous rumble burst through the woods. The ground was in an uproar, knocking me over and fracturing beneath me. I dropped the bow and fiddle as my spine cracked against the icy ground. My heart raced, the blood chilling in my veins.

Then the rumbling stopped, and all I heard was breathing. Deep, low, heavy breaths, warm against the nape of my neck.

And then a voice.

"Hasn't anyone told you not to disturb me?"

His voice was so deep it thrummed against my spine. Nausea formed a heavy rock in my gut. I knew I had to turn around. To look at him. To face him. That's why I was here. But—

"Answer me, little dove," he whispered, a caress in my ears, though something unnatural crackled with his words.

"You've been disturbing us," I said, trying my best to keep my voice steady. I couldn't turn around. Not yet. I couldn't face the monster yet.

A rush of air whipped around me, sending my hay-colored curls skittering above my head as they wriggled free from the intricate nest Ms. Tomlin had fashioned them into.

"Look at me," he hissed. The voice had an echo, like two beings in one. Spindly fingers clutched my jaw, but I refused to look. His hand was massive but rough and unnatural. Each finger was a thick twig pricking my skin. I squeezed my eyes shut from the gust of wind accompanying his movements. I couldn't open them. Not with him now in front of me. He jerked my chin up, and I heard creaks as his face lowered. "Look. At. Me."

My heart raced so fast, pumping so fiercely, that I couldn't feel anything else. I swore I could even hear it.

The twiggy fingers relaxed.

"I know." His voice was calm. "Maybe you'll look at me in another form." His hand didn't leave my face as it changed. Where once were long, prickly sticks were now soft, uncalloused skin. A human hand, large but smooth as silk. "Look at me, little dove," his voice was just as human as mine, and though it was still deep, it was soothing. Seductive.

I had to look. I wouldn't accomplish anything if I didn't take that first leap. Besides, I only had to talk with him. That's it. I just needed to survive this encounter, plead my case, and then I could go home. There was no need of anything else Ms. Tomlin had warned me about while she readied me to face him. Her precautionary words about seduction and sacrifice were merely to prepare me for the worst.

All I had to do was survive.

Slowly, I opened my eyes.

For the briefest moment, my heart stopped.

Before me was no mossy creature or frothing beast. Grasping my chin was a man. One with incredibly broad shoulders and thick hair as dark as untouched soil deep beneath the forest floor. His body was a sculpted mass that was hard to ignore, especially since all he wore was a drape of moss hanging from his lean hips. The sight was both shocking and intriguing; I'd never seen a man so bare. But what was most striking about him were his eyes. As he gazed down at me, a canopy of shadow, his eyes pierced mine, locking them in a deep trance. The striking green of his irises was mesmerizing. Unhuman in the way they shone, sparkling in the glinting light of the new autumn sun.

Those sultry eyes reflected a glow so intense I couldn't look away.

His full lips cracked into a half smile. "What is your name, little dove?" His hair framed his face in thick, inky waves, perfectly swept back and cropped at the base of his neck.

"I-I didn't come to discuss me. I came to discuss my people."

His hand was still on my jaw, but as he answered, he stroked his index finger along my cheek. "You mean the trespassers. Do discuss."

"Y-you have been stealing from us. It's gotten so bad that people are getting hurt. Wheels have been broken off our carts, food has either been spoiled or stolen, and villagers have gone missing. *Children* have gone missing."

His eyes fell to my mouth. He brushed it with his thumb, and I shivered at the fizz of his touch. "You have such a beautiful mouth."

My skin flushed, but I ignored the rising heat. "A woman, her baby daughter and teenaged son, and two children—siblings—haven't been found. What did you do with them?"

"I did nothing," he said coolly, still running his thumb along my lips. Each touch ignited a spark impossible to ignore.

"Liar," I whispered, but I couldn't stop my eyes from fluttering closed.

"Tell me your name," he purred.

"What will you do with it?" My breath was ragged, my eyes still shut. Hypnotic heat and emotions I couldn't place pooled through me. Something like candy and magic bubbled through my veins, skating from my tongue to my toes. He leaned in and smiled against my ear. A fire blazed deep within me.

"I want to get to know you. No mortal woman has ever summoned me before." He nipped at my earlobe, and I let out a gasp. My eyes shot open as I staggered back, falling against a tree. His eyes bored into mine in a sultry stare as he slowly crept toward me.

My chest moved in fast, uneven motions. Cold air stung my throat as I sucked it in, desperate to breathe. *What do I do? What do I say? What—*

He stalked closer, his arm grabbing a branch above his head. I'd never seen a man like this—so bare and beautiful, with a body somehow oozing with both masculinity and vulnerability. I swallowed and tried looking away, but he leapt in front of me and grabbed hold of my jaw. He craned his neck, then bent forward until his face was level with mine. He let out a low hiss as he bared his teeth.

"Tell me your name." The sound was like rustling leaves. The wind roared around me, encasing us in the eye of a miniature dust storm. His gaze fell to my mouth. He leaned in closer. "Tell me."

"Leena," I breathed. The briefest flutter flickered along my lips as his mouth barely brushed mine. They didn't fully touch, but he was too close for me to think of anything else.

"Leena," he purred, and again, that heat bloomed within me. "Come with me, Leena. I have things to show you."

# CHAPTER FIVE

## LEENA

H E TOOK MY HAND, guiding me from the tree scraping against my back. His eyes held mine with ferocious intensity. My heart raced. What was I doing? This man—this *monster*—was dangerous, yet here I was, entranced by his every move. Liquid at his every word.

He stopped and turned so suddenly I bumped into him. My cheeks set fire at the feel of his bare chest on what was exposed of mine. He guided my hand to be at my side, but he didn't let go. He laced my fingers in his and took a step closer so nothing was between us but our breath.

"Do I scare you, Leena?"

I opened my mouth, but I couldn't speak, and I didn't know what I'd say if I could. He did scare me, and he knew it. He chuckled, low and deep, and unlaced his hand from mine to trail it up my arm and onto my bare shoulder. I couldn't move. I didn't want to. Every place his fingers touched went aflame, sending shocking waves across my flesh. I wanted to melt into the sensation.

He swept the back of his hand down the slope of my neck. "Don't be afraid." His fingers fell down my throat; I had to force down the shaky breath crawling from my lungs. "You're safe with me." His eyes flicked up, and when they met mine, they were feral. It shook something in me—something primal from a forbidden place I'd never dared investigate.

"You're dangerous. You're killing innocent people," my words tumbled out with a bite, but he didn't so much as flinch.

"I haven't killed one innocent creature. My very job is to protect the innocent in my forest." His face was barely a finger's length away, and his voice was so deep it rumbled against my chest.

The air hitched in my lungs. "Y-you don't consider my people innocent, and you may not have killed them yet, but you've at least stolen them."

"They're not—" he snapped, baring his teeth. "The ones who have gone *missing* are children and victims. All were innocent. Children are always innocent. I would never harm one. And I didn't steal them. I rescued them."

My head jerked back. "What? But—"

"Are you almost done accusing me?" Something close to rage swirled in his eyes, but that feral look of hunger was too powerful to replace. "I'll lose my patience soon, even if you are so..." he smiled on his way down to my shoulder, where he pressed a kiss to my skin. I let out a sound as he trailed his bottom lip along my collarbone. When I started to fall, he caught me by the small of my back with one large hand.

His lips didn't move from my collarbone. He gently scraped his teeth against it until his mouth was at the base of my throat. I let out a gasp and jumped back, trying my best not to fall as I composed myself.

"Don't touch me!" I pulled at the silk of my dress and attempted to cover myself. It was no use. The cloth remained firmly beneath my shoulders, refusing to cover anything it didn't have to. That was probably the exact reason Ms. Tomlin had chosen it.

Something darkened in his eyes, and suddenly, everything that had transpired in the village flashed before me. The reason I was here.

I needed to be on his good side if I wanted to save my grandmother and stay alive.

And I was screwing it up.

Being accepted by him was the only way I could live and the only way my people would be safe. No matter the danger or cost, I had to push past the fear.

I was doing this all wrong. I had to be seductive in return to survive.

Shifting my weight, I tried looking more confident, but the corner of his mouth curled, and the foxlike way he watched me sent that warmth rushing through my blood again.

"I've heard all about you, but I'd like to learn more," I said, immediately cringing. *How was that seductive?* Trying to recover, I offered him a smile, but when he chuckled and shook his head, it dropped, and my hands curled into fists. "What's so funny?"

"You're adorable." He crept closer. I had to avoid his gaze so I could collect my thoughts. "Why are you looking away? I won't hurt you. I promise." The deep hum in his voice begged to differ.

He couldn't be trusted. My semi-seductive façade immediately crumbled. "How can I believe you?" I looked up at him, inhaling sharply. He was a lot closer than I'd thought.

He caught a loose strand of my hair between his fingers and bent down to smell it, his eyes closing as he breathed in the scent. I swallowed and ignored the dizzying sensation that followed.

"Why would I lie to you, little dove?"

"Because you're a monster."

His eyes flicked to mine. "Is that what I am?"

"Yes," I said firmly, planting my back against the tree and slapping his hand away from my hair. "Now tell me the truth."

He rose to his full height, his emerald eyes gleaming.

"I am, little dove. I don't only play games with you lot, you know. I'm capable of good deeds, too." He cocked his head playfully. "Besides, I'm far too powerful to give a damn about lying to you."

I scoffed and looked away, but his grasp found my chin. He forced me to look at him. "I mean it. I *am* capable of good." Those unearthly eyes shone with something no mortal could possess. A light like crystal stars. They appeared sincere, but he could easily be casting a spell on me—the same one he was clearly casting on my body. I felt strange like there was something burning deep within my bones. It heated my skin in a way that made me want to fall into his arms against my better judgment. Luckily, my head was at least somewhat clear right now.

"Your definition of good is entirely different from mine," I said.

"Is that so?" he purred, and I had to look away again. No part of him was safe to look at. His eyes, his arms, his exposed torso and legs. It all sent strange bouts of fire whipping through my blood and skating across my skin.

"And what about you?"

"What about me?"

He leaned in until his nose was almost on mine. My eyes shuttered, but I kept them open this time.

"Why are you here?"

"To help my people," I whispered, barely able to speak.

"But why you? Besides your obvious bravery."

Pain tightened my face as I thought of everything that had happened these last few days—my unsuccessful hunts, the cruelty of my uncle, Ms. Tomlin's stony face as she laced up my corset, my grandmother's gut-wrenching expression, Casimir's disgusting leer. Of this stupid gown and this treacherous man or monster. Whatever he was.

"I'm a protector," I said, and the Leshy laughed a low, sultry chuckle.

"Now who's the liar."

"I am *not* lying."

"I can feel your heart." He slid his hand down my arm and tucked his fingers beneath the lace of my glove. He pressed against the inside of my wrist. "You're lying. I can feel it. I can smell it. It radiates from you like a perfume."

I jerked away. "Fine. If you must know, no one in the village was doing anything, so I was chosen to find you. Are you happy?"

He frowned, crossing his arms as he studied me. "Why you? Surely, you have a family to protect you—one who wouldn't want to send you to a *monster* like me. You mortals breed like rabbits." My blood boiled, but something ached in my chest. "Ah," he said. "You have no one."

"That's not true," I grumbled.

"No one who cares then."

"Shut up," I growled. "You have no idea what you're talking about." Without thinking, I shoved him, and then was immediately horrified that I had. This wasn't Casimir or some village brute. This was the monster of these woods.

His brows shot up.

"Oh my. She has a temper." His lips formed a wicked curve. "How delicious."

My hands formed fists at my side, but I was relieved that my sudden bout of bravery—or stupidity—hadn't left me dead. Shifting uncomfortably, I suddenly realized my body was itching with sweat. My fingers uncurled. *What's going on?*

It only took a moment for my answer to come. One look at my surroundings left me gaping.

Just mere minutes ago, the forest was a sea of dying trees with spotty, claw-like branches. Now, each tree was vibrant and alive with wild heads of green, the most magnificent shade of the color I'd ever seen, save for the Leshy's eyes.

"What—How did you…"

"Can't you see I've turned it into spring for you?" His wicked grin remained as he hooked his finger inside my glove, gently gliding against the center of my palm as he tugged it off. "Would a monster give you spring?"

"Get away from me!" I hissed, pushing him away and stumbling back. Distance. I needed distance from him. To leave his stare. His spell. His body.

"My, my," he said, sauntering closer. "Come now, is that a way to treat the Keeper of the Woods?"

"Just bring those children back, and the woman—"

"You know I can't do that." He craned his neck, and I was once again shadowed by his massive frame.

"Why not?" I glowered at him, keeping my eyes on his face, refusing to let them linger on his physique. Whenever my gaze flickered to his form, it set off a deep curiosity I wanted to satiate. I couldn't deal with it right now, and it was embarrassing. I desperately wished he had more clothes on.

A chuckle rumbled from his throat. "I can tell what you want."

"And what's that?"

He stepped closer. "You want to touch me."

My face burned. "I do not!"

He took my gloveless hand and placed it on his chest, but I instantly snatched it away. "That is completely inappropriate," I said, holding my hands across my chest and turning from him.

"Do I intimidate you, Leena?" His voice was a dark song. I longed to close my eyes and listen—to drink it like a poison. To let it infect me.

I had to keep it together.

"No," I snapped, but it came out the way a pouty toddler might have said it, which made him laugh again.

I shot him a glare over my shoulder and peeled off my remaining glove, tossing it to the side, but my eyes widened at the clothes forming on his body. A black tunic stretched across his muscled form, with matching tight, black trousers replacing that tattered cloth. "Is this better?" When I didn't respond, he said, "I want you to look at me more. I love those eyes of yours."

He was trying to capture me. He was trying to trick me.

"That won't change anything," I said, then remembered I was supposed to be playful. Sultry. I was very bad at this.

"Please come with me, Leena. I have a whole forest to show you."

"I would like to stay here, thanks."

"Leena," he breathed my name against the back of my neck and slid a finger down my spine. Goosebumps blanketed my

skin, and my head fell back against his chest. I didn't care that
it was irresponsible; I closed my eyes. I let myself revel in the
black magic of his touch. He wrapped his arms around me.
"Let me show you my palace," he whispered, "and then I'll tell
you where the missing villagers are."

My eyes shot open, and I turned around. "Really?"

"Really." He offered me his hand, and this time, I allowed
my hand to curl into his. His fingers were long, his palm enormous—my whole fist could easily fit inside.

My body was still warm as I followed him, and I stared at
the muscles of his back through the thin tunic. I was able to
admire his form with less embarrassment this way, watching
his muscles move, the way they tightened and relaxed. My gaze
wandered to his hair. I'd never seen someone with hair such a
dark shade of brown that it appeared black; it only revealed its
true color when the sun hit it just right.

It was impossible to take my eyes off him until we reached a
thick wall of moss, vines, and leaves. Upon further inspection,
I realized that beneath the green was a long rock wall with a
gray slab of stone embedded in the middle. Across the stone's
surface were strange, ancient markings and insignias that created a border around an emerald gem that matched the Leshy's
eyes.

"Are you ready?" His eyes shone brighter as if being in close
contact with the gem lit something within them. I nodded,
and he put his hand on the stone.

Beneath our feet, the ground came to life, growling and quaking as branches soared through the dirt and pulled on the mossy wall. The leaves trembled in a shaky dance before falling away, and as the vines curled in, the branches pulled at an opening in the middle of the slab. The emerald stone cracked in the middle, and light poured out as a doorway appeared.

My free hand clapped over my mouth. A rounded entryway now gaped in the center of the wall, and through it was a scene I couldn't believe.

"We're here," he said, but I couldn't take my eyes off what lay beyond the rocky maw. He gently tugged on my hand and guided me through. "Welcome to my kingdom."

# CHAPTER SIX

THE VILLAGE WAS LIKE a fairy tale. Every color imaginable painted the houses, plants, and even the wildlife. Sheets of moss of matching hues laid across rooftops, each one vibrant and alive. The spongy material covered small, neatly arranged cottages of dark burgundy and polished wood, some oak, some pine, and some I didn't recognize. Some were brightly pink like the blush of a flower, while others were ruddy and elegantly smooth. Paired with the moss's lively greens, yellows, and unearthly pinks and deep-sea blues, the cottages looked more like a scene from a picture book than the body of a village.

This had to be a dream. How could it not be? This enchanting man—this being, whatever he was—swept me away into a place so unlike the one I was used to, so unlike the one that caused me so much pain. A place I wasn't sure really existed. The more I looked at it, the harder it was to believe.

The colorful homes and thick blankets of grass over paths and hills wasn't the most unbelievable part of this pocket of the woods. The most beautifully peculiar part of this world was the town's occupants. There were tiny faeries of all shades of the rainbow, flying with brightly colored dust falling onto the lush blanket of grass in their wake. There were similar-looking beings that were tall, thin creatures with pointed ears, and others that blended into the shrubbery and flowers. There were even adorable pets that reminded me of the dogs back home—small, friendly log-like creatures trailing at the feet and calves of those walking by.

There were even more beings, whose origins I hadn't read about in storybooks. Some were made of wood, others of grass or another form of plant. Some I did recognize—beings who looked more human. They appeared almost like anyone else back home; the only differences were their pointed ears and noses and the vibrant skin tones and hair colors that matched their effervescent town. From what I'd learned in books and over late, story-filled nights with my mother, these creatures had either branched from humankind or were at the beginning of everything. They were known as fae. Though varying in color, size, and any attribute a human may vary from the next, the identifiable traits they all shared were their ears, noses, and youthful appearances.

I still wasn't sure if I was dreaming. It was all too fantastical. This odd, breathtaking world of magic was so far from the dreary, broken world I'd left behind.

"How do you like my home?" The Leshy asked, his fingers entwined in mine. At first, I didn't want to look away, but his voice drew me in. When I looked at him, the muscles in my chest relaxed.

"It's beautiful," I said, and he smiled, which didn't help the gooey sensation gathering in my chest. Our eyes stayed locked until a voice squeaked through the silence.

"Your Majesty," it said, and we both looked down at a tiny creature with a body made of rounded wood. It looked like a wooden toy for a child but big enough to be a child itself. Only, from the cantor of its voice, I could tell it was an adult. Its eyes were amber buttons, and its mouth was a slit, like someone started carving a smile but gave up before they could finish the edges. Its clothes were made of leaves so glossy they looked like candy.

The Keeper's demeanor changed. His face hardened, and his eyes turned cold. "What is it?" The words were curt and venomous. It was hard not to react, but I remained expressionless.

The creature bowed its spherical head. "We can't find Melora, Your Greatness."

"What?" he dropped my hand and grabbed hold of the creature's arm. "What do you mean you can't find Melora? I just spoke with her this morning."

The creature quivered, his leaves shimmying. "Her visits are unpredictable. We—"

"I need to speak with her." His voice was quieter now, a cold hiss, and I wondered if I was supposed to have heard the words at all.

"Yes, Your Majesty. We're scouring the nearby villages for her. She—"

"Don't dawdle," the Leshy snapped, straightening his back. "Find her, and then report to me. Immediately."

"Yes, Your Majesty," the creature said with a bow, then scuttled off into a nearby bush. There were a few seconds of silence before I looked at the Leshy again. He was staring ahead.

"Who's Melora?"

He bristled, then straightened and turned to face me. His eyes were suddenly gentle, his voice soft. "No one to worry about." His deep voice fell into my ears like a spell. "Now let me show you more of my kingdom." He offered me his hand, and I took it without hesitation.

As he led me along a sandy path deeper into the belly of the forest, I looked up at him. "You know my name, but I haven't asked for yours." I kept my eyes on his thick, dark hair as he led me along. He didn't turn to me or answer right away, and when he did, he still didn't turn to face me.

"You can call me Bratan."

My eyes focused on the road ahead as his name etched itself into my mind. *Bratan.* We turned a corner into a place overgrown with plants and brush. I lifted my hand to shield myself and prepared to crouch through it, but with one sweep of his hand, he moved it away. Branches thickly filled with large leaves and plump fruits draped to the sides, clearing the path ahead.

I gawked at every inch of the world around us, but my eyes always ended up making their way back to him. He helped me over a slight incline. I watched his bicep move effortlessly with the weight of my body and remembered the tightness of his muscles and how the rich, sun-kissed glow of his skin glistened as he stalked me in that thin curtain of moss.

"We're almost there," he said, causing me to jump. My face must have been as red as the cloak I now had tucked between my arm and hip, but fortunately, his focus remained ahead as he lifted one last branch to reveal a crystalline pond in the middle of a rounded area free of trees, weeds, or unwanted eyes.

"Wow." Roses and daisies bloomed together next to a pond littered with fish and cattails. The water was so clear it looked like glass. I never knew there could be bodies of water in the forest. Although, I never knew a town of woodland creatures could exist here, either.

"You must be tired," he said, leading me to a soft patch of grass. "Would you like to rest?" He gestured to the ground. I couldn't take my eyes off him as he helped me down. Had I nodded? I wasn't sure. Something about this man made my brain turn to goo.

He smiled and let out a long sigh, falling onto his back. I watched the way his muscles tightened with every movement, studying the godlike construction of his body. He *was* something like a god. He was a guardian spirit, perhaps even something more. He turned onto his side and stroked the side of my face. "Lie next to me," he purred, and as if on command, I did. Even if I hadn't wanted to, my body gave me no choice. His request turned every part of me to gelatin.

When my back fell to the grass, I was instantly aware of how close his body was to mine. I could feel the heat of it against my shoulder and arm. He must have sensed it because when I looked at him, his expression was wicked. "Am I making you nervous again, Leena?"

My face heated. "What? No..."

He turned to be on his knees and knuckles, and I had to scoot away. The heat rushing through me was too intense. Air. I needed air.

"I'm fine, really." I quickly crawled away. It probably wasn't the daintiest sight, but the power he had over me whenever I so much as gazed into his eyes or lay next to him was frightening. I couldn't risk losing myself. I had to have my head on straight if I wanted to survive. Yes, I needed to be seductive—I needed him to like me—but if I was nothing but mush in his hands and there was no chase, a predator like him would move on without a second thought.

"Is that so?"

I tried not to look at him, but...

The moment I turned to peek, I promptly regretted it. The wind whispered through his brown-black hair, and still on his knuckles, he prowled closer. Something vibrated in my bones, extinguishing any thought that was still in my head, burning my good sense to ash.

"I..." The word caught in my throat. He was in front of me now, and he wasn't smiling. I shouldn't have liked it, but I did. His eyes were dark with something wild and hungry. A primal starvation. Like I was his next meal and nothing else would satisfy him.

Slowly, the words I knew I should say jumbled into a mess of letters and fell to the back of my mind. I let myself drop onto my back and watched him crawl over me. My nerves lit up with each of his movements, especially when he leaned in until our noses touched. "Say my name," he said, the warmth of his breath parting my lips.

I couldn't utter a sound. He leaned in closer. My eyelids fluttered, then closed. His lips brushed against mine, and it was like he'd sucked the air from my lungs. "I—" My mind went blank, and when he dove into my lips, my consciousness left completely, and I lived only by feeling. My body sparked with tiny bolts of lightning as I tasted him. It flushed my skin and shook my bones, and when I felt his tongue swipe against mine, I had to stifle a moan.

I loved it. I loved the way my mind stopped whirring and the way my body was water beneath the heat of his flesh.

He kept kissing me, and I hungrily kissed him back. One of his hands gripped the back of my neck, the other grabbing hold of one of my hips. He held me tight against him like I was the only thing tethering him to this world. Like he couldn't let anyone else have me.

He pressed his thumb into the hollow of my hipbone, and my head fell back, releasing his lips. I didn't have time to move before I was immobilized by a kiss he pressed into my collarbone. He stroked it with his bottom lip and then licked up the side of my neck, making his way to my earlobe with the tip of his tongue. He bit gently, and shivers sparked all the way from my lips to my feet.

"Say my name," he whispered. It was hard to breathe, let alone speak. He kissed me again, letting the warmth of his breath fall slowly against the space behind my ear and then down my neck. "Say my name."

"Bratan," I gasped, and I felt his lips curve into a smile.

"Good girl." His deep voice rumbled against my throat. Although he purred the words, there was something off in the way he said it. I opened my eyes, still dewy from his lips on my neck, when the ground trembled. He backed away and got to his feet. My mind was still a foggy mess as the earth quaked beneath me. I frowned, confused and dazed, but the monster of the woods just stood above me, watching me with an unreadable expression other than a faint spark dancing in his eyes.

The ground thundered more violently. It rattled against my back with such violence that I thought my spine might snap.

"What—" I was cut off by a sudden pain snapping across my wrists. I looked down to find vines tying me to the earth. Then, another lash of pain wrapped around my ankles with matching restraints. The Leshy walked closer, smiling down at me as my heart raced. He touched the crown of my head and slowly stroked it until his fingers unpinned my hair and slid down the waves as they rippled down and over my shoulders.

"There's no escape for you now." His voice was a cold whisper against the nape of my neck. "You belong to me."

# Chapter Seven

BLIND PANIC FLASHED THROUGH me like a whip. "What are you talking about?"

He grinned with wicked delight. "You're mine now, little dove."

"What are you—Why?"

He looked to my side and lifted one hand in a curved, up-side-down motion like he was grabbing something and pulling it up. And he did precisely that. Through an invisible power, the vines jutting from the soil moved with the motion of his hand. Slowly, my body rose from the ground; he pulled me forward until I was standing right in front of him on the soil that now held me prisoner.

His eyes fell to the exposed skin of my thigh. At some point, a vine must have whipped against it, slashing it in just the right place so my entire right leg was left without cover. I tried wriggling my wrists and ankles free, swaying my hips to also get the skirt to cover my leg, but none of it amounted to anything.

All it did was give a new look of hunger to the monster's eyes as they swept up my body before meeting my gaze.

"Why what?" His words were clipped, but I could tell he was baiting me. That he was playing some kind of game.

"Why are you doing this to me?"

He stepped so close that it hurt my neck to look up at him, then bent his knees so he could whisper in my ear. "I was told you'd be a perfect companion for me." His breath was hot on my skin.

"What? By who?"

"The matriarch of your village. When the arrangements were made, I was told of your character." I'd been so stupid. Ms. Tomlin had played dumb. I'd already been arranged to be a sacrifice. "Thank you for coming to me." His finger traced my jawline. Even after capturing me and proving that he truly was the monster I'd thought he was, I couldn't help the involuntary heat that rushed up my legs. And for one brief second, I longed for those lips to once again find my skin. To linger and explore.

I turned away, refusing to look at him. Refusing to feel this way. I had to stay strong. "You're wrong. I'll be your greatest antagonist. I'm not a good companion for anyone, much less you."

He paused before grabbing my chin and forcing me to look at him. His green eyes bore into mine. "I'm never wrong."

I scowled and jerked from his grasp. "There's a first time for everything." A new look of excitement ignited in his eyes.

"Not today." He stroked up my throat with one finger, flicking it off at my chin, then took a step back. "Now, I have business to take care of, so you be a good girl and wait for my return or to be fetched by one of my servants."

Fury shot through me like gunfire. I tried lunging forward but was kept back by the vines. "You're vile. You're such a..." I gritted my teeth. No words would wound this man. This ghoul. I couldn't find a word strong enough to satisfy me, but there were a couple my mind kept gravitating to.

He leaned in closer. Something darkened in his eyes. "A what?" My heart sped. My eyes burned. The glare I shot at him would have killed anyone else, but he simply moved closer, challenging me as he said, "Say it."

"You're a sick bastard. A monster." A tear skated down my cheek; he swept it up with a finger and studied it as he rubbed it between his thumb and forefinger.

He swallowed, his Adam's apple bobbing as he continued to stare at his fingers. Then his eyes met mine. "You're as feisty as she said," he chuckled. "Anything else you care to say?"

"Many things."

After his eyes lingered on me for one more moment, he was gone. And I was left there, alone and confused.

And very, very afraid.

***

*Bratan*

*You're a sick bastard. A monster.*

My teeth clenched as I weaved between the trees. I gritted them the entire way to the village, my jaw tight and aching when I finally got there. I'd been told the maiden would be wild and that she wanted things a certain way, but the way she acted and what she called me...

I didn't care for it.

"Master," a female called out. Her long, earthen hair covered a spherical wooden head; it creaked as she bowed. Others behind her followed her lead. "Are we to believe you have found the maiden you've been searching for?"

I thought of the girl. *Leena.* I thought of the curves of her body and the violent ferocity in her eyes. I'd never seen anyone quite like her before.

"I found *a* maiden," I grumbled.

The female creature might have cracked a smile if she hadn't been so frightened.

"We should set up a bed for her, then. A nice warm meal, too." The creature glanced behind me. "Where is she, master?"

Chewing on the inside of my cheek, I tried formulating a response. "She's tied up at the moment. Make the preparations at once. And find Melora. I have questions for her." I started walking away, but the creature's voice made me stop. "But Your Majesty, you haven't even wooed her—"

"Quiet!" I spun around with a look so fierce that the leaves across the female's head shook uncontrollably. I bent down to look at her, but she didn't return my gaze. "I said, make the preparations at once. Is that clear? Or are you going to insult me further by questioning my orders?"

"No, Your Majesty. I'll tell the others."

I straightened. "Good." Heart racing, I spun back around, trying not to think about the words my subject had spoken, but it was impossible. I needed a companion. Not a captive.

The thought had already crossed my mind. I required the help of a maiden to keep the forest, and I'd been told it had all been arranged. I was supposed to find one centuries ago, but I didn't feel it necessary; I'd been told that we leshies—and many other deities—each had a mated soul in our world. I figured that one day I would find her, or she would find me, and that would be that. But centuries had gone by, and no one so much as tempted a second glance.

Until now.

I thought of Leena, the softness of her skin beneath my touch, those full lips, those fleshy hips. Love was the last thing on my mind, especially with a human, let alone one from a village so carelessly desecrating my home. But I couldn't help indulging in whatever this was. She was to be my companion, after all.

The male Leshy before my father had been wed for millennia, and the forest never had trouble. Things had been growing worse for a long time now. I needed help. It couldn't be any maiden; no matter how dire things got, I had to be choosy. The Leshy bride had to be someone I could form a strong alliance with. Someone who could do the job right. Despite my strong attraction to her, what made this girl worthy?

My bride would need to both tempt me and be my queen. I could have taken whomever I desired, but none had been suitable. But there was something promising about this girl. Despite only knowing her for a sliver of time, there was something about her I couldn't shake. She was strong, protective, and she'd been so eager...

The memory of her taste teased my lips, and I could still feel the warmth of her skin. The way her body felt beneath mine. My blood turned white-hot. Maybe I'd been too hasty tying her up. Maybe I should have wooed her as my subject suggested.

I winced. I'd never wooed a maiden before, but...I swept a hand through my hair. No. I couldn't risk it. Things were escalating with her village, and odd things were happening all throughout the woods. I needed a companion, but I had to be sure she wasn't a threat—that she was worthy of being in this realm with my people.

I didn't have a choice. At least, not for now.

# Chapter Eight

I TUGGED ON THE vines at my wrists, pulling them with every ounce of strength I had. I tried planting my feet, pulling from the depth of my strength, but it only caused me to trip because of my shackled ankles. And because I couldn't really fall, it just tightened my restraints further.

I threw my head back and screamed.

Crows cawed and fled from far-off branches, and something in the pond dipped beneath the surface. I took a deep breath, exhaling with a groan.

"How could I be so stupid?" I closed my eyes and felt the warm sun against my skin. At least the weather was nice. The Leshy probably had it all planned. The warm temperature, the soft whispers against my neck, the seduction.

The sensations of his lips on mine and his steady breaths against my neck were feelings I'd never be able to forget. I hated that I couldn't fight the longing I had for him or the heat that rose when I thought of his hands exploring my body. The gentle scrape of his teeth. The way my breath caught in my throat when I relived each second of it in my head.

I swallowed, steadying the rapid rising and falling of my chest as I tried focusing on the feel of the sun—on the comforting beams of light soaking into my every pore. When a small voice rose from the wind, I jumped. My eyes shot open.

A thin woman with a human-like figure but green skin and wooden eyes peered down at me. Her eyelashes were unusually long and as dark as her evergreen hair, which flowed down her back. When I didn't respond to whatever she'd said, she spoke again. "You must not have heard me. I said that I was sent to fetch you, my lady."

I didn't mean to stare, but the female was uncanny and beautiful. A living doll. There was still a slight possibility that I was dreaming.

The most unbelievable part of this wild dream was that I was falling for such an ass just because he stoked such an intense desire in me. Every time I thought about it, I was immobilized. The way Bratan had kissed me was too overwhelming to be peeled from my mind. I'd never been kissed like that before. The only times I'd been kissed had been in small, hurried pecks by a young man I once knew ten years ago. It was nothing like the way I'd been kissed by the Leshy. I didn't even know it could feel like that. That I could feel a thousand bursts of fire skating down my limbs, sending me somewhere far away.

"My lady?"

I snapped back to the physical world. "I'm sorry. What were we talking about?" She opened her mouth the moment I remembered. "Oh, right, we need to leave. Thank goodness. Let's go then." The woman nodded and bowed as she scuttled to my side. Slowly, she waved at each restraint without touching them, and they fell back into the soil.

The vines moved slowly, squirming like eels as they were swallowed into the earth. "Wow," I said, rubbing my wrists, though they were surprisingly not sore. "How did you do that?"

"Woodland magic, my lady. You'll have it too. Actually, a far more powerful magic will be bestowed upon you, from what I've been told."

I frowned. "How would I possess such a gift? I'm a human. Just a peasant from a small village. I'm nobody important."

"Nonsense," the woman cooed. "Now come along. We must get you ready." She nodded toward the way Bratan had left just a few minutes before and walked into the trees. With a deep, anxious breath, I followed.

I couldn't bring myself to ask the obvious question as we wove through the trees. Even when we entered the picturesque, albeit unsettling, village, I kept my mouth shut. There was a big part of me that didn't want to know.

The village was bustling with creatures of all shapes and sizes moving about in haste. Something important must have been going on. It was hard not to stare; I couldn't help watching in awe as they hurried along from hut to hut, gathering different materials, from chairs to leaf-wrapped gifts. I kept walking behind the woman who'd fetched me, scanning the crowd as I went. Until I saw him.

I couldn't help the sudden inhale of breath I took when I saw him. Just a few paces off, looming over a man with the same form and skin tone as the woman leading me through the village, was Bratan—the Keeper of the Wood. As if he could feel my gaze, he turned to look at me, his eyes piercing mine with an intensity that brought the heat back to my skin.

He lifted a hand to the male speaking to him, all the while keeping his eyes on me. I stood frozen in place, unable to look away as he approached, cursing myself for the excitement that fluttered through me. It was short-lived, though, because the incident of his betrayal was still fresh, and I was still beyond angry.

"How could you leave me tied up like that?" I spat, but his composure remained, though, for a fraction of a second, he winced.

"I did what I had to," he said. The words were calculated but strained. "Though I was told you humans liked that sort of thing."

My eyes bulged. "*What?*" I laughed in disbelief. A man behind the Leshy swiped a hand down his face with the shake of his head. I almost thought he'd say something. "You are so..." I groaned, still reeling from what he'd said.

"I don't have time for this," he said with a bored wave. "Nor do you. You need to get ready."

I couldn't take it anymore. I had to know what everyone was talking about. "Get ready for what?"

His eyebrows shot up. "You don't know?"

My heart somehow managed to race even faster. I didn't respond. Not even with a shake of my head. The world around me spun, and I didn't even know the answer yet.

His mouth curled into a wicked smile, and he approached me once more. When he got so close I could feel that familiar breath against the tip of my nose, he leaned forward. His lips pressed on the space behind my ear, and I had to resist the urge to close my eyes and see what would happen if I collapsed into him.

I was torn between kissing him and slapping him in the face. Depending on his answer, I was inclined to do the latter.

Finally, the rumble of his voice sounded in my ear. "Our wedding ceremony."

The words made my heart stop. My stomach sank.

"What?" I could hardly say it.

He chuckled into my hair, smelling it and kissing it as it flowed between his fingers. "You are going to be my bride."

My blood boiled, and this time, it wasn't from anything pleasant. "You're vile. You're despicable. You're—" He placed a finger on my lips and leaned in.

"Let's get through the ceremony first, shall we?" His voice was a low purr. "I'd rather you save that fire for tonight." He winked and turned around.

A low growl crawled up my throat, and before I could think better of it, I stepped right up to him and slapped him across the face.

The creatures around us gasped. I nearly did, too. This man was powerful. He wasn't human. What possessed me to slap him?

The village around us was so still I could hear every sound that rattled from the forest. Even Bratan didn't move or speak until he lifted his hand to the side of his face, staring at me with wide eyes. "You really are strange, aren't you?" There was no hint of anger in the words. He almost sounded impressed.

I waited there with bated breath, as I'm sure the villagers were, too. Bratan's hand dropped to his side. He continued to stare at me, looking me up and down.

"Get ready. We will be wed in one hour's time." With that, he was gone.

No one else could move, least of all me. Everything Ms. Tomlin had said was veiled in lies. I had no autonomy—no choice in the matter. If I wanted to keep my village's end of the bargain and keep them safe, I had to go along with this. I had to get married to the Leshy.

\*\*\*

*Bratan*

"You really tied her up?" Damir asked as we headed to the house. The half-elf, half-fae male was the only being in the world I trusted. He was my oldest friend; we'd grown up together, though most of the villagers didn't know it. I thought it was best to keep that particular piece of information to only those who needed to know.

My friend had bronze skin and thick black hair that stopped just above his pointed ears. His eyes were dark and shaped like the blade he kept strapped to his back. He was the kind of friend anyone would want by their side, and I was lucky to have him as my servant, though I didn't see him as one.

"What about it? It's what we do with all trespassers until we know they're safe." I opened the door to the home I'd be sharing with Leena and trudged up the stairs. "Plus, Melora said human women like that sort of thing."

Damir cast me an annoyed glance. "Do you really think Melora knows what human women like? And this girl isn't a trespasser; you're to wed her. A deal was struck. We were expecting her."

"So? That doesn't mean she isn't dangerous." I threw off my shirt and opened the wardrobe, looking for a decent ensemble to wear beneath my wedding robe. "You saw how she slapped me. She isn't afraid of me."

"And that means something's wrong with her?"

"It means she's suspicious." I took out a few pairs of trousers and some tunics until I found a couple that seemed suitable.

"We don't know anything about her. Just because she's human doesn't mean she's dangerous."

"I suppose Melora *is* the one who arranged this," I muttered. "She has her issues, but she's been around longer than any of us."

"I'm not convinced that crone can be trusted."

I closed the wardrobe doors and shot him a look. "If you don't trust Melora, how can you trust the maiden?"

He leaned against the wardrobe door beside me. "I guess she did hold up her end of the bargain." He sighed. "That must mean something."

I stared at the fabric in my hands, trying to allow Damir's words to convince me, but I couldn't stop thinking of the woman and children I'd rescued and of the bruises littering their arms and backs. Humans were brutal. "None of us know her true character. Not even Melora. Regardless of her being my bride, Leena is still human. Until we know she's safe, we can't take any chances."

"Bratan, come on. If you wed her, you have to trust her."

"So, what, I have to give her free rein around here and let her traverse around both realms? She could be plotting something with her people."

Damir placed a hand on my shoulder. "No, I just don't think you should tie her up." He clapped me on the back and handed me a cloak. "You're not a charmer, my friend. Either wed her and trust her and treat her like our own or send her back."

"I am *not* sending her back." The ferocity of my words surprised even me. The pull I had toward this human wasn't normal. Touching her, kissing her, whispering in her air, caressing her skin—all of it came naturally. I couldn't stop thinking about her. Sending her back wasn't an option. "I guess she doesn't seem dangerous..." I mumbled. Damir laughed.

"There you go. Trust her and don't do anything stupid, or she may go back to her old village on her own."

I frowned. "She'd leave? But we're to be wed. It's why she came to me."

"Then you better stop being an ass." Damir handed me my cloak and wedding robe. "Now, let's get you ready. We'll work on your people skills later."

# Chapter Nine

"You look lovely already, My Lady," the woman who'd freed me and whom I now knew as Theodora said as she continued lacing up the corset, squeezing my waist. I stared at my reflection in the mirror, not completely present. My body was in this new realm, but my mind was elsewhere. I barely registered that I was the one staring back from the other side of the glass—the pale maiden whose hair was getting pinned into intricate ringlets atop her head while simultaneously being dressed in a black-and-green gown of fine silks and golden accented leaves. The mirror was an oval portal to another existence, or maybe just one welcoming me to this strange new world.

The intricate wooden patterns surrounding the glass held me in place as everything finally sunk in. In the small dressing room within the hollowed quarters of a large pine tree was the first step into my new life as the bride of the Leshy—the creature in charge of the life and well-being of the forest.

The strings on the outer corset and bodice of my dress tightened against my ribcage, and I was reminded of those vines on my wrists and ankles. Would I be a slave? Would my sole purpose be to let him use me as he saw fit? I shuddered at the thought.

My mind drifted back to when I'd slapped him—those striking eyes blinking down at me, wide and impressed, and his broad, looming figure towering over me.

Frustratingly, I thought of his lips again and how they knew exactly where to go to make my mind go numb.

*I'd rather you save that fire for tonight.*

My face burned. I couldn't think about what tonight might entail and whether or not I'd have a say in anything that transpired. If his kissing and soft caresses were any indication of his lovemaking, it may not be so bad...

I couldn't meet my own gaze in the mirror.

"Lift your arms, My Lady," Theodora chirped, and I did as I was told, soon being covered by another layer of dark green, and then a matching veil was placed upon my head. After two golden leaves were tucked behind each of my ears, Theodora and the small female who'd still not told me her name held out a hand to help me off the stump in the middle of the hollowed tree.

"You look absolutely breathtaking. Doesn't she, Ani?"

I peered surreptitiously at the female to my left. Ani. A fae-like creature half the size of Theodora but larger than the pixies fluttering around the realm in various colors of pastels.

She had cropped black hair and sad, drooping eyes. Her lips were a tiny bow in the middle of her blue face. Her skin was the shade of an icy lake, but her eyes were as dark as the depths of the ocean floor. At first glance, it looked like she had no eyes at all. Somehow, the look worked for her, though there was something unsettling about her countenance. I tried not to think too deeply about it. I was hardly in a place to judge anyone or think clearly.

"I suppose," Ani sighed.

Theodora cast a disapproving look at her companion, then turned to me and took my hands in hers. "Come. I'm sure His Majesty is waiting for you. He's awfully excited about this."

I swallowed a snort. *I'm sure he is.*

"Melora will be excited, too," Ani grumbled. "Their little plan will finally come to fruition." She shot me a glare. "As long as this human isn't completely useless."

My stomach dropped. "What plan?" I turned to Theodora, whose eyes were wide with what appeared to be both shock and rage as she stared Ani down. "Theodora?"

"Don't talk about this maiden like that, Ani," she hissed, her voice low as if she'd get scolded if someone heard. "You know she is to be our queen."

"She will never be my queen," Ani scoffed.

"She sure will, and do you really want to be on the receiving end of His Majesty's wrath when he finds out you insulted his bride *and* were spreading rumors before his wedding?"

"It's not a rumor, and you know it."

"Hush!" Theodora said, then turned to me with a forced smile. "Come, My Lady. I will show you to the willows where you will be crowned our queen."

I wished I could speak, but my voice had abandoned me. Too many questions were warring in my mind. Slowly, my body went numb. Theodora draped the veil over my face and guided me out of the hollow tree.

I floated along, unable to see anything as Theodora shuffled me to my fate. I stumbled on rocks and almost fell on my face a number of times, and the corset made it hard to breathe. Worst of all, I couldn't get Ani's words out of my head. This was the second time I'd heard the name Melora, but it was the first I'd heard of a plan. Did Bratan have more up his sleeve?

Light warmed the top of my head, beating through my veil until, finally, I could see through the gossamer fabric. "Are you ready, My Lady?" Theodora asked when we approached a similar curtain of vines as the one Bratan and I had walked through.

*As ready as I'll ever be* was what I wanted to say, but I opted for a polite nod instead. This woman was the only one here who'd been nice to me, at least without a jagged edge. Of course, I knew that nice people weren't always *good* people, so I couldn't trust her yet, but I at least needed to be nice to her. She was the only person close to a friend I had, and I needed someone on my side.

Theodora swept her hand along the curtain of green and revealed a scene I had a hard time comprehending. Sparks of fireflies buzzed around the darkened sky and moonlit ceremony like dancing stars ready to lead me into my new life.

To lead me to him.

I looked up at the sky and wondered what magic could make the moon feel like the sun, because it was indeed the moon that had warmed my head and cast beams against the trees to guide us here. I scanned the small clearing, passing various fairies and woodland creatures seated in neat rows of wooden stumps fashioned into chairs. Sprouting from the backs of the stumps were intricate patterns of woven branches adorned with cherry blossoms, whose petals slowly drifted into the wind and then re-grew in place.

At the front of the clearing was an arch of the same intricately woven wood with matching cherry blossoms, but it was adorned with a variety of other flowers as well, sitting like jewels encrusted overhead. The most striking were the blood-red roses and the occasional black one, outlined with matching rubies and onyx.

The only thing missing from the grand display was the groom.

Fireflies gathered and illuminated the path stretching from me to the arch. It was awkward walking down the path of fallen cherry blossoms with no one at the end of it, and the only music playing was the chirps of birds nestling into their beds for the night. I kept walking in awkward, near-silence, staring straight ahead. There wasn't even a priest at the end of the walkway, though such a thing was probably unnecessary when wedding a deity. But I did need a groom.

Unease twisted my gut. I'd only known about the Leshy for a short time, but what I did know was that his absence could mean something malevolent—something that would make my life even more of a mess. I cringed at the endless possibilities. As the unease spread, each of my footsteps was heavier than the last. The sensation felt so physical that I had to look down to make sure I wasn't treading through mud.

I was almost to the end of the aisle, naively hoping he'd changed his mind, when a gust of wind rushed through the clearing, spinning cherry blossom petals into a whirlwind and shaking the flowers along the wooden arch. As if summoned by my thoughts, there he was. Standing in a finely crafted suit, double-breasted with long sleeves and buttoned cuffs, with a thick, regal black cape thrown over it all. The sight of him sent a warm shiver across my skin, and the tightness in my stomach eased. His intricate attire was impressive, and I found myself inspecting it before reaching him. When I did, his floor-length cape fluttered by his feet like a train moving with the wind. I couldn't help noticing the way it also swept through his dark hair, which was styled in neat, shining waves and tucked behind his ears. His back was rigid, but his face was soft. He offered me his hand with a smile that made my insides liquid.

Theodora nudged me forward as I momentarily forgot how to move. There was something about him that sucked me in and immobilized me. Something that made me want far more than I was comfortable admitting. I couldn't let him notice the redness inevitably creeping up my face. "Do you always make such a dramatic entrance?"

His smile widened, and he grabbed a loose curl atop my head, pulling it softly as he glanced down at me. "Only when such a beautiful bride awaits me."

I rolled my eyes, trying to formulate a snarky response, but a shimmer of dust fell from the sky, and harps began to sing. The colorful powder fell like shooting stars, twinkling against the harps' strings and the gentle whistles of the accompanying flutes. It was like magic captured in a bottle, shaken to brilliance. A wedding present just for me.

I looked back at Bratan and at his hand once again outstretched instead of playing with my hair.

"Come, little dove, our new life awaits."

The words carved into my chest. *Our new life.*

Thoughts and memories of my old life shuffled through my mind like playing cards. I didn't have much in Woodsmeadow and hadn't known happiness for years, but being married to a monster had to be worse.

I had no choice, though, not one I was satisfied with anyway. If I wanted my grandmother to have that better life I so desperately wanted her to have—one free of starvation and abuse—this was the only way to do it. And if I wanted to stop the torment of my people, I needed to take this crucial step.

"Will the bride and groom please step forward?" a creature resembling a mole said as it stood at the end of the aisle. It looked disturbingly human, like an old man with small spectacles and a worn-out suit. A minute ticked by and then another. I couldn't move. When another went by, the mole officiant cleared his throat and repeated, "Will the bride and groom please step forward?" Bride. I was the bride. Still frozen in place, I couldn't even beg my legs to move.

After another long moment, Bratan grabbed my hand, placed it on his large bicep, and ushered me to the center of the odd stage before the human-like mole. I would have been irritated at his forcing me forward, but I was caught in a daze from the impossibility of everything around me, still unconvinced I wasn't dreaming.

The mole priest uttered a long string of words in a language I didn't understand, but even if he'd been speaking my native tongue, he was going too quickly, and my mind was too foggy for me to comprehend any of it. Until I swore I heard the word "eternity" and then "immortal". I blanched, suddenly reminded of all those fairytales and stories I'd heard of beasts, demons, and deities. I would be bound to him for eternity. Of course I would. What was I expecting? To go home?

At some point, my brain stopped trying to wrap itself around what was going on or what would come. It was hard enough to keep my eyes away from my groom, but when those dreaded words came, I had no choice. "You may kiss the bride."

My heart pounded as my eyes flicked to Bratan's. Without hesitation, he grabbed me by the nape of my neck and kissed me, one large hand sliding down my back. He pressed me against him, and my breath went ragged, my blood warm. I shouldn't enjoy this. I really shouldn't enjoy this.

But I did, and I felt guilty that it didn't feel wrong.

This was my life now, though. I might as well enjoy it.

My fingers moved up his chest, linking behind his neck as I kissed him back. He tasted like sunlight and morning dew and something so primally male, matching his scent, that it sent me into a ravenous flurry. I clutched his shoulders, kissing him more deeply. His hands roamed my body, his fingers finding my thigh beneath the layers of fabric. The sudden heat that shot through me pulled a gasp from my throat, forcing me out of his spell. Remembering we were in front of a crowd of our subjects, I looked out in bashful horror, but no one was there. Not even the mole.

Bratan tilted my chin until I faced him, and he kissed me again.

This time, I pushed away. "No. You're a monster. I can't—"

"You're my wife now, Leena. And the ceremony isn't over."

"What's that supposed to mean?"

His mouth pursed like he was trying not to laugh. "It's not what you're thinking. It's for your reign."

I lifted a brow, surreptitiously trying to cool myself down. "What about my reign?"

"Come. We scared off the officiant before the most important part." He grabbed my hand and pulled me into a portal between vines and trees. "You'll be filled with powers beyond your comprehension," he said, leading me through the thickness of the forest.

"What?" I jumped over a rock before tripping over another and tried to keep up.

"You are the wife of the Leshy. You have duties to perform."

I dug my heels into the dirt and slid my hand from his grasp. "Don't I get a say in this?"

"You've already had your say. You've given yourself to me." He turned around and grabbed my wrists, getting far too close. "I told you before. You belong to me." He might have been scowling with fire in his eyes, but I shot him a glare fierce enough to burn down the woods with him in it.

"I may have wed you, but I have not given myself to you." I ripped my wrists away and eyed him up and down with disdain. "Nor will I." I expected him to bite back, but he didn't, and I couldn't tell what he was thinking. He stared me down in what looked like puzzled awe.

"Is that so?" The impish grin he gave me spoke of what I already knew: that I was doing a poor job at keeping my desires for him at bay.

"Yes," I said, but his grin didn't move, and I hated how immature I probably looked with my chin up in the air. "You and I will be cordial companions, but I like my independence." I tried not to let the fear creeping up my spine stop me from speaking my mind. I wanted to feel out his expectations and see his reactions. I needed to understand the way his mind worked.

"Well, you still need your powers. Let's hurry. That damned mole is hard to track down, and I want to get this over with."

I barked out an appalled laugh. "You want to get this over with? What about me?"

He didn't look at me. "Why don't you talk to me after you get your powers? Then tell me what you do or don't want." I narrowed my eyes, but I was glad that he wasn't biting back as hard as I'd thought he would. Was he not taking me seriously, or was he as apathetic of our union as I was? Other than the obvious physical temptations...

I needed to stay strong and show him he would never fully have me. We may be wed, but I would never be his. Not fully, not truly.

"Fine," I grumbled, which appeased him enough for him to grab my hand and continue forward. There was so much unknown in my future, but for now, I let him drag me along to find that blasted mole and to find out what lay in store for me in this odd life I would share with the monster of the woods.

# CHAPTER TEN

I COULD BARELY FEEL my feet as Bratan led me deeper into the woods. A dark chill tumbled down my back at the disconcerting shift in the realm. With each turn, the trees grew more warped. Less natural. Something sinister out of a storybook. Branches reached out to me like claws. I swore they moved as if to rip me apart and taste the blood of their new queen.

"There he is," Bratan grumbled, pulling me forward and sending me stumbling toward the shivering mole. I glared at him, to which he muttered, "My apologies." I couldn't tell if he was being sarcastic or not, but it didn't really matter. His eyes fell to the creature behind me. "You fled before the most important part, mole." The creature bowed, still shivering.

"I'm sorry, Your Majesty. It appeared you wanted a moment alone with your bride."

*Bride.* My fists clenched at the word, but my stomach leapt. I grumbled at my body once again betraying me.

Bratan grabbed the mole by the shoulders. "Did I ask for a moment alone with my bride?"

The creature frantically shook its head. "No, Your Majesty."

He tossed it back onto its feet. "Then finish what you started so we can be done with it."

"Yes, Your Majesty." Without skipping a beat, the mole cleared its throat and looked between us. "Step forward, My Lady."

I did as I was told, trying my best to hide the wringing of my hands as I made my way to the creature. It then looked at the Leshy. "Now you, Your Majesty."

Bratan stepped forward, his eyes still shooting daggers at the officiant. "Why are you not calling my bride by her proper title?"

The mole's black eyes blinked. I was just as dumbfounded.

"Is she not 'My Lady'?"

Bratan hovered over the creature. "She is your queen. You will address her as such."

My heart flipped, and I had to look away to hide the color rising in my cheeks.

"Y-Your Majesty?" the mole asked, peering over at me; it was still peculiar to see it standing there, looking straight at me and speaking.

"That's correct," Bratan said, straightening. "Now proceed."

The mole quickly continued. "Your Majesty, take your king's hands."

I chewed on the inside of my cheek. He was *not* my king. Begrudgingly, I turned to face him, unimpressed and annoyed at the smirk plastered on his face. He extended his hands, and when my eyes flickered to them, I suddenly remembered the rush of blood at their touch just minutes ago. Why did I succumb to him so easily? What was wrong with me?

Something in the woods must be influencing me, making me act out of character because wanting a beast such as him was never something I'd want of my own volition. I slapped my hands in his, half-expecting his eyebrow to twitch, but he slowly closed his fingers around mine, warm and steady, and that blasted heat buzzed through me again.

I glared harder.

"Repeat these words," the mole said, "and keep your eyes on each other." Bratan's face turned serious, which made me nervous. My heart raced as the mole rattled off a series of words. "I am now one with these hands."

Silence.

The officiant cleared its throat and repeated, "I am now one with these hands."

More silence.

"Leena," Bratan grumbled. "Repeat the words."

I narrowed my eyes at him and mumbled through gritted teeth. "I am now one with these hands."

Bratan winked. I scoffed and looked away. "Return your eyes to your husband, Your Majesty," the creature said. I rolled my eyes over to the Leshy, trying my best to ignore his smug expression. "To tend the trees."

"To tend the trees," I mumbled.

"And everything within them."

Bratan's eyes softened, which teased something in my senses. "And everything within him," I repeated.

"*Them*, Your Majesty. And everything within *them*."

My face burned. "O-of course. And everything within them." I hated that I had to keep my eyes on Bratan's. What I would give to sink into the dirt right now.

"And he and I will be one."

The warmth on my face spread down my neck. "And he and I will be one."

Bratan's expression was no longer smug. The intensity of his gaze peeled back the layers of a shield and made it impossible to stand without trembling. I was twenty-six years old; I knew myself, but something about this man made my body foreign to me. From the moment I saw him, every part of me had been at war with itself. Even now, my stomach was twisting, and my chest ached.

"Now you, Your Majesty." The mole turned to Bratan. "She and I are one."

His eyes stayed on mine. "She and I are one." His deep voice rumbled in my ears, falling through them like silk.

"I will stand beside her."

Bratan's voice was soft as he repeated, "I will stand beside her."

"And protect her."

The sounds of the forest faded away. All I could hear was the rich cadence of his voice. "And protect her."

I swallowed, still unable to look away.

"No one will break this bond," the mole recited.

Bratan's head shook ever so slightly as he repeated the words, his soothing voice untangling the knots in my stomach. "No one will break this bond." It was nearly a whisper, and as if he knew what the mole would say next, he finished his vows: "And I will bestow power upon her and connect us as one."

Something buzzed in my hands, but my eyes stayed locked on his. Neither one of us looked away, even as the mole said, "This vow to be one is complete with a kiss." The wind whipped around us, sending curls loose from the pins atop my head, and then Bratan took my face in his hands and kissed me. Gently. Carefully. Before pain rattled me to the core.

Flames tore through me. I screamed as it spread, shooting light from my fingers, the tips burning like I'd just touched a hot iron. I fell to my knees as the fire raged. It felt like the flesh was being shredded off my bones. Sweat ran down my face in sheets, mingling with the tears sliding around my still-screaming mouth.

I could barely make out Bratan's muffled voice. "What's happening?!"

The question was frantic, but the mole calmly replied, "She's receiving her powers, Your Majesty."

Bratan asked something else, but I couldn't hear it. My ears were filled with invisible cotton. My body fell hard to the ground. The burning sensation oozed from my fingertips and branched through my legs. I screamed until my voice was hoarse.

The pain only grew. I no longer had any control over my body; it writhed on the cold, hard forest floor in involuntary spasms. A final rush of incomprehensible pain shot through me. My back arched, my body convulsed, and the back of my head slammed into the earth.

Then silence took over.

And quiet darkness as cool as night.

***

The first thing I noticed when I finally came to was the splitting headache cracking my skull. My temple throbbed, and it took way too long for my hand to reach it. My arms were sorer than they'd been when Vasska started working me to the bone after my parents died. That week was brutal, as if losing my parents hadn't been hard enough.

Dropping my arm, I looked around, blinking until my vision was clear enough to take in my surroundings. I didn't recognize this place. Beneath me was a soft bed of curated grass, with violet and pearl flowers blooming all around it. The trees were close enough to offer shade but far enough away that I could see everything in the small clearing, including the dark-haired man lazily sitting with his back against a log, sharpening what looked like a scythe with a long, silver blade.

I winced as I rose to my elbows. The movement must have caught the Leshy's attention because he was at my side before I could take another breath. "Are you all right?" He gently grabbed hold of my forearms and helped me into a sitting position. His fingers brushed the hair from my face. "Your head hurts." It was a statement. Not a question.

"How did you know?" My voice was still hoarse, and I wondered how long I'd been screaming.

"I can feel it."

I frowned, confused, and opened my mouth to ask about it, but he was already closing his eyes and placing his fingers on my head.

"What are you d—"

"Shh! I'm trying to concentrate."

I looked at him flatly but resigned to whatever he was doing to me. I didn't have the energy for banter right now. After only a matter of seconds, warmth pooled through my skull and healed my headache. I looked up at him, confused, but his eyes remained closed as he laid me back on the grass. His large hands swept down my limbs, skating down my arms and falling to my ankles. With each stroke, the pain lessened, except in my legs.

"Your dress is too thick," he said, finally opening his eyes. He moved to hover over me, examining me and gently moving my face and neck to inspect every muscle. I was about to ask him another question when he slid to my feet. "I need to take off your dress."

I bolted upright, my muscles surprisingly relaxed. "Absolutely not!"

There was no lust in his eyes. Just irritation. "Your legs will be useless for days if I don't help you. Maybe longer."

"If I have my own powers, why can't I help myself?" I knew it was a stupid question, but I couldn't let him take off my dress. The thought of him undressing me...

My body ached, and I had to shake my head to snap myself out of it—to continue to object. "You can't—"

"We're one now, remember? I have to help you." He glared at me. "Stop being stubborn and let me do this."

"What if I say no?"

He sat back and scoffed. "Then you can suit yourself and lie here useless until the pain wears off. But I won't bring you any food or drink, so I don't know how long you'll last."

I glowered at him before looking down at my wedding dress, following the vines of embroidery crawling down the skirt. "Fine. Good luck taking this thing off, though. It required more than one person to fit me into it. I don't think you'll be able to take it off on your own."

"I assure you I won't have any trouble."

My eyes made the mistake of meeting his and seeing a glint in them that set fire to my blood. "Tch." I crossed my arms and lay back. "Good luck," I grumbled, and before I could prepare myself, he was hovering over me again.

"You want to be lying down for this?" he asked, an impish gleam in his eyes. I scowled at him and slid backward until I was sitting up again.

"No!"

He chuckled and moved behind me. "Wow, you weren't kidding. It's a maze back here." His fingers found the lace of my outer corset. I had to force my eyes to stay open—to force defiance and resist these maddening urges that kept intruding on my good sense.

The lace whipped free of its first loop. Both the sound and feel of it made me jump. Something fluttered in my stomach. His breath was warm against my neck as he leaned in. "Are you okay, my queen?"

That familiar heat continued to spread, now rushing down my torso and filling my legs.

"Of course," I whispered, immediately clearing my throat. He chuckled and leaned back, continuing to pull the lace free. I had to concede that I wanted him. I had to admit it so I could be strong against it.

*I want him, but he won't get me. I won't let him.*

I sat as still and platonic as I reasonably could while my corset loosened, doing everything I could not to let myself go and do whatever my body wanted to do with his. Then, at last, the corset cracked open from the back, and he whipped it off, which only made everything worse. He turned me around with no effort at all, and to my surprise, the slightest tinge of pink was dusted across his cheeks.

I wanted to tease him about it, but I didn't dare to. Plus, all my energy was being spent keeping my own desires at bay. If I acknowledged his, and he decided to act, then what? I would be putty in his large, stupidly attractive hands.

Since when did I find hands attractive? I didn't know if I wanted to scream in frustration or indulge in the desire to watch his fingers work as he pulled the string of my bodice free. They were so masculine. So much different than my dainty ones. His knuckles grazed the top of my breasts, and I shot back. "You don't need to take off my top! Just focus on the bottom half. The outer corset is off, so you can...you can just lift my dress." I couldn't look at him. My whole body was aflame.

He sighed. "Pity. I was so looking forward to looking at your breasts."

I gasped and burned at his statement. "What? I-I—How dare you!"

He chuckled softly and stroked a finger down the side of my face. "You'll want me soon, little dove. You're mine, remember?" He leaned forward, grasped my hips, and pulled me onto his lap. His face was so close our noses almost touched, and his breath brushed against my teeth. "We are one in soul and purpose now." His voice was low, husky. "Aren't you looking forward to being one physically as well?"

My heart pounded, and I knew he could feel it against his chest. I was pressed so tightly against him I yearned to follow his lead and go wherever his hands took me.

Instead, I managed to swallow and shake my head. "N-no, I'm not."

His lips curled into a wicked smile. "You're not curious?"

"No." The word was an unconvincing whisper.

He leaned back, slowly pushing me onto the grass. "You'll change your mind." He winked, and I growled in irritation, which he ignored as he crawled down to my feet. "I want you to want me."

My stomach flipped, but I stayed flat on the grass, waiting for him to heal my legs so we could move on, and I could be as far from him as possible. For as long as I could, anyway.

"Because when you finally admit it to yourself, and we become one, I know we'll set this world on fire in a way nothing else has before."

I couldn't resist the small sound that escaped my lips. I finally let my eyes flutter closed for a moment before composing myself and getting up on my elbows. "We'll see about that." I forced a glare, which made him chuckle.

His hands fell to my ankles and started trailing up my legs. "Tell me when to stop."

# Chapter Eleven

## Leena

**M**Y FACE BLAZED AS his fingers grazed my thighs. I gave him a quick nod, and I swore I saw the flicker of a smile before his hands roamed higher. Was this proper? I'd never let a man touch me like this before. *He is my husband,* I thought, *and as for being a man...*

I focused on the dark hair spilling onto his face as his eyes closed and something warm radiated from his fingertips. I found my own eyelids closing as I lay back in the grass. My dress went higher, and I sucked in a shivering breath, but as soon as excitement pulsed through my veins, my dress lowered back to my ankles.

"There. You should be able to move without issue now," he said, getting to his feet. My eyes followed him, catching on his muscles as he rolled up his sleeves. The fire raging in my core was less than ideal, and despite wanting to look away, I had no choice when he bent down and offered me his hand.

"Where are we going?" I asked.

"Don't you want me to show you around your new king-dom?"

I crossed my arms and looked away. "No. I'd rather be alone." My heart raced. I didn't want anything to do with this man right now—or whatever he technically was. I didn't like how he made me feel and how I felt such little control around him. It was unsettling.

My fingers curled over my biceps. I didn't know what it was that he made me feel, but I wanted it to stop. I had to gain control of my mind—of my body—or this would all go up in smoke. My plan to save my people...to save Grandmother...

The Leshy's fingers slid up the slope of my neck. "What are you thinking, little dove?"

"Nothing that concerns you."

"I find that very hard to believe."

I scoffed. "Why? Because you're so thrilling that my mind could only possibly be consumed with thoughts of you?"

He let go of my face and smiled. "You said it. Not me." I let out a low growl, and he continued. "But that isn't why. You just went through quite the ordeal, and we're married now. Today has been a whirlwind, has it not?"

I studied his expression. "What of it?"

"How could you be thinking of anything else?"

It strained me not to roll my eyes, but I was acutely aware of how dangerous this man was. Of course, what he was saying was true, but I didn't want him to know that. "I'm tired. It's been a long day, as you said." I looked up, noticing the darkened sky for the first time—a sheet of black buttoned by stars. I'd never seen the night sky so clear; it would have been beautiful had my circumstances not been so bleak. The cold wind also nipped at my fingers with an added sharpness that only came with twilight, and I had to shove them beneath my arms to stop them from shivering. The sun must have fallen hours ago. "How long was I asleep?"

"Not long, but if it's a bed you're after, you could have just asked." My eyebrow twitched, but once again, my face burned until it was a mask against the chilly wind. Not again. He couldn't see me like this. I tried stepping away, but he caught me by the wrist. I lifted my other hand to slap him, but he easily stopped it. A chuckle rolled from his throat. "I married a feisty one."

I yanked both wrists free with a growl. "You're vile. Do you know that?"

"Because I want to be with my wife?"

"Stop calling me that!"

"You *are* my wife, aren't you?"

Silence filled the air. The birds were asleep, and oddly, no owls made themselves known. All I could hear was the breathing that filled the small space between us—his breath mingling with my mind, brushing against my lips. When did he get so close?

"I'm going to bed." I started to turn when his low chuckling stopped me. "What are you laughing about now?"

He spun me around and trailed a finger along my jawline. "I like the way you say what you want, Leena."

My fists tightened at my sides despite the thrill buzzing through me. "I don't want company," I hissed. "I want to sleep alone. Get that through your thick skull, will you?"

He grabbed my face with one hand. It was so large he could hold so much of it with just his palm, his long fingers curling over my jaw and against my cheeks. He loosened his grip and then gently grabbed a loose strand of my hair. "There are so many things I want to do to you." The words were both a purr and a threat.

I scowled at him again, pushing down the other feelings brewing below the surface. "Good luck trying because I want nothing to do with you."

"Is that so?" He eyed me carefully, dragging his gaze slowly over my body and then scanning my eyes as if peering into my mind to detect any lies. One side of his mouth turned up. "I think you want everything to do with me."

My heart raced. "I..." He inched closer, and panic lit within me like a torch. I pulled my face from his grasp. "Think what you want, but you're wrong." He took a step closer, and I spat at him, but he dodged it before it could land on his boots.

"What a bolt of lightning you are." He stepped forward and stroked the side of my face. "How lucky I am to be tied to such fire." I shot him one last glare before turning on my heel and heading into the woods. "Where are you going?"

"I'm finding a bed."

"You don't know your way around these woods." His voice was suddenly not trimmed with sarcasm or some form of teasing, and I briefly wondered if that should make me worried about wandering the woods alone. But then I remembered the pain that had wreaked havoc on my body and what the Leshy had said about giving me powers before I felt them flood me. Bratan wasn't the only one with powers anymore, and the creatures of the forest were my subjects, too. I should be able to do everything and anything on my own from here on out.

"I'll find my way," I said, and I heard him let out a sigh as I walked away, accompanied by the crinkle of footsteps upon the thick grass below. "Don't follow me," I said without turning around.

"You do what you want, and I'll do what I want."

I groaned and picked up the pace. "I can't do what I want if you're anywhere near me."

"Don't you want me to show you where you can find a bed?"

"I'm not falling for any of your tricks."

A rush of wind caressed the nape of my neck. It was so shocking and sudden and oddly pleasant that it caught me off guard and allowed Bratan to take me by the shoulders and spin me around. "I wouldn't dare trick you." His eyes were unreadable, but the one thing I knew about him was that he couldn't be trusted.

"Somehow, I doubt that."

The mischievous glint in his eyes dimmed, replaced with something more serious. "You know I would never touch you against your will. Don't you?" I paused, studying him and chewing on any words I could think of. "You saw me ask your permission before healing you. Surely, you know I could have done whatever I wanted. And while you were asleep—"

I pulled away again. "It doesn't make you a gentleman just because you resisted laying a finger on an unconscious woman."

"There was no temptation," he said, irritation clear in his voice. "But you don't seem the type to believe what people tell you."

"Not when it comes from a monster who would kill my people and leave me for dead." His head jerked back, and my stomach sunk at his wounded expression. If I didn't know any better, I would think there was sorrow somewhere in his eyes.

I waited for him to speak, and when he didn't, anxiety gnawed at me enough to quickly break the silence. "What? No coy remark?"

His eyebrows fell on his glaring eyes. His jaw clenched. "You can find your way back on your own." My mouth opened in surprise, but before I could think of what to say, he was gone. And I had no idea what to do or where to go. Or what had just happened.

# Chapter Twelve

I walked through the woods until a cluster of cottages spilled color through the trees, revealing a hidden edge of town I hadn't seen upon my arrival. It should have been relieving, but I couldn't stop thinking about Bratan. I really didn't want to, but I couldn't help it. I tried not to let it bother me that I'd somehow wounded my new partner because even though he was a vile monster, I was not. Guilt was a natural, human response that he seemed incapable of feeling, but I felt it, regardless of whether or not he deserved it.

The stretch of cottages looked like a cluster of pastel candies; there were so many of them, but there was no one in sight. I was starting to lose hope when I spotted a female fae with light blue skin stoking a fire beside one of the houses.

"Excuse me?" I said.

The fae turned. Her lashes were a dark green that matched the irises in her otherwise black eyes. Her hair was the same deep blue hue of her skin, save for the yellow smattering of freckles across the bridge of her nose.

She gasped, dropping the metal object in her small hand before bowing and falling to her knees. "Your Majesty. I apologize for not addressing you sooner. I didn't see you there."

The display was disconcerting. I wasn't any more special than anyone else, and I firmly believed that no one deserved to be waited upon by any other being, no matter who they were or who they were married to.

"It's all right. There's no need to bow."

The female didn't budge from her lowered stance. "I am beneath you, Your Majesty. I will serve you and accept any punishment you see fit."

"Punishment? There's no need for punishment, and please, you don't need to bow."

"I must—"

"I command you not to." I felt a twinge of guilt saying it, but I was hoping my "command" was used in a way that justified it. Hesitantly, the woman straightened, still bowing. "What's your name?"

She tentatively met my gaze. "Judith."

"It's nice to meet you, Judith." I smiled, but she didn't return it with one of her own. She simply bowed her head again. When she remained silent, I continued. "Do you, by chance, know where I'm staying tonight?"

This caught Judith's attention. "The home you share with His Majesty, my queen."

I tried not to grimace. I was afraid of that. The last thing I wanted was to deal with Bratan again tonight. "Could you take me there?" I continued smiling, pushing out the thoughts of my new groom. Whatever palace I'd be sharing with him should be large enough for me to easily avoid him, so long as I didn't have to share a room with him.

"Of course, Your Majesty." Judith dipped her head again and started into the woods. I followed, torn between wanting to see Bratan to push through the awkwardness and wanting to never see him again. I was so wrapped up in my thoughts that I accidentally bumped into the fae when she came to a halt. It seemed like only seconds—maybe a minute or two—since we'd left, but when I looked around, there was a two-story building behind her.

It wasn't huge, but it was bigger than any of the other homes in this realm or any cottages I was used to seeing. It was surrounded by trees, tucked away like a hidden fortress, though there weren't any guards or butlers. Surely, this wasn't the palace I was sharing with Bratan. It couldn't be.

"I'm so sorry, Your Majesty." Judith fell to her knees in another deep bow. I was starting to worry about what my new husband had done to make his subjects so frightened and ready for punishment.

"Please, Judith. Don't worry about it." I offered the young female my hand, and to my surprise, she took it. My eyes returned to the house. "This is the palace?"

"Palace, Your Majesty?" Judith's small face pinched in confusion.

"Yes, where a king lives."

"Oh. No, he used to live elsewhere. This house was created and furnished for the two of you to live in just this morning."

I blinked. "What? How is that possible?"

She seemed just as confused as I was. "What do you mean? We all worked together, and with our individual abilities and His Majesty lending some of his magic, it didn't take long at all."

"I see..." Apparently, I had a lot to learn, but it was hard wrapping my head around any of it. It took our village weeks to move somewhere new, and our huts were not nearly as well constructed as this house.

"Is it to your liking?" Judith asked, her eyes edged with worry.

I placed a hand on her shoulder. "Yes, it's wonderful." Judith audibly sighed, her shoulders dropping with relief. My eyes returned to the house; I couldn't remember the last time I saw a house made of stone. It was large for a regular person's house but much too small for a king or forest deity. It was two stories with five windows and a flat roof made of some sort of dark material. Onyx, maybe? The door was made of thick, dark mahogany, which surprised me. I would have thought they'd make a more secure door for their king, especially since there were no guards. Then again, he *was* a powerful deity, and considering Judith's behavior toward me, no one would likely dare trespass upon the Leshy's territory.

My stomach lurched at the thought of sharing the home with Bratan for even one night, let alone for eternity, if that really was what the mole had said. I really hoped it wasn't the case, but hoping the Leshy and his bride wouldn't be immortal or at least live for centuries was a lost cause.

I looked back at Judith. "Thank you."

"Of course, Your Majesty. Your husband wanted it to be perfect for you. He's been quite flustered about getting married." The fae giggled. "It's been endearing to see."

"What?" The Leshy was flustered to get married? Considering how he'd acted to me so far, I found it hard to believe. "Are you sure we're talking about the same person?"

"No one could confuse him with another, Your Majesty."

"I suppose that's the truth. He's a brute, no doubt."

"Oh no, My Lady, he has always protected us. We are very grateful to him."

My eyebrows shot up. "Isn't he bad to you?"

"Never. He's a little rough around the edges, but he has a good heart."

Again, hard to believe.

"I guess I've only seen his rough edges."

"You'll see his true self soon, I'm sure of it."

The true softness of the Leshy? I doubted there was such a thing. Still, this young woman was a greater authority on my new husband than I was by far. Maybe I'd misjudged him.

"Thank you again, Judith. I hope you have a lovely evening."

"Of course, Your Majesty. You as well." She bowed and went back the way we'd come

With my stomach still twisting, I swallowed my nerves and entered the building. To my surprise, it was dark. No one appeared to be home, and I couldn't see a thing. It was like walking into a shadow. The floorboards creaked as I crossed the threshold and closed the door. For such a thin wooden partition, it made an impressive slam as it shut, and I swore I heard a chain jingle and then slide once it had.

I looked around, but all I saw was black. I was shrouded in complete darkness. Blinking didn't help either; my eyes couldn't adjust to this depth of darkness.

"Hello?" I called out, walking slowly with my hands splayed out to avoid bumping into anything. "Is anyone here?"

No answer.

My heart started to race.

I swore someone locked the door. Someone had to be in here.

A floorboard creaked behind me. I spun around, my breath catching, fear pricking my skin.

"Hello?" I wasn't sure why, but tears burned in my eyes. "I-I have powers. I can hurt you." I backed up, taking one step at a time until my lower back hit what felt like the flat edge of a table. My fingers curled around it as if holding onto it would keep me frozen in place and unable to be abducted. "I-I can hurt you! I'm warning you!" A tear slid down my face.

Light flashed, momentarily blinding me. My eyes squeezed shut, and I heard his voice before I saw him.

"If I were indeed someone who came to hurt you, you'd already be dead."

I had to blink a few times before the room came into view, as did he, arms crossed in his dark attire, face held in that same scowl he'd worn when he'd left me in the forest.

"Charming as always," I said flatly.

His expression didn't change as he walked to a wall on one side of a simple staircase. Everything about the house was simple. Around me appeared to be a small kitchen, complete with a stove, sink with washing basin, a small counter, and dishes hanging on the back wall. Against my lower back and still curled in my fingers was the edge of a long table that stretched into the kitchen. I turned my attention back to Bratan; I didn't want to let my guard down around him, especially now that we were alone in an enclosed space.

Despite everything, I had to admit that the adjoining parlor he stood in was cozy, and although it was simple, every piece of furniture appeared carefully crafted with rare materials. Straight across from where I stood was a fireplace carved from marble and flecks of silver. I'd only seen fragments and scraps of such materials before.

In front of the fireplace was a thick rug woven from the finest sheep's wool. Looking around, I noticed that that was the only animal product in his home, at least that I could see. It was understandable, though, since he was the protector of these woods, and I knew from growing up around animals that taking wool from sheep was a blessing to the creature. Anything made of leather or other animal skin probably wouldn't be found here, though I couldn't help wondering what the slick couch was made of. It had the appearance of leather, at least upon first glance, but there was something off about it. Maybe I shouldn't ask.

My gaze finally landed on the staircase, passing over Bratan in the most nonchalant way I could muster. Apparently, it didn't matter because as soon as my eyes landed on him for a fraction of a second, he snapped his fingers, and a fire roared to life within the marble alcove. The garnet flames crackled, and Bratan moved his hand around the living area until plants appeared in decorative patterns along the walls, falling like vines on the outer side of the marble fireplace.

"What are you doing?" I asked, tearing my eyes from the magnificent weaving of vines.

He was still scowling, even when his dark eyes shifted to mine. "Don't you want this place warm while you reside here?"

"While I reside here?" I didn't comment on his interior decorating since he seemed to purposely evade it. "Won't you be here too?"

The muscles in his jaw tightened. "I haven't decided yet."

"Why not?" I asked, irritation rising. Part of me didn't want to ask because, now that I was thinking sensibly, I could care less if I hurt him, but the bigger part of me was terrified that I was going to screw this up.

His eyes narrowed on me. "You're extremely aggravating, Leena. I'm not sure how much time I want to spend around you."

"Likewise," I snapped. The blood pounded in my ears, and I was more confident than ever that I hadn't misjudged him. He crept closer, his eyes boring into mine, darkening in a way that made my flesh go hot. I wasn't sure if he wanted to hurt me or do something else entirely. The way he leaned in made me think the latter, but he did nothing more than study my gaze.

"You're going to be a pain in my ass, aren't you?"

"If you continue being one in mine, then yes."

He smiled. A wicked, sultry smile that caught me off guard. "Good."

"What?"

He wrapped his arms around my waist and pressed me against him. His forehead fell against mine, and I could hardly breathe. The world around us fell into a blur. I couldn't even hear the crackles of the fire. "Will you forever be bent on being my foe, Leena?" The words rumbled from his throat. His breath was hot on my skin. I involuntarily lifted my head to meet his eyes, but I could hardly breathe and was reeling from the jarring shift and what was transpiring. His fingers grazed my lips. "Well?" The words were deep and slow, calculated with a precise sensuality. I could somehow feel them hot against me.

"Y-yes," I replied, but it was an unconvincing, broken whisper. "I *am* your foe," I tried again. It was a little stronger but still quiet. There was no way I'd convinced him of anything, nor could I. Not when I turned to liquid when he held me in his arms and spoke to me in such a sultry caress.

"So you wouldn't like it if I did this?" He tugged at the top of my dress; my corset was missing from when he'd healed me in the clearing. His fingers pulled at my sleeve, pushing it lower until it was off my shoulder. My breathing quickened, and something warm pooled through my legs. "Or this?" He pressed his lips against my shoulder, and I let out a whimper. He smiled against my collarbone.

How was I supposed to resist him when he did things like this? I had to get away. I had to stay away from him at all costs. He was an evil monster, and what would it say about me if I let him take my body when he'd already taken my freedom?

"You...you're my enemy," I said shakily, pushing away from him. I was dizzy and warm. I could barely see or think straight as I backed away.

To my dismay, he stood at his full height and moved closer, each step slow and precise.

"Is that so?" He towered over me, his shadow engulfing me as he bent over me and peered into my eyes.

"Yes," I rasped, pushing past him. "I'm going to bed now." I was only one step up the staircase when I felt his fingers trail between my shoulder blades. A shiver of excitement sizzled through me, continuing as his hands wrapped partially around my neck, the tips of his fingers grazing my throat.

"Are you going to kill me, Leena?" His lips pressed against my ear before trailing beneath it. The tightness in my shoulders eased, the muscles loosening as I nearly fell against him. His hands moved up my arms, slow at first, but then he grabbed my sleeves, pulling me in and gripping me in a way that made me weak. And when he kissed the crook of my neck, my composure finally crumbled.

I let out a sound and fell into him, my back relying on his chest to keep me upright. He softly bit my neck, and my legs trembled. I lifted my hand to his face, eyes still closed and back still against him. All I had to do was touch him, and he was unleashed.

Tearing the sleeves clean off my dress, he turned me to face him. His eyes were feral, which lit something primal in my core. He grabbed me with a snarl and kissed me, sucking on my lower lip and sliding his tongue into my mouth. I grabbed his face, hungry for every part of him. He grabbed my hips and lifted me up, my legs wrapping around his waist as if we knew the other's desires without speaking a word.

That's exactly how it felt, too.

Like he knew my body with just his hands.

I threaded my fingers in his hair, pushing so hard into him that he fell against a wall. We kissed and touched as his back slid down the tan surface. The moment he hit the ground, he pushed me onto my back. I caught myself by the elbows and watched as he crawled over my body, eyes vicious and starving, a growl rolling from his throat.

His breath was hot as he guided his tongue up my neck and into my mouth. I could only kiss him back once before my head fell back. I ached when he touched me, and I went limp as he kissed my throat, melting from the fire between us. My arms lay at my sides while his fingers trailed down my chest. My back arched. He pulled my dress lower. He hooked a finger around the string holding the top section of my bodice together and untied it with one snap, and then, with no effort at all, he ripped it off, kissing me while he did it. Fire ignited in my veins, pulsing up my legs. He licked up my throat and bit my chin before grabbing my face and pulling me back into a feverish kiss.

The surge of desire bursting through my blood forced the strength out of me. I pulled at his shirt until I ripped it off his body. Our hands moved quickly, mine clawing up his back and his moving down my arms until our fingers laced together. His mouth let go of mine, and I stared at him breathlessly while he lifted himself up on his knees, one on either side of my waist. His fingers traced loops up my stomach, playing with the remaining material of my dress, and then he looked into my eyes as he ripped it in half. My teeth buzzed as I pounced on him, kissing him viciously but still yielding to his touch.

We kissed and bit and clawed at each other in a foggy mess of passion until he opened his eyes to drink in my naked body, which only made me ache for him more. He prowled over me until his lips brushed mine.

"Are you sure you don't want anything to do with me?" He leaned back, and that mischievous gleam sparked in his eyes.

He must have been loving the feat, but I couldn't care less. "I want you to do anything you want with me."

A look of pure desire replaced the wickedness in his eyes, and excitement surged through me. "Ah," he said, placing a finger on my lips. He trailed his fingertip slowly over my bottom lip until I bit it, licking it as he let out a low, sultry laugh. "Oh, little dove. I don't know if you could handle all the things I want to do to you."

"Try me," I breathed. Something ferocious escaped his lips before he took my mouth in his. We kissed in ravenous fury as I pushed thought after thought of what was right and what was wrong out of my head.

"Are you ready to be mine in every way?" he teased. And then it hit me. If I did this, if I gave him this last part of myself, there would be nothing left of me to have as my own. If I could, I needed to keep this part of myself as long as I could. Now that we were wed and I had added strength and possibly immortality, I had more pull.

What would it say about me if I gave myself to a monster so easily?

"No." The word caused a fissure in the moment, cracking the tension and heat between us like an ax.

He blinked down at me. "What?" The unguarded expression was almost endearing. I had to slide away before getting caught up in him overrode my senses again. I wasn't sure I had the strength to snap out of it again.

"I-I can't. I need to sleep," I said. He stared at me, confused and nearly frozen by the sudden halt on things. "Today has been too much. I'm in no shape to do anything rash." Spotting a blanket from the corner of my eye, I plotted a swift exit. My heart rate was slowing back to normal, and my head had screwed itself back on. The complete state of nakedness I found myself beneath my new husband was both too much and not enough—I needed to cover myself while I still felt some embarrassment and before I lost my head again.

I slipped from beneath him and snatched the blanket from the nearby couch. Wrapping it around myself, I weighed my options. I could go upstairs to sleep in the bed, but that was asking for trouble. My eyes landed on the thick rug in front of the fireplace.

That would have to do.

I padded over to it without a word, and I could feel Bratan's eyes follow me in my wrapped cocoon as the plush rug embraced my feet. It was softer than any bed I'd ever slept on, so it would be more than adequate for tonight. I'd figure out a long-term solution in the morning.

"Good night," I said, curling up on the soft carpet.

"We have a bed."

"I don't need it."

"Why not?"

*Because I can't think straight when you're near me*, I wanted to say, but instead, I said, "I need to be alone tonight."

"You can have the bed, and I'll sleep down here."

"No thanks," I said, restraining myself from adding *I don't trust you*.

"But—"

"Good night." My clipped words cracked with the fire. The radiating heat of the embers made me a little too hot, but I couldn't turn around. Not until Bratan left. But I didn't hear him move, nor did he speak. Fortunately, the exhaustion of the day hit me like a sudden lashing, and I fell asleep, waiting for the sound of his footsteps to start and fade away.

# Chapter Thirteen

## Leena

T HE FIRE SNAPPED, JOLTING me awake. It took a moment for me to remember where I was, and when I did, it all came flooding back. The heated blood, the passionate kisses, the near connection of our bodies.

I cringed, tucking myself deeper into the blanket. I'd succumbed to his spell, and I hated myself for it. At least I stopped myself before I passed the point I could never turn back from. But now I had the rest of forever to resist him. It seemed impossible. I'd never been so attracted to someone, and I was married to him. We were to live in the same space, and sure, I evaded the bed last night, but what about tonight? Maybe it would be better if I just accepted how I felt and let myself succumb to him again and again. Grumbling, I rolled to my other side.

I gasped at the sight of Bratan lying asleep on the couch. What was he doing there? Why didn't he go upstairs? I crawled closer, holding my blanket against me with one hand as my knees and other hand shuffled me to the couch.

His breathing was even, and he was still in the clothes he'd been wearing the night before with no pillow or blanket. Quietly, I pulled my blanket off and draped it over him. It was hard not to stare at his face. The contrast of how he looked now versus what he looked like in the hours he was awake was so stark. It was odd. Awake, he held such anger and venom in his features, but while he was sleeping, his face was soft.

He made a grumbling sound and adjusted his position. Jumping to my feet and not wanting him to see me, I tip-toed up the stairs.

To my surprise, the staircase led to only one spacious room. A space with light green wallpaper and plants hanging from invisible hooks in each corner. They weaved around the ceiling and walls like the vines downstairs. Sharp emerald leaves created patterns against the shadows. To my right was a wide window spilling early sunlight onto the enormous bed that covered a large portion of the loft. It was big enough to fit a family and was in a frame crafted from fine oak. Swirls topped the posts, and two tan waves met in the middle of the headboard.

The room was a palace of its own.

I padded to the bed and sat on the soft surface, feeling it mold to my shape. It was the perfect combination of soft and firm, and weariness from the day before was still heavy in my bones. It was too early for me to start my day, and I was exhausted. Who knew being made immortal came with some of the bonds of mortality? Yawning, I slipped into bed, tucking myself beneath the white duvet, and fell asleep without another thought.

Sleep was mercifully restful, but I wished it could have gone on a little longer. Such was not the case, though, as the biggest problem in my life decided to pester me further. The first thing I heard as I roused from sleep was Bratan whispering my name.

"Leena?" Bleary-eyed, I looked up, blinking until the Leshy came into clear view. He was still completely bare from the night before, and in the daylight and my right mind, it made me crimson. My eyes quickly met his; I begged them not to wander. "Was it too warm downstairs last night?" He pointed to the blanket folded over his forearm.

"No, I just...I thought you might want it." The words came out quiet, and paired with my eyes looking up from beneath my lashes; he must have mistaken it for an invitation.

His wicked smile returned.

"You naughty creature," he said, and my body went ablaze. I quickly turned around, tucking the duvet tight around me, but I felt the bed sink behind me, and the blanket billowed up. His body curved on mine. Before I could scoot away, he kissed the nape of my neck, and my mind fizzed to a stop. I tried not to utter any noises or give any indication that I wanted more, but I *very* much wanted to.

He wrapped his large hand around my middle and kissed down my spine. His fingers stroked my stomach in tender circles as his lips trailed lower, and my mind went numb when his mouth parted in the middle of my back. The warmth of his breath hot on my skin made the blood rush up my legs far too precariously.

I really should tell him to stop...

He teased my lower back with his tongue before licking up to my neck and biting it. I let out a noise just before my breathing ceased. My heart pounded wildly as he licked to my shoulder, sucking on the bone and then kissing up my throat to my chin. He turned me slowly toward him, his body moving on top of mine. When he reached my lips, I welcomed him, and, to both my dismay and intense pleasure, we picked up where we'd left off last night.

Passion radiated from every part of him as we let our kissing deepen. He released my mouth and snarled before nipping at the curve of my neck. My head rolled back, my spine arched, and my nails scraped down his back.

I ached for him. I *hated* that I ached for him—that I yearned for him in every possible way. Most of all, I hated that I didn't care what was right or wrong. I wanted him to swallow me whole.

His teeth trailed down my legs, and his hands grasped my hips, thumbs pushing into the hollow of my hip bones. I let out a small sound at the feeling. Did he know everything I liked through our new connection, or was he really this good at guessing how to make me wild?

My mind was a haze as we moved by sensation.

He growled in my ear, "Do you still think I'm a monster?"

"Yes," I breathed, my eyes still closed.

A chuckle rumbled from his chest. "You think I'm a monster." The statement wasn't spoken in dismay but in delight.

"I-I—" I kept my eyes closed. "Yes." The word was a breathy whisper, and I didn't expect the excited growl or nip of my collarbone that came as his response. "Yes..." His hand slid down my thigh. I wanted nothing more than for him to keep going, but...

My eyes shot open, my good sense returning. "W-wait!" I pulled back, pushing his chest away from me. He fell back with a frown.

"You liked it a minute ago. Did I do something wrong? I can do whatever you like." His offer sent my yearning through the roof, but I had to stick to my good sense.

"No, I...I really enjoyed it..." I laughed awkwardly, then cleared my throat and composed myself. "I just can't do this. I can't be with you like this." *At least not yet.*

He blinked. "Why not?"

"Because I don't like you."

He snorted. "Is that why you told me you wanted me to do anything I wanted with you last night?"

My cheeks burned. "I wasn't in my right mind."

"I thought you just said you really enjoyed it."

"Yes, but I don't like *you*. There's a difference."

"Ah." He crossed his arms and legs, completely bare, and leveled his gaze. "Because I'm a monster?"

"Yes. Because you're a monster." I challenged him, refusing to break eye contact. Refusing to give up or give in.

"You wanted me a moment ago. You don't want me to finish what I started?" He cast me a mischievous grin, a dark sparkle in his eyes that turned my insides to goo.

"Not anymore," I said, steadying the quiver in my voice. "I don't want anything to do with you."

His venomous grin only widened. "You could have fooled me when you were gasping for breath a moment ago."

Somehow, my skin managed to flush more. "I was an idiot for falling into your trap. You...you caught me off guard in bed with no clothes on. I wasn't prepared."

"Prepared for what?" He lifted a brow.

"Um...I-I..." My brain was hazy mush, and I was still groggy from sleep. I had no good excuse. I *did* want him. That was the fact of the matter, and he knew it.

His head fell back with a laugh. "Oh, little dove. You're so cute when you're lying. Just admit that you desire me." His voice was intoxicating, low and rich in its deep thrum and seductive cadence.

"Fine! I did desire you. I admit that I wanted you to bed me both last night and moments ago. But not now!" I groaned. "You're so frustrating!"

"I'm frustrating?"

"Yes!"

He leaned forward, crawling to me on the bed. "And what about you?"

My cheeks reddened, but I couldn't look away. He was too close. "What about me?"

"*You* are incredibly frustrating."

"I am not!" I squeaked.

He sat back, crossing his arms again. "You have been hot and cold for the last twenty-four hours. One moment, you say you want everything to do with me, and the next, you say you want nothing to do with me."

I chewed on the inside of my cheek. "Fine. I understand. I won't frustrate you further. This will never happen again."

I turned to scoot off the bed when he caught hold of my chin.

He gritted his teeth. "You've woken the beast in me, Leena. I have never desired someone the way I desire you." His eyes were primal, and I hated the thrill it sent through me.

It took longer than I cared to admit to snap out of the trance left by his gaze, but once I did, I jerked my chin free and slid to the edge of the bed, pulling the duvet over my chest. "Well, I don't desire you anymore, so you'll have to get over that."

I finally snapped out of it. I'd been a fool to be tricked by the Leshy. I knew he was mischievous and cunning, but I'd assumed I was clever enough to resist anything he threw at me. Every time he looked at me, got too close to me, or touched me—*especially* when he touched me—I was turned into a slave to lust. If I didn't want to succumb to my desires, I had to avoid him at all costs.

"You're a monster," I reiterated, this time with venom in my bite. "And I want nothing to do with you. So stop trying to seduce me." Our eyes stayed locked as he studied me, perhaps searching for a lie, but I could tell he was frustrated, maybe even shocked I'd resisted him.

I wasn't sure if it was due to my newfound powers or something between us that assured me I was in no danger from him—or maybe it was the lingering influence of Judith's words—but I was surprisingly brave against him now. This time, when I walked away, I didn't attempt to hide my nakedness. Dropping the duvet, I proudly strode past him, reveling in the bliss of my victory.

The stairs were cold against my feet, but I was in triumphant spirits as I walked down and found pieces of my wrecked wedding gown and threw on the slip that had been attached to the insides. It would have to do until I found proper clothes, but I assumed those clothes were upstairs, and I wanted to leave Bratan stewing a little longer.

"You cheeky devil," he said. I turned to find him smiling, and he at least had underclothes on as he threw clothes at me.

I accepted the red silk dress with wide eyes. "You're not attempting to seduce me anymore?"

"What? Disappointed?"

I glowered. "*No.*"

He chuckled and walked closer. My eyes instantly fell to the movements of his muscles. His legs were impressive, to say the least. They were nothing compared to his arms, though. His biceps were hard and tight, and I was instantly reminded of how he'd held and touched me, and how he'd held his weight by his knuckles as he hovered over me. I hated how much I loved having him near, even if it was from the primal part of me with no proper intelligence.

I didn't grant him a response and instead turned to leave, but he cupped my face and forced me to look into his eyes. Neither of us made a sound. There wasn't even the crackle of the fire now that it was out. I wanted to reach out and touch him but had more motivation to resist now. I had to show him that I was stronger than him and his advances.

Still, I couldn't help melting in his stare.

He leaned forward, letting his fingers trail down my neck. "If I continued my efforts in seducing you now, I know I'd succeed, and where's the fun in that?"

My jaw clenched. "This was your last morning of fun and the most you'll ever get from me. I won't be so unguarded anymore. I won't be so stupid." I escaped from his grasp and stomped away to get dressed and start over. I had to be better—do better than let myself succumb to a monster.

"We'll see," I heard him say as I ascended the stairs. I didn't miss a step despite the flurry of mixed emotions fluttering low in my gut. "I like a good challenge."

# Chapter Fourteen

## Leena

M Y DRESS WAS ONLY partially tied as I made my way to the hollowed tree, where I hoped I'd find Theodora. Holding onto the neckline of the sagging gown, my hopes lifted when I heard the wooden door creak open. But as I saw the small maid exit the quarters instead of Theodora, I instantly deflated. Our eyes met, and Ani paused, eyeing me as if deciding what to do and whether she'd judge me for my current state of partial dress.

"I just need help lacing my bodice," I said, forcing a smile. Her expression didn't change, and I had a feeling that she was trying hard not to roll her eyes. She sighed and gestured for me to follow her. "Thank you," I replied with a long exhale, but the maid didn't say anything. She wordlessly took the strings of my bodice and started lacing it up.

She was halfway through helping me with the dress when her hands stilled. "Where is your corset? And," She pulled the back of the bodice open, tugging on the ripped black slip that lay beneath, "what is this? Isn't this your slip from yesterday?"

"Yes..."

She grabbed me firmly by the elbows. "You're supposed to be a *queen*. Didn't the servants provide new underthings for you? Where is Theodora? She should have dressed you at the house."

"I'm not sure—"

"You're not *sure*?" Ani's voice was loud, and I suddenly wished I had run into any other female in the realm.

"I didn't have time to look for new underthings or to call for Theodora."

Ani let go of my arms and let out a bitter laugh, shaking her head. "But you had time to tumble with His Majesty by the look of it."

My face burned. "I did not!"

"Enough, Ani," came a voice that relieved my coiled nerves. Theodora shot a look at her fellow maid and uncurled her hand, to which the smaller female slapped my bodice strings and grumbled as she walked away. "Where are you going?"

The smaller fae whipped around. "I'm not going to sit around while you treat this worthless human like the queen she so clearly isn't! You may have accepted her wrongful place here, but I never will. She's nothing more than Bratan's whore." The word rang in my ears, and though I should have been mad, I found self-loathing in its place. "Melora will soon hear of it and—"

"Enough!" Theodora shouted. Ani clamped her mouth shut, but there was fury in her eyes as she spun around and left without another word. The awkwardness between the kinder maid and me was thick and palpable. I wasn't sure what to say to break the silence. Luckily, Theodora spoke first, turning to smile a little too sweetly. "Let's fix your dress, and then I'll show you around. Does that sound good?"

I forced a tight smile and tried forgetting what Ani had accused me of being. Is that what all the others would think? Would I start off as a ruler of this realm as nothing more than a bedmate for their king?

I couldn't allow that.

If I hadn't been motivated to resist his advances before, I sure was now.

"Yes," I said. "That sounds perfect."

Theoroda spent a good part of the morning brushing through my tangled knots and fashioning my hair into a sleek, regal updo. She had guided all of it into an intricate style atop my head, with small curls twirling loose at just the right angles to accentuate my features. The last thing she did was tie a thin band of braided hair from one side of my head to the other in a makeshift crown. Once I was presentable, we strolled into town, Theodora introducing the various townsfolk to their new queen and me giving them slight bows and awkward smiles.

Fortunately, it didn't seem that Ani's sentiment was shared by anyone else, but perhaps that was because I no longer looked like I'd just emerged from the act of lovemaking.

I was with one group of woodland beings, some green and some blue, but all with the heights and features of human beings—save their pointed mouths and black eyes—when the mood instantly shifted, dropping like a sudden flurry. Where chatter and laughter had been whistling in the air like the sweep of a breeze, there was now nothing but the sound of rustling leaves.

The air was thick, and a shadow cast over us, eclipsing the small group that had gathered around me. I didn't have to turn to know he was there.

His achingly deep voice hummed in my ears. "I see your new queen has graced you all with her presence this fine day."

"Your Majesty," a female creature said, her voice trembling as she bowed. All others in the vicinity followed suit, including Theodora, who also gave a deep curtsy.

Bratan's hand found the small of my back, and it took more self-control than I cared to admit not to let it do anything to my mind. I couldn't control the sensations it fueled in my body, though, especially as his fingers slowly stroked their way to my hip when he pulled me against him like we were indeed a royal newlywed couple to be respected and adored.

"May I steal her for a while?" Everyone knew it wasn't a request.

"Of course, Your Majesty," Theodora said sweetly. I weighed my options. I could pull away from him now and shatter the illusion of marital bliss in front of everyone, or I could ensure more respect wouldn't be lost and reject him when we got a moment alone.

I bowed my head in a slight, graceful motion before waving a gentle goodbye. Bratan led me deeper into the forest by my waist, and as soon as we were deep enough in the ocean of trees, I pushed him away.

"I told you I want nothing to do with you!" I glared up at his amused expression.

His fingers found my chin, and his gaze lingered on my lips before lifting to my eyes.

"I only remember select moments from this morning." His voice was low as he stroked the back of his hand up my jawline and down the back of my neck. It found its way to my sleeve, which hung delicately over my shoulder, and he grabbed it, holding onto my small bicep as he leaned forward and kissed my shoulder. "You've stoked a desire in me that can't be satiated. At least not without you."

The burning was mutual, but the desire to be seen as more than a concubine was far greater than my lust, even if it was only by Ani. I shimmied away and tried not to think about how he'd gripped me with those same hands in the early hours of the morning. And late last night. The wine-red dress was gorgeous, and I loved how confident it made me feel, but now, with Bratan eyeing me so hungrily, I regretted not asking for more conservative attire. This one fell off my shoulders in thin, sash-like sleeves and exposed the entirety of my back. There wasn't even a slip beneath. You could see everything from my shoulder blades to just above my backside. It was similar to the dress I'd come here in, but it was more elegant and from finer material.

His eyes went wild, and a wicked thought surfaced in my mind. I could use this to my advantage. It could be fun driving him absolutely insane.

I gave him an impish grin and laced my fingers behind my back. "I'll admit that I enjoyed our mutual passion last night and this morning," I said, trying my best not to think of said passion, "but I don't need any more of it, and as I told you earlier, you won't get to touch me anymore. Our marriage need not be consummated. We have no use of each other, other than whatever obligatory duties we have to this forest."

Bratan attempted to close the gap between us, but I gracefully slid away, side-stepping his advances and causing him to trip. He caught himself but heard my quiet snicker. A fire ignited in his eyes. He stalked me, his thick, black boots squelching against a thick patch of mud.

"I have so much more use of you, little dove." He leapt at me like an animal. This time, I couldn't trip him. He was too quick. He grabbed me by the shoulders, but I pushed away.

"Get off of me, you brute!"

Surprise widened his eyes, sending his brows shooting up. "Wha—"

I couldn't help but laugh at the surprised look on his face. I shifted my weight to one side. "What? Did you think I was teasing? That I would beg for you night and day? I'm not playing a game with you." He still gaped at me, confused, as I walked away. But I had to give him one last dig. One last piece of bait. "You can try if you want, but you will *never* get to bed me."

I didn't look to see his expression, but I could practically feel the wheels in his head turning through our connection.

"We'll see," he called out, which only made me snort.

I shot him a playful look over my shoulder, very aware that from this angle much of my body was bare to him.

"I guess we will," I said with a wink. Red flashed across his face, and triumph soared through me.

This could be fun.

***

I managed to avoid Bratan for the rest of the day, internally reciting a mantra that I didn't need him in any way and that he was a monster of the worst kind.

*I'm better than him. Act like it.*

I followed Theodora around as she introduced me to more of the townsfolk and showed me around the innermost parts of the forest. But when we made our way to the edge of the secluded realm, I tensed. "Are we going out there?"

"Not without His Majesty."

My stomach dropped, as did my patience. "When will he be joining us?"

"Miss me already, my love?" The richness of his voice pooled through my ears, but his charm was already starting to wane.

I spun on my heels, a sticky-sweet smirk plastered on my face. "How did you know?"

He obviously wasn't expecting this response, and I swore I saw the side of his mouth momentarily twitch into a smile. "So cheeky."

"Let's get this over with." I shot him an annoyed glare before turning to face the entrance to my old world—the forest that lay beyond.

*Why am I so scared? This should be the scary side.*

Bratan stepped in front of me and waved a hand around the circular exit like he had when he'd brought me here. I was surprised he didn't try to touch me as he passed. Maybe he'd grown tired of banter, or maybe he respected me enough to stop trying.

Neither was likely.

As the vines and leaves parted and an entrance opened to the world beyond, Theodora took a step back. "I'll leave you to it, Your Majesties." She gave a deep bow, and before I could beg her to stay, she was off. It was obvious that the maid wanted no part of our venture. I couldn't blame her.

I tried not to look at him, but there was no point dragging this out longer than necessary. I reluctantly looked at Bratan, and when our eyes met, he offered me his hand. I pushed past him, walking through the exit on my own. I was petrified to go through it in case his magic had kept things together the first time in a way I wouldn't be able to manage on my own, but I couldn't imagine he'd let anything happen to me. At least not until he'd succeeded in his plan of seduction, which, of course, he wouldn't. But he didn't know that.

Holding my breath, I took the first step, wincing and praying Bratan didn't sense my trepidation. Then I took another step, and then another, moving through the realms with no ill consequence. It was dark at first, but the day was at its brightest, so it wasn't long before the pitch-darkness subsided, and I walked into the ordinary beauty of my old world. The magic of the forest's door didn't phase me. Perhaps it was due to my newfound powers. I didn't need the Leshy. We were one now. I was connected to him and his powers. I may have even been as powerful as he was, though I didn't know how to wield my powers, or how to control them, or how much I could actually do.

Was I as powerful as he was? My hope that I was sunk the more I thought about it, especially considering his true form and how easily he could shift into it. All I had done was get overrun by an agonizing force that was supposedly power. So far, all it had done was give me pain and make my body useless until Bratan healed me enough to move again.

Twigs snapped behind me as Bratan entered the human realm. I did my best not to look back at him; I didn't want to look at him for many reasons, but I was genuinely annoyed with him at present.

We walked through the woods in silence until I realized that I had no idea why we were out there, what we were doing, or where we were supposed to go. I whipped around, catching Bratan staring at me.

"What are we doing out here? Are you supposed to show me around the forest or something?"

His stoic face lifted slightly before dropping again. Like he was trying not to laugh. "Yes and no."

I groaned. "Please don't be cryptic. Just tell me what we're doing out here. I'm too tired for your games."

He gave me a coy look. "We did have a marvelously frenzied night."

I chewed on the inside of my cheek, begging myself not to blush. When I was composed enough to speak, I shrugged and said, "I don't know about marvelous. It was all right." I reveled in the drop of his jaw. His offended expression. I stared ahead, striding through the woods. "Tell me what we're doing here so we can eat supper, and I can get some rest."

The human forest was duller than I remembered, even though it had only been a day since I'd seen it. The leaves weren't as vibrant as the Leshy's realm, and things didn't feel as alive. When the silence stretched on without a quip from my husband, I finally turned. His face was inches from mine in an instant. Had he been that close the whole time? I hadn't felt him.

He grabbed my face and leaned forward, his grip tight. "If it was anything less than marvelous," he said in a near-whisper, his deep voice even lower, "then we should do it again, and this time finish it. I can't marvel you until I can properly show you what I can do." He leaned in until his lips were nearly on mine. "I want to please you until you can't think straight." His grip on my face tightened, and despite my better judgment, I loved it.

His fingertips curled into my hair, pulling me closer. Strands came loose from the back. My head tilted up, and I lost myself in the intensity of his gaze. "I want to make you writhe for days, unable to think of anything but me and what I did to you. That's when I'll know I've done my job right, and you will finally know what a truly marvelous, frenzied night entails."

My toes curled in my satin slippers, but I tried my best not to show it. "You'll be waiting an awfully long time because I keep my promises." Something in his eyes shifted, and I knew he saw straight through me. "You can't get me to break that promise."

Fire ignited in his eyes. "You will break it," he whispered, "and you'll beg for me."

I bared my teeth. "The only begging I'll do for you is to beg you to leave me the hell alone."

"Is that so?"

I nodded, to which he cocked a brow. I would be strong and keep my promise. I would refuse any tenderness from him in any form. Any contact. Any whispers. Anything.

I wanted nothing to do with him.

At least, I had to keep telling myself that until I believed it.

I inched closer, tilting my chin up in defiance. "I don't sleep with monsters."

The muscles in his jaw tightened, and finally, our eye contact broke, and he stared straight ahead. "Let me show you around the woods. You need to know every inch of it like the back of your hand."

"Why?" His quick change of subject was jarring, but I was glad to move on. I wasn't sure how much longer I could keep up the facade.

He scanned the trees as if looking for something. "You'll have to do things from time to time." I ran after him as he started walking.

"What kind of things?"

No answer.

I leapt in front of him, causing him to skid to a halt. "What are you doing?" he barked. "I almost—"

"What kind of things do I have to do?"

He studied me for an uncomfortably long time. I tried to focus on the sounds around me—the rushing of wind against blades of grass, the swirling of leaves, and the cawing of crows as they made their last calls before sleep—but I couldn't break from his stare. And my stomach was in knots about what he might say.

He looked down, chewing on his words, then met my eyes again. "If the villagers hurt our animals or any part of these woods, you have to join me in retaliation."

The air left my lungs. I staggered back, my knees almost buckling as I violently shook my head.

"No!"

"You *have* to." His voice continued to rise. "It's your duty as the Leshy's wife."

"I am not your wife!" I knew it was a childish response and stupidly false, but I couldn't take it anymore. "I didn't want this life! I didn't want to be married to you! I didn't want any of this!" My chin quivered, and as he took a step toward me, his arms raising from his sides, I pushed him. "Get away from me!" I screamed. "I don't want anything to do with you!"

My cheeks were hot and wet with tears; they spilled like rainwater down my face, sliding down my throat. I angrily swept away the moisture and ran into the belly of the forest.

"Leena!"

I didn't look back. I kept running. My legs wobbled, but still, I ran. Faster.

Faster.

I had to get away.

"Leena!"

"Leave me alone!" I screamed, and suddenly, lightning cracked across the sky. The world around us clapped with deafening thunder. The ground beneath us quaked as rain poured down in sheets. I only faltered for a moment and then kept running.

I didn't look back. I kept going, even after his voice was drowned out by thunder and I couldn't hear anything but the violent hiss of rain.

Then pain struck me to the ground, and my spine pounded as it made contact with the hard earth. The rain made it too hard to see, but I could make out that I'd run into a man, his shape unidentifiable. But I could tell by the height and shape that it was no woodland creature or tree.

"I told you to leave me alone!" I cried, wincing as I got to my feet. But when I looked up, it wasn't Bratan I saw. It was a familiar redhead leering at me.

"Hello, Leena," he said. My mouth went dry. I knew what Casimir had always wanted to do with me, and now we were alone. Everything I'd learned to protect myself against him was out the window in this situation, and I didn't know how to use my powers.

He grabbed me by the sash-like sleeves and pulled me off my feet. My underarms stung at the pain of the fabric digging into my skin.

"Fancy seeing you out here."

I thought I might vomit. No matter how hard I tried, I couldn't free myself from his grasp. He was deceivingly strong, and as he threw my back onto the ground with tremendous force, I suddenly wished I hadn't pushed Bratan away.

# Chapter Fifteen

F EAR SWELLED IN MY chest, and a throbbing pain pounded in my spine. Did becoming immortal give me any useful abilities? Other than when my new powers, or whatever it was, first rushed through me, I hadn't felt any different. To me, I was still the breakable mortal girl I'd always been, vulnerable and weak.

My stomach sank. Maybe the tales weren't true, and maybe I'd heard the officiant wrong and wasn't immortal. What if the ceremony had been a ruse? That wasn't out of character for the Leshy, and his subjects would have done and said whatever he told them to.

Then I thought of Ani and how she was bent on driving me away. *She will never be my queen.* Her words had been a stinging wound, but they seemed to be the truth. From the disdain she held for me, and her acknowledgment of my becoming queen, the ceremony had to have been real.

Pain pushed against the soft underbelly of my forearms. I let out a cry, the rain pouring harder, pelting me with icy drops and shards of hail.

"After all these years," Casimir snarled in my ear, "I finally have you where I want you." My fingers dug into the thick mud in desperation to crawl away, but he was stronger than he looked. And the pain was deepening, especially as his kneecaps dug into my thighs.

"Please," I begged, choking on rainwater. "Please stop—"

He put a hand over my mouth, and with the rain filling my nostrils, it was impossible to breathe. I wiggled and fought, thrashing as hard as I could, but it only made the pain worse.

"Don't worry. I'll knock you out when it's over."

Tears burned against my icy cheeks. Fog crept into the corners of my eyes as my vision blurred at the lack of oxygen. *Why can't he knock me out first?*

My dress rose to my knees, and I squeezed my eyes shut, desperately hoping I'd pass out before anything happened. As soon as the cold air sent gooseflesh across my skin, a great *boom* rattled the ground, violently shaking the trees. Their leaves hissed wildly as Casimir's hand peeled from my mouth. His body flew away with a crack of thunder.

I gasped out a breath, my body violently shivering. Fear wrapped around me, suffocating me more than the pressure of the man's slimy hand. I was so cold and in so much distress, but I had to know what happened. There was no way Casimir would have stopped of his own volition. Especially not like that.

My body ached. My head throbbed. But still, I tried rolling onto my side. A man's ear-splitting wail cut through the storm, and I immediately knew it belonged to my assaulter. I heaved, trying my best to sit up and see what was going on. The man wailed again, and the earth shook.

Finally, I managed to push up on my palms and hip to see what was going on. My sharp gasp was swallowed by the storm.

Casimir had been propelled a good distance away, but he and Bratan were close enough that I could see the rage on my husband's face as he struck the redhead for what looked like the second or third time. A wave of emotion crashed against my chest, along with an acute sense of shock.

"You think you can touch my wife, you sick bastard?!" he roared. He grabbed Casimir by the collar and threw him with inhuman strength.

Casimir looked like a ragdoll as he skidded across the ground, creating a groove in the mud beneath him. Bratan stared at the man's crumpled form and advanced, keeping his blazing stare on his victim. The display was so incomprehensible it was hard to remind myself I wasn't dreaming. Shadows squirmed at Bratan's feet, leaving black mist in the wake of each step. The trees and shrubs around them shook, and the ground was unstable. There was a wildness in his eyes I'd never seen anyone else possess. A thrilled shiver shot up my bruised bones.

Bratan grabbed the man by the scalp, and his human form melted into something else—something that chilled the already icy ground and worsened the sick feeling in my stomach. My husband no longer looked like a man. He grew and shifted until he was an enormous creature taller than the massive trees around us. A monster so colossal that Casimir looked like a toy in Bratan's large, branch-like fingers. I couldn't make out exactly what he looked like through the thick sheet of rain, but from any distance or angle, the sight was terrifying.

I fell against my side, still unable to stay upright. The Leshy let out a splintered roar and threw the man against a tree.

"You're dead." His voice was partly his own and partly something else's.

Casimir was a bloody heap at the base of the tree, wobbling as he attempted to stand. It didn't take long for Bratan to reach him in his monstrous form. He grabbed him again, and my stomach sank.

I didn't want this. Casimir was vile, but I didn't want someone to die because of me. I didn't know if it was right or wrong to spare his life, but I couldn't help the guilt building in me.

"Wait!" I cried, but the word was a whisper in the rain.

I pushed hard against the ground, desperate to get to my feet. I'd never sleep again if I witnessed a murder and knew I had a connection to it—if I felt it was even remotely because of me. I didn't want his blood on my hands.

"Wait!" I called again. This time, the Leshy stopped, one large claw hovering above Casimir's head like the unhinged jaws of a beast. "Don't do it!"

Limping closer, I saw that Bratan's skin was made of thick layers of bark, each finger a jagged branch that looked like it had been ripped from the trees. His mouth was a gaping hole, and his eyes were almost the same: large black holes that were too lifeless to belong to any mortal. There was a red light in their depths that became more apparent as I got closer. Limp black hair hung from his head, falling loosely around two horns that curled up at least six feet from his temples.

"What?" His strange new voice was steeped in frustration.

It was hard to look at him like this, but it beat the alternative of looking at Casimir, whom I'd accidentally caught a glimpse of and was subjected to his bloody state of half-consciousness.

"It'll only cause more problems," I said, "and I don't want you to be a murderer because of me."

A pause. His gaping mouth moved. "I have killed many before." My blood turned cold, though I wasn't sure why I was surprised. He could be thousands of years old, and he was a deity in these woods not known for his kindness. I also wasn't sure if I believed him that he'd saved the villagers who'd gone missing. But I did want to know what had made him kill and when and how many times it'd happened to make it so easy to do it now.

"Please," I whispered. He probably couldn't hear it, but he must have read my lips or understood because his form shrunk back to the man I recognized. As he did, Casimir gasped a relieved breath. I paid him no mind. He deserved to be punished. To be locked up. I just didn't want the blood of his death on my hands. My eyes fell on Bratan, my muscles relaxing slightly as he walked away from my attacker. The feral look in his eyes was still there, but his expression was softer as he approached me.

During the transformation, his eyes never left mine, and now he was searching me like he was trying to understand. "Why would you want to let him live after what he did to you? After what he was going to do to you?" The memory reignited the wildness in his eyes. His shoulders rose and fell in rapid, ebbing waves with his quickening breaths. He was going to lose control.

"Because I don't want any part of this. I know he's despicable, and we should somehow make sure he never does this to anyone else. But I wouldn't be able to sleep at night if I stood by while someone was murdered because of me. No matter who it was."

Conflict tightened Bratan's face, along with his fists. The muscles in his jaw tensed as he picked Casimir up by the shirt. He bunched the cloth in his fist and brought the man's face close to his.

"If you so much as breathe her air or come near her again, I *will* kill you." He pushed him away, and we both watched him flee, limping and skittering like a newborn foal back to Woodsmeadow.

We watched in uncomfortable silence until he was long gone, and even then, I kept my eyes from Bratan's. I didn't know where to go from here. I wished I could avoid this whole situation. I didn't want this new life, but I didn't want my old one either. Everything happened so fast, and I was still shaking from the attack.

The rain slowed to a stop, and I heard the squelching of footsteps approach me through the mud. "Are you all right?"

I swallowed and looked up at him. Those wild eyes were gone, and the tenderness that replaced them made me want to crumble into his arms. I was so scared. Casimir almost succeeded in his horrid attempt. All my life, I'd managed to evade him. And if it hadn't been for Bratan...

"I'm fine," I said, but instantly winced when I tried to walk.

"You're not fine." I opened my mouth to protest when he swept me into his arms, one arm beneath my bent knees and the other holding me against his chest. "Leena." His face was so close. His eyes were electric, the green more vibrant now that the darkness was gone. "I'll never let that happen to you again."

A lump bobbed in my throat, and I cursed the tears that wanted to spill down my face. I blinked them away and broke eye contact. "What have you done in your life that made it so easy for you to kill him? To want to kill him."

There was a beat of silence. "Oh, Leena." Reluctantly, I looked up. "Even if I'd never harmed a single creature in all of my life, I'd have killed that man in an instant if not for your protests."

"What? Why? What made you so..." I didn't want to finish the thought, but he finished it for me.

"Crazy?"

I nodded.

"You."

My lips parted as I let the word sink in. "Me?"

"Yes, little dove. You drive me mad. Absolutely insane."

I hated the look he gave me—full of passion and longing. "I-I don't..." I fumbled for the words but couldn't think of anything to say, and despite the freezing wind, my skin burned. "Let me down." I could barely breathe. My body was weak, I was fatigued and in pain, but I didn't want him to hold me. Or maybe I did. Maybe too much, which was precisely why I needed him to put me down.

He did as I asked and set me back on my feet. I stared at my satin shoes, now covered in mud. One of them was torn on the side. His fingers found my chin and lifted my face like he always did. In his eyes was that same passion, paired with the tenderness that left me confused and melting inside.

"Don't you know that I'd kill anyone who hurt you?" His gaze fell to my lips and then quickly returned to my eyes. "You are precious to me. From the moment we met, there was something about you that drove me mad. Then after the ceremony bound us together and you received your powers, that feeling intensified beyond comprehension." The words struck my every nerve, every bone. Because I knew what he meant. I'd thought it was lust, but there was something pulling me to him, and I couldn't explain it. "I may have spared him this time," he continued, "but I don't know if I could hold back if he tried again. I wish you hadn't stopped me tonight."

"I don't want you to be a murderer on my account, even if you've done it before."

"It wouldn't be on your account, Leena. He made his bed, so he can lie in it. Anyone who so much as scratches you deserves to be punished. But him? He deserves to be dead."

A torrent of conflicting feelings warred inside of me. Part of me believed he was right, but another part believed he was crazy—completely bonkers. And I'd be lying if I said I didn't like the passion in his words and the feral protection between them.

"Why do you care about me so much?"

We stared at each other as the rain continued to pour. I earnestly wanted to know. What made this man I just met want to kill someone on my behalf? He gently took the side of my face in his hand. "Don't you feel it?" His voice melted like warm caramel, and though it was soft, I could hear it through the rain. "An inexplicable connection? A strong thread that guides us together?"

"Yes," I found myself saying. "Like I've known you longer than a lifetime."

His eyes searched mine. "We were meant to be one, Leena. You are my mate."

His mate. The Leshy's mate.

"I don't know what you're talking about." I pulled away, but he caught me by the wrist before I could flee.

"I see right through you, Leena. A feeling like this can't be faked. I know you feel it as I do."

I wanted to move. I wanted to be anywhere but here, but I also didn't want to leave him. The contradictory feelings ate at me. "It's a trick. You're tricking me."

"Do you really believe that?"

"No. I..." I winced and shook off his hand. "I don't know."

"Leena." His low voice caught hold of me before his hand did. He whipped me around to face him. Putting his forehead on mine, he whispered. "You are good. So very good. I think you were always meant to be the better part of me."

"I don't know," I whispered, but the feeling that tethered us together convinced me otherwise. Or at least tried to. I still didn't know what to think; everything was happening too fast.

"Let's get you home," he said. "You need to rest."

# CHAPTER SIXTEEN

## LEENA

I COULDN'T STOP SHAKING, recounting the events in my mind over and over—Casimir's limp, bloody form thrown to the trees like a ragdoll. The angry fire in Bratan's eyes. Why was he so protective of me? Was it truly due to some cosmic bond? It was as good an explanation as any, I guessed. There was no better one. It also explained why I couldn't resist him, no matter how much I tried.

The last couple of days had been too much to take in. My brain was struggling to keep up, always springing from one thought to another. No matter what train of thought it led me on, though, it always drifted back to the violent occurrences of the night and the healing balm of Bratan's touch.

But the pleasant memories were quickly replaced by the painful images of the night—Casimir's knees digging into my thighs, the fear that bubbled like acid up my throat.

Was letting him go the right call? Up until now, penalty by death was clearcut to me, but the more I thought of Casimir's devious nature and what he might go on to do, I wasn't sure anymore. Hopefully tonight would set him straight.

It was the right call, I assured myself, though I couldn't shake off the uneasy feeling gnawing at me. Curling up tight, I decided not to think about it. I didn't have the mental or emotional capacity to wonder if I'd made the right choice. All I wanted was for sleep to take me away. Maybe I'd wake up to a better life free from despair and forced marriages, and Casimir almost getting his way with me.

Our front door creaked open. My face brushed against Bratan's damp chest. Halfway home, I'd decided that I needed help after all and didn't fight him carrying me. The rain had been dreadful, yet he moved like it was nothing and was already nearly dry. I peered up at him—at the man who'd saved me from Casimir's horrendous attempt. I was acutely aware of his muscled arms, strong against my shoulders and back and beneath my legs where my scraped knees poked out from tattered silk.

I winced as he carried me up the stairs. Each slight bob of my body left me aching with pain. He looked down at me, frowning. "Are you badly hurt?"

A muffled groan escaped my lips as my body bounced at his next step. "Obviously."

Fully expecting him to bite back some sort of retort, I was surprised to see his frown deepen. "I'll walk more slowly then." Surprise sparked through me, and he clutched me tighter and moved slowly up the stairs.

He gently placed me in the bed; the warmth and delicacy of the mattress were sweet relief to my aching body. "We should get you out of those rags," he said. I wanted to protest, but I could tell by the concern in his eyes and the puckered space between his brows that this wasn't an attempt to see me naked.

"Okay." My voice was hoarse, but he didn't seem to notice. I watched as he took off my shoes and pulled at the loose, dirty cloth that had once been the most magnificent and decadent dress I'd ever worn. It slid off with ease, and the cold sharpened against my skin. I reveled in the warmth of his hands as they brushed against my thighs. Once again, I couldn't help the heat rising at my sudden vulnerability.

If he noticed, he didn't say anything; he only took off my underskirt, slid the damp silk off my chilled body, and tossed it in the pile of my other soiled clothing. I very much noticed—and loved—the red that dusted his cheeks, but his expression didn't change. I was only in my underthings, yet he didn't do anything but pull the duvet to my shoulders and gently tuck it around me.

"You should get some rest. You can talk to Theodora about bathing in the morning. I'll have her fetch you new clothes, too." He glanced at the wardrobe across the room. "I'm not sure what's stocked in there for you, but I imagine it isn't anything practical for daytime activities." His eyes roved to mine again. "I'll take care of all that. You just focus on sleep." He turned to leave when I did something that surprised even me.

I grabbed his hand, catching him by the fingers. He looked at me with wide eyes.

"Stay with me," I said, and the surprise further showed on his face in the furrow of his brow and in the way his lips parted slightly. Without a word, he slipped beneath the covers and nestled in beside me. Even in my current state, it was hard not to giggle at how awkward he acted lying next to me. Like he didn't know what to do with himself, and he was so much larger than me. To me, the bed was enormous, but when he lay in it, it looked like a bed made for a child.

I looked up at him, my near-naked body against his black, villainous suit that smelled of sweat, cloves, and something masculine. "Hold me," I said, "until I fall asleep."

His Adam's apple bobbed, and then he nodded. "Okay." His voice was quiet, and unlike the tone he usually spoke in. It was tentative. Nervous. I smiled and stroked a hand down the side of his face. He studied me, peering into my eyes. I knew I shouldn't be like this with him after what I'd promised myself, but I couldn't help it. What he'd said was true—there was something about our connection I couldn't deny. Something strong. Passionate. And watching him protect me without a second thought made that feeling inflate beyond measure.

I combed my fingers through his hair, then brushed my lips against his. "Good night, Bratan."

He swallowed. "Good night, Leena."

I gave him another smile before turning around to lie on my side. He immediately wrapped his arms around me, pulling me into him, and I fell asleep in the curve of his body, feeling warmer and safer than I ever had in my entire life.

*** 

*Bratan*

Her body was warm against me. I stroked her bare arm as she fell asleep, nuzzling my face in her hair and breathing in her sweet, citrus scent. She smelled of so many things—oranges, dewy grass, and fresh apples. Beautiful and hopelessly sunny. Not knowing when I'd feel this closeness again, I held her tighter. I hadn't felt warmth from someone in centuries, and it had never felt like this.

As I felt the rhythm of her breaths change, those feelings intensified until I was reminded of what that disgusting sack of flesh had done to her. I could feel the throbbing pain in her bones, but I couldn't do much about it, no matter how deeply I wanted to. All I could do was lessen the aches and intensify the effects of the power flooding her newly immortalized body. I tried my best, moving my hand over the curve of her hip, pushing my power into her muscles and bones until I was sure some sort of healing power had transferred to her, lessening the pain in one way or another.

Sliding my hand back around her waist, I pulled her in tight and rested my lips against the top of her head. The intensity of my warring feelings took hold, as they'd done in the forest.

It was time.

My hand slid away; I lifted the locks of hair cascading down her back and pressed a kiss against the nape of her neck. Then, carefully, I crawled out of bed, wrapped a cowl around my neck, and walked out the door.

I didn't bother being quiet as soon as the door shut behind me. My focus was on one thing and one thing only, and as I walked there, as I thought of that piece of shit human who'd put his hands on Leena, the furious fire inside of me raged. By the time I left my realm and got to the humans' village, that anger was a blazing wildfire. It quickly took over every part of me as I searched.

I stormed through the village, not caring who saw or heard me. Most of the villagers were in their homes, likely asleep in the cold slumber of night. But that bastard had to be awake; it hadn't been that long since he'd scrambled away, and I doubt he'd be able to sleep tonight.

I'd find him. No matter how long it took or how many houses I had to break into. I *would* find him.

There were only a few huts with orange lights still flickering through their windows due to the time of night. I kicked each door open, one by one, until I burst through the door of a seemingly empty house. My boots crunched against broken glass from the window my power decimated on my way in. The house was more of a large room—an open living space with two closed doors fixed against the back wall. A small clatter sounded behind one of them as if someone had accidentally knocked something over.

The power and rage burning my nerves seeped out of my body in black mist as I moved toward the room. Blood boiling, my powers rose to the surface. I erupted through the door, blowing it off its hinges. It flipped forward and crashed against the adjacent wall, snapping into countless shards of wood.

A yelp squawked in the opposite corner. There he was. Swollen and bloody, but alive.

I walked to him slowly, stalking him, my shadows skittering across the floor and climbing the walls. They skated to the redhead like moving charcoal along the polished wood. I bore my eyes into the insignificant human, baring my teeth as I moved my hand, guiding the shadows to clutch the man's throat.

They sprung into silent action, coiling around his skinny neck. He gasped until no more air could enter his shriveling lungs. I took another slow step forward, this time forming a satisfied smile as I looked down at the pale creature. The man squirmed violently, kicking out in every direction. His hands tried and failed to grasp the shadows, but of course, his fingers moved through them like smoke, so all he did was scratch his already bloodied neck.

"You're pathetic," I said. My voice was surprisingly calm, but when the man's bulging eyes met mine, that rage burned brighter, and I grabbed him by the tattered shirt and lifted him off his feet. "My wife may wish to spare your life, but I want to see you die." The man kicked in the air as my true form took shape. My rapidly growing body broke through the ceiling. Splintered wood and loose thatches of hay rolled off my shoulders. I leaned in. "And I want it to be by my hands."

The shadows slithered away, releasing Casimir's throat, but just as the man gasped for air, I took my claw and pierced him in the gut.

Gasps and cries from villagers who'd gathered sounded in the distance, but that didn't stop the smile that stretched across my face as I watched the life slip out of this monster's eyes.

The pale man mouthed something, floundering until he finally sputtered out, "G-go to hell."

My smile widened. "I'll see you there." I opened a claw and finished the job.

# CHAPTER SEVENTEEN

## LEENA

I WOKE UP THE next morning to a female voice. "Rise and shine, Your Majesty." My eyes peeled open, blinking to focus on who was standing at my bedside. The first thing I saw was Theodora's smiling face, accompanied by the sulking Ani, who wasn't attempting to hide her scowl or the look of disgust scrunching her nose. "Did you rest well?" the kinder of the two asked. I gave an "mhmm" and ran my fingers through my hair. It was too early to talk to anyone, especially after last night. "We have the things for your bath all ready, and we brought you new dresses, all stocked in your wardrobe."

Behind them stood a large oak wardrobe, hand-carved designs of curving vines and blooming roses snaked up the sides. I could have sworn a different wardrobe had been there the night before, but I was in a realm of magic, so why shouldn't an enormous piece of furniture change in appearance? It was the least strange occurrence that had happened to me this week.

I let out a yawn, stretching my arms until a familiar scent wafted through my nose. I closed my eyes and breathed it in.

Bratan's scent was still on the pillow next to me. Images of the night before teased my mind, as did the feel of his hands on my bare waist and the warmth of his embrace as I fell asleep. I thought of him gently taking off my clothes, and my face went crimson. "Where's my husband?" I asked, clearing my throat and tucking my knees to my chest.

"His Majesty had some business to take care of this morning and left before dawn. He sent word for us to bathe and help you today because he will be gone all day and possibly into the night."

I frowned. What kind of business did he need to take care of? "Isn't he supposed to show me around? We were supposed to go back to the village last night but didn't make it."

Theodora's face held a peculiar expression as she replied. "I think he decided to do some other things first." Her voice was odd and wobbly, and I swore she flinched. I wanted to press the issue, but I was too tired, and my bones were still throbbing.

The flashes of Casimir's attempt resurfaced, and I curled into myself more. A delicate hand placed itself on my knee. "His Majesty was very worried about you when he came to us this morning," Theodora cooed. "He wants us to stay with you today and make sure your needs are met." My heart skipped, but Ani's look of disgust only deepened as she crossed her arms and looked away.

*He's worried about me?*

"Ani," Theodora turned to the smaller woman, "Fetch the medicinal herbs. We'll place them in her bath."

Ani grumbled something under her breath and padded down the stairs. Theodora offered her hands to me. "Come with me, Your Majesty. Let's go to the washing room and soothe those aches."

"Thank you," I said, taking her hands and sliding out of bed. As soon as my feet touched the floor, my legs were on fire. "Ah!" I cried, then let out a quiet whimper. A blade-like sensation tore through my muscles. They ached even more than yesterday.

"Whoa, be careful. Don't push yourself. I'm here to help you."

I steadied myself by clutching Theodora's arms, letting the maid guide me to the washing room. But as I limped along, I realized something.

"Wait, I didn't see any other rooms downstairs."

The maid chuckled.

"There's a room behind the stairs, and don't worry Your Majesty, immortals have no use of the washing room other than to bathe."

*So I* am *immortal. I was right.* "At least something good comes from immortality," I muttered under my breath. Theodora seemed at a loss for words as she continued ushering me along.

*Note to self: introduce sarcasm to this realm.*

A newfound strength would have been better than not having to use the bathroom, but I'd take what I could get. I shuffled into the washing room, ignoring the slight humiliation I felt when these maids I hardly knew had to not only see my naked body but help me into the tub. I felt useless. Pathetic. No wonder Ani thought I wasn't fit to be queen.

All those thoughts fizzed away as soon as I sunk into the bath. The warm water was a dream. Sighing, I plunged deeper until only the space above my nose was visible. I breathed steadily, not sitting up straight until I noticed Theodora placing flowers along the surface of the foamy bath. They looked like white lilies but with a slight shimmer to them—like little stars floating on the glassy water. I smiled in delight at the rainbow dust falling from the petals as each lily sunk and dissolved in the water. I ran my fingers through the bright kaleidoscope around me, musing, "How magical."

When they'd all disappeared, Ani poured an olive-green liquid into the tub.

"The flowers will numb the aching," Theodora explained, "and the potion will give you strength to walk. I think it'll help if you at least walk some today, or you'll cramp up in bed and be in an even worse state tomorrow, especially with the potion. It's kind of fussy that way. It likes its user to put in the effort."

I stared at the water. Despite knowing magic was all around me, a sentient potion was a little unsettling. But the magic in the water soothed my body, wrapping me in healing warmth almost instantly; it couldn't be too bad.

I fortunately didn't need help out of the tub after the tonics worked their magic, so I was able to dry myself off and mostly dress without the maids' aid. I had to relent when they showed me the gown I'd be wearing, though. Another fine garment of silk, this time a green as dark as the trees at midnight. The silk wrapped around my shoulders, and beneath them were nets of complementary shades of green, contrasted from light mint to dark pine. Floral designs were woven all the way down to the loops that wrapped around my middle fingers on each sleeve. The neckline was low enough to be sexy but high enough not to be too revealing. The bodice had to be laced in the back, which accentuated my form.

In the reflection of the mirror, I watched in admiration as the two women styled my hair in pins and combs. I appreciated that some of my hair fell over my shoulders today instead of resting completely atop my head. I turned to admire every angle. My current situation wasn't ideal, but I did enjoy the perk of looking like royalty every day. It gave me a newfound confidence that didn't come from being treated like a slave in Woodsmeadow.

Theodora placed her hands on my shoulders, bending down to look at me through the mirror. "You look beautiful, Your Majesty."

"Thank you, Theodora." I smiled, but I couldn't help looking at Ani, who just snorted and rolled her eyes. My cheeks reddened, nausea filling my stomach.

"Ani!" Theodora clucked, but I waved a hand in the air.

"It's okay. Let's go. I could use a good walk."

"All right," Theodora said. "Let's go to the main square and get you some food, and then we can show you around a little."

The smells of the forest were divine. It was clean and earthy; the rain had brought out a fresh scent that accentuated the sweet aroma that reminded me of Christmases spent with my parents. As I licked my fingers to finish off the residue the glazed scone had left behind, I found that I was actually enjoying myself until Theodora gasped.

"Let me get you a napkin, Your Majesty. It isn't proper to lick your hands like that."

"Oh, I'm sorry." I started wiping my hands on my dress, which made Theodora's jaw drop. Frantically, she took my wrists and placed them gently at my sides.

"It's okay. Just...wait here." She lifted her skirts and scuttled away, leaving me alone with Ani.

After an uncomfortable amount of silence, I turned to Ani, hoping to break through her hard exterior. "How are you today?"

"Don't try," she snapped. "I don't like you."

Hurt cut through me like a knife. "Why not?"

She rolled her eyes. "You're nothing but a worthless human brought here to sleep with the king. I will never respect you."

Embarrassment turned to frustrated anger. "I don't—" I started, but Ani lifted a hand to silence me and walked away, apparently not caring what her duties were for the day. I hated that I felt like crying. Hoping to spot Theodora, I scanned the village, but all I saw were the merchants and their booths with wares, treats, and produce. Beyond them were some of the woodland people's homes, children playing, and adults going about their day-to-day tasks. It reminded me of Woodsmeadow, but I recognized no one, and the kind maid was nowhere in sight.

Ani was getting to me, messing with my head and feeding on my anxieties—some I already had and some I didn't know I had. As different townspeople walked by, occasionally glancing at and bowing to me, I couldn't help but wonder if they saw me as Bratan's bedmate too. A disgusting human unworthy of being their leader.

Was it me or were they whispering and giving me dirty looks?

Tears stung my eyes. I had to get out of here.

Leaving through a dense cluster of trees was my best option, so when no one was looking, I rushed in, moving along the edges so I didn't get too far from the clearing in case Theodora came back. I tried my best to avoid the mud or anything that would ruin yet another new pair of shoes when a familiar voice made me halt.

"I know that," he hissed, and even without seeing Bratan's face, I knew he was saying it through his teeth. Someone else spoke back, but I couldn't make out what they were saying. I crept closer, listening and hoping he wouldn't spot me.

"Leave her out of this," he growled. The other person grumbled something, and he shouted. "I know! Do you think I'd—" A twig snapped beneath my foot when I almost lost my balance. I winced.

Bratan's face was drained of color when he turned to face me. "Leena? What are you doing here?"

I straightened, deciding to be confident, and quickly ran to see who he was talking to. I craned my neck to peer behind the tree, but all I saw was smoke.

"Who were you talking to?"

"No one you need to worry about. I was taking care of business."

"That doesn't answer my question. I know someone was there."

"Don't worry about it." His tone was terse, bordering on condescending.

When he turned to walk away, I cut in front of him, glaring up into his stupidly handsome face. "You do *not* talk to me like that!" I spat. His emerald eyes widened. "I'm not your servant. I am your *equal*, and you will treat me as such." He stared at me, dumbfounded. I was on a roll, but I didn't know what else to say. I needed to make a triumphant exit. "So...respect me! Or you'll regret it." I wanted to smack myself in the face.

*Really, Leena? That was the best you could do?*

My glower was strong despite the pang of embarrassment digging into my side. He didn't seem fazed by my awkward comment. He continued staring at me, speechless, so I spun on my heel and left, leaving him to think about what a jerk he'd been.

I wasn't expecting the gloved hand that met my chin, turning me around. His eyes were somehow darker as he gazed down at me. "There's that delicious fire," he growled, and my heart tripped. "What else would you like to tell me, little dove? Keep going."

Now I was speechless, blinking up at him like a doe. "You're stubborn. Arrogant. You treat everyone around you like they're inferior." The more I said, the more excited his expression became, his teeth baring like he wanted to eat me. "Things are going to change around here. No one is going to grovel at your feet anymore."

His hand curled around my face, sliding to the back of my neck. He grasped it just tight enough that I had to suppress a gasp.

"You're the only one I want groveling at my feet." His voice was low, sultry. The excited fire he often sparked in my blood came to life.

"You're vile," I hissed, but he only smiled wickedly and pulled me closer. For some reason, I let him.

He leaned forward. "What do you desire, Leena? I will do whatever you want. Say the word, and I'll do it."

I ignored the heat in my body and pushed him away. "Why? What have I done to make you so smitten? What could I possibly be doing that makes you act like this?"

His eyes darkened, and his hand fell down my back, pressing me against him by the hips. "You enrapture me simply by breathing," he purred, and the air whisked from my lungs. "The moment I saw you in the woods, I knew you were mine." He leaned even closer, brushing his lower lip against the top of my breast. I failed to suppress a gasp, which only made him more eager as he licked up the slope of my neck. My eyes closed. "And I was right. You're fire itself. Ferocious. Sensual." His hands roamed my waist before gripping my hips. My head fell back in longing as he breathed on my throat and kissed it. "Come home with me, Leena. Put that fire to good use."

I opened my mouth to protest, but he began slowly kissing down my chest. The warmth of his breath on the top of my breasts made my toes curl.

"I want you," he growled. "You're the only one I desire. The only one who can match me." His fingers found the top of my dress, curling into the front of the bodice. "I want you in every way each time I wake and before we go to sleep." He pulled my dress lower, and I heard Ani's words echo in my head. *Bratan's whore.*

My eyes snapped open.

"No! Let go of me!" My body was dangerously warm, my mind precariously fuzzy. "I want nothing to do with you! You can't distract me from your lies with your seduction."

"What lies?" He grabbed me by the wrist before I could flee. "I haven't lied to you."

"You wouldn't tell me who you were talking to and I have a feeling you're keeping things from me."

"There are a lot of things you don't know yet, Leena. In time, you'll know them all. I promise"

His face was unreadable, and I had no clue where to go from here. I kept getting caught between wanting this man and remembering he was a monster, and then wanting to believe that he'd saved those missing villagers, and then not trusting him. It was giving me a headache. "How can I trust you?"

"Ask me anything," he said. "What do you want to know?"

There were so many things I wanted to know, but I started with the one weighing heavily on my mind. "Did you really save the woman and children who went missing in my village? We were under the impression you'd hurt them or stolen them. I haven't seen them since my arrival; if you didn't hurt them, where are they? And why would there be a need of a deal between you and my village?"

He leaned his back against a tree. "Did you know those villagers?"

My head jerked back. "Yes, why?"

"Then you must know why they were freed."

"Well...you had said they were being abused and that you'd saved them, but I haven't seen them."

He pushed off the tree and walked closer. His size was intimidating, but I didn't feel scared as he approached me. On the contrary. He made me feel safe.

"I can feel every creature in this forest, as I'm sure you will start to, too. I can feel every person, animal, plant, and creature's pain. Including humans. That woman was getting beaten by her husband regularly. I felt it. I heard her cries." His eyes stayed fixed on mine, and I couldn't look away, even when the clouds overhead covered the sun, creating a momentary blanket of darkness above us. "I freed her," he said. "I have a designated group of subjects who look after such affairs. They brought her food and clothing for her and her child. They did the same for the other children who were being hurt, including that adolescent boy."

"You sent them all off on their own? That boy and those twin children won't survive on their own."

"No, I arranged for them to leave together," he said. "My subjects who took care of them provided them shelter in the human realm of the woods for as long as possible. When my people were approached by your town's matriarch to stop the disappearances and other actions I was taking to push those horrid people out, my subjects helped them escape. They brought them somewhere safe. They will be okay. I've made sure of it."

I searched his eyes for the truth, but I could feel it. Every word he spoke was true. "How will you help anyone now? What do you want from me?"

Finally, he broke our gaze and stepped back. A cold ripple shivered between us. "That part is complicated," he said. "I'm still figuring some things out myself." He took a deep breath in and let it out in a loud exhale. "What I *can* tell you is that I hope you will help me. The rest will come later."

I looked away, but I couldn't stop thinking about the villagers he'd saved. We'd all thought they'd been stolen, killed, or both. But he'd liberated them. There were things he wasn't telling me, though, and I had a feeling they were an important piece to the puzzle. "You can't tell me why you need me or why you agreed to this arrangement?"

"I already told you, Leena, I'm still figuring things out. But if you're worried about anyone back in your village, I assure you that I'm keeping my end of the bargain. Their crops are growing back, and things will soon be back to normal." He huffed. "They don't deserve it, and I don't want them in my forest, but a deal is a deal. As long as they don't do anything stupid."

A wave of relief washed through me at the hope that Grandmother would be safe and taken care of, but something wasn't right. "You're the one who made the deal. What's in it for you? Surely you didn't just want someone out of loneliness."

"I don't have all the answers you want, Leena, so stop asking. I'll tell you when I can."

Fury flashed across my skin in waves of heat. "Why can't you tell me now? You're the one who made the deal!"

"It wasn't like that! I—" He grumbled under his breath and scratched the back of his head in frustration. "Can't you trust me for now?"

"How can I? You won't answer the most important questions I have!"

Stepping forward, he got as close as he could, shooting daggers into my eyes. "Do you know how frustrating you are?"

"Do you know how frustrating *you* are?"

His jaw clenched. "Go busy yourself with something to do. I'll find you later." He took a step back and turned to leave.

I swore I saw flames in my eyes. "I don't want you to find me later!"

"Fine!" he said, throwing his hands up as he walked away.

"Fine! Go tend to whatever business you have today! But don't expect me to be waiting up for you!"

"I wasn't going to!" he said without turning around.

I let out a loud, frustrated groan and stomped away.

This man would be the death of me.

*** 

*Bratan*

"You seem to have the girl's mind properly muddled," the woman croaked.

My fingers curled, then released. "What do you want? I thought you'd left."

A cackle like a creaking door escaped her shriveled lips. "I wanted to make sure you weren't catching feelings for the girl."

I shot her a look, wishing I could throttle the old hag. "Why shouldn't I catch feelings for my own wife?"

She laughed again, louder this time. "We both know what this marriage is." The withered woman approached me with those disturbingly hollow eyes—ones that reflected no soul, only shadow. "We both know you cannot love."

My breathing quickened, fury ripping through me. "You lied to me, Melora," I growled. "Leave. NOW!"

The old crone laughed so loud I panicked, looking in the direction Leena had fled. I let out a sigh of relief at the empty path. "You know she cannot love you."

An involuntary, untamed yell roared from my throat as my true form started to show.

"LEAVE!" I opened my claws, my shoulders scraping against treetops. The old woman cackled again—the sound of glass against a chalkboard—and slipped away in a wave of shadow.

The sounds she'd silenced upon her arrival resumed—the chirping of birds, the wind skating against the leaves—but a heavy sense of dread fell over me as I returned to my human form.

Shadows bled from my feet as anger and panic swelled. Tears burned in my eyes, which only angered me more. I threw myself at the spot the woman had just been and let out a wail of rage. Wildlife fled from every direction, crows cawing as they flew away.

And for the first time in a very long time, true fear sprouted in my chest.

# Chapter Eighteen

Leena

I paced around the village with balled fists until Theodora called out to me. "What are you doing, Your Majesty? I was looking everywhere for you." I couldn't stop thinking about Bratan, fuming and wishing I'd added more to my retort to humble him a little. I couldn't stand his arrogance and tyranny and how everyone I encountered trembled in his presence. What could I do to get under his skin?

"Your Majesty?" Theodora repeated, handing me a napkin that I no longer needed.

Then a brilliant idea bloomed to life. "I want to throw a party."

"What?" Theodora fidgeted nervously and looked around as though afraid Bratan might overhear.

"I want to throw a party," I repeated, more insistent this time. "I want to introduce myself to everyone, and what better way than to gather everyone together and have a good time? I looove to dance. And music brings people together, doesn't it?" I laced my fingers behind my back and scanned the square.

"I think the middle of this section of town will do, but we could always go somewhere else." The maid continued to stare at me, speechless. "Though you were going to show me around the forest. Perhaps there's a better location?"

"Um...well...we've never done anything like that before..."

"And you've never had a formerly human queen before either, right?"

"Well, we have...but it was long ago and wasn't with His Majesty. But still, this is highly unusual."

"None of the beings alive now has ever had a queen, correct?"

The maid sighed. "Most of us, no, but—"

"This place needs a woman's touch, and I'm taking the lead. As queen." I lifted my face triumphantly.

Theodora sighed again, rubbing her temples. A group of children skipped by, chasing each other in glee. "I want more happiness like that around here. Help me prepare. Please." I nodded toward my house but then realized there wasn't much there. "Um...could we gather some seamstresses and other townsfolk to help with food and decorations? And party favors?"

Theodora dropped her worried hand and shrugged in defeat. "Of course, Your Majesty."

"Leena. Call me Leena." I smiled brightly, but the maid shook her head.

"That is something I cannot do. I think His Majesty would have my head."

The thought of Bratan and his tyrannic rule made me fume again. "Fine. But we are throwing a party whether he likes it or not."

Theodora scanned the square, inspecting the area and landing on a cottage on the far side of town. "Very well. Follow me."

*****

The seamstresses worked with the fabric like magicians. The fine material wove through their hands like sheets of soil scooped fresh from the earth. I marveled at the way they worked. I was always impressed with the seamstresses back home, but these otherworldly creatives were on a level a human simply could not match.

"Your Majesty." The voice came from a female who looked human but with two small horns protruding from her temples. "The bakers want you to test the pastries."

My face lit up. "I'd love to!" Anything food-related was where I loved to be. Following the girl out of the seamstress' tent, I marveled at the newly decorated town square. Streamers of every color were strung across the village from tree to tree, covering the square in a rainbow canopy.

"Over here," the seamstress called, motioning for me to one of the long tables off to the side. I wondered how they'd found tables so long on such short notice. They were each easily half the length of the forest's trees, and various sweets were patterned like confetti along the surfaces, no empty space to be seen, and no color was next to itself twice. It was a beautifully curated mosaic.

I scanned the delicacies covered in frothy icing and scoops of caramel and fudge. I ran my hand along the table. It was smooth and polished and felt completely new. Did carpenters make them specifically for this event? These people—or creatures, or whatever I was to call them—were amazing. Such talent with eyes for creation.

"We have a few desserts we'd like you to try," a raspy voice came from below. I looked down at a male troll—his nose was round with little wart-like bumps; his skin was a dark green, matching his fuzzy head. He held a large wooden platter of a colorful arrangement of cupcakes, custards, breads, and treats I'd never seen before.

I took bites of each one, ascending to heaven with every smack of my lips.

"This is incredible," I said with a mouth full and crumbs bouncing off my chin.

"How dainty." The deep voice instantly soured the mood. I shot Bratan a glare as I swallowed a hunk of cupcake.

"I didn't ask for your opinion, my dear husband." The last few words held a particularly large amount of venom, but that didn't stop him from chuckling.

"I like the sound of that on those pretty lips." He leaned in close, but I scoffed and quickly turned my back to him.

I plucked a small cookie in the shape of an acorn and popped it into my mouth. My eyes rolled back, and I made a sound of sheer delight. "Mmmm."

A hand caressed my shoulder. "You're making me jealous, little dove."

I swatted Bratan's hand away and pretended he wasn't there, taking another sweet. He grumbled behind me, intensifying my satisfaction.

"Please ignore my husband," I said with a saccharine smile; the troll looked up at Bratan in fear. "He's probably never indulged in such treats before, or else he wouldn't be able to resist." I winked and took a bite of what appeared to be a sugared donut but ended up tasting like maple candy.

"I wouldn't say that," he purred, moving a sheet of my hair from my shoulder, "there's a particular taste I rather enjoy."

I whipped around with a venomous glare before assessing what he was wearing. He wore a thick black vest with matching trousers, gloves, white tunic, and cape. He seemed to alternate between black and white. I'd yet to see him in anything else.

"Go home and get changed," I said.

He lifted a brow. "Why? What are you doing anyway?" He turned, motioning around him with an outstretched arm. "What is this?"

"A party, sweet husband. Now go get dressed into something more casual."

"A party? Why? What are you up to?"

I rolled my eyes and wiped my crumb-covered fingers off on my skirt, hoping Theodora didn't see.

"You know, not everything has to have an ulterior motive."

"No, but it often does."

"Not with me." Not bothering to face him, I turned back to the baker. "These are all very lovely, and I'm sure the rest are just as good. Please continue." The man bowed and skittered away. I narrowed my eyes on Bratan. "You see what you do to your people? This is exactly why we need a party."

"I'm not supposed to be liked," he said, bored. "I'm supposed to run this place and keep them safe."

"That doesn't mean you have to be cruel. Besides, I'm running this place now, too, and I say we're having a party." I pointed in the direction of our house. "Now go get changed into something you can dance in."

He barked out a laugh. "Dance? You can't be serious."

"Go! Now!" I stared at him with complete composure and confidence until, to my immense shock, he grumbled something under his breath and left. His cape billowed behind him as he strolled home. I stood frozen, stunned, but then realized I hadn't given him pertinent information. "Come just before sundown!" I yelled, and he lifted a lazy hand without stopping. I couldn't tell if I was annoyed or feeling something else...something positive? I was almost happy at the thought of him coming, which was annoying.

Taking a deep breath, I wondered what tonight would be like. "Your Majesty?" I turned to find Theodora with a black, lacy curtain of fabric hung over her folded arms. "Are you ready to be dressed?"

"Yes, of course," I said, but my mind was elsewhere. I couldn't stop thinking of Bratan and what was going through his mind. I truly didn't understand him, though I wasn't sure I wanted to.

Still, I couldn't deny that I was excited to see what the party would be like with him so grumpily out of place in a field of song and laughter. I could hardly wait.

***

I was in a daze as I stood on my usual stump in the unofficial dressing tree. Butterflies bumped against the walls of my belly, and I found myself smiling as I was fitted into a new gown—a black one with gold embellishments. The dress was the color of night at its darkest, with netted sleeves and a lace collar that weaved up my neck. Golden thread snaked around the bodice, which had an outer corset made of black leather. I wanted to make an impression—to radiate like the sun amid shadows to signify my place as queen and equal to Bratan. This was perfect.

I'd also insisted on getting ready here and not at home so I didn't run into him. I wanted to surprise him—to make him want me so desperately he couldn't breathe. Of course, I wouldn't cave into my desires, at least not yet, but I wanted to be sexy. Beautiful and desirable. A carrot he couldn't reach.

Then, a thought dawned on me.

What if he didn't show up?

It was highly unlikely that he would. He was the monster of the woods, after all. But he did begrudgingly go home to change. Maybe he went somewhere else and didn't listen. A heavy weight sunk into my gut.

"Oh no," Theodora muttered, going through the drawers of a jeweled armoire. Her hands sifted through each section. When she got to the bottom drawer, she forced it shut. It jingled like a wind chime.

"What is it?" I asked, following the maid's movements as she fetched her cloak.

Theodora sighed and then forced a smile, meeting my gaze in the mirror. "You look beautiful, Your Majesty, but I want you to look absolutely perfect. Just as you requested."

"Oh, I didn't mean to put any pressure on you."

"Nonsense. You're my queen. It's my duty to serve you." She slung her cloak over her shoulders. "I have to get hair ornaments from my cottage. I thought I'd brought them, but I must have forgotten. Ani will finish lacing you up and getting your hair ready. I'll be right back."

That small bit of excitement fizzled away as Ani took her place. The grumpy maid had been, thankfully, sitting quietly on a stump in the back of the room. I was hoping I wouldn't have to deal with her today, especially not alone. "Thank you,

Ani," I managed to say. The fae woman didn't respond. She took two golden combs and fitted them into my hair. "Isn't Theodora fetching hair ornaments?"

She ignored me, so I stopped trying to speak to her and watched her work in the mirror. Despite my dislike for her, I couldn't help smiling at the hairstyle she was fashioning for me. I liked that my blonde waves were partially down; it made me feel a little freer and accentuated one of my favorite features of myself. I loved my hair's volume, and I liked that Theodora had curled the ends with another source of magic in an oil she'd brushed into it moments before.

Ani's hands left my hair and roughly grabbed the cords of my outer corset. I suppressed a wince as she started, surprised at her strength. "Are you really going to keep pretending you're equal to His Majesty?"

I tried not to give her a reaction, at least not a flustered one. "I *am* equal to him, and I plan to change things around here." To my dismay, I couldn't hide how furious I was, which wasn't typical of me, but I'd had enough of Ani's attitude. The maid snorted, her fingers working more quickly on the back of my dress.

She pulled at the cords a little tighter than necessary. "He won't keep you for long. He only needs an heir. Once you give him one, he'll leave you."

The blood drained from my face. Nausea replaced my frustration. "He what?"

Ani pulled harder. "Why do you think he wants to bed you so badly? Do you really think he wants to lie with human trash?"

"Ani!" Theodora snapped, snatching the cords from the smaller woman's hands. "What venom are you poisoning our queen with?"

"The truth." She shifted her vicious gaze to meet mine.

"Leave," Theodora commanded. "*Now.*"

Ani chortled and walked past the maid who I was starting to realize held a higher position, or else Ani would likely not have listened. But she seemed to stand by tradition. Before leaving, she shot one final glare at me. "Remember my words, human. He will cast you aside the moment he gets the chance."

"She's speaking lies, Your Majesty. He needs you."

"Until he gets an heir," Ani spat.

"He *wants* you," she said, taking hold of my hands. "Trust me." I ignored Ani as the infuriating maid left, pondering Theodora's words.

I didn't know who to believe. What Ani said made sense. He wanted to bed me so badly. There was nothing special about me. But I thought of the gentleness of his hands as they pulled off my clothes the night before. The way he'd held me close as I'd fallen asleep after rescuing me from an attacker. And of the heat that continuously roared between us—a special fire that wasn't just lust. Sparks like that couldn't be fabricated. I was sure of it...but...The nausea swelled in my stomach.

Theodora squeezed my hands tighter. "Don't listen to her," she said. "I've learned that she's a stickler for tradition and has a prejudice against humans. She knows nothing of His Majesty. She only speaks for herself and a small group of zealots. All right?" Her eyes held such sincerity that I decided to believe her. If I had to believe someone, it might as well be her.

"All right," I said, though it held no conviction.

Theodora smiled and released my chilled fingers. "Good. Now, let's finish lacing you up. The town's preparations are ready. All we need now is the guest of honor." She winked, but as she finished lacing up my dress and removing the combs to put the hair ornaments in place, I couldn't help but wonder if Bratan did have an ulterior motive and what I could do to keep myself safe.

# Chapter Nineteen

S TRINGS FROM WOOD-CARVED INSTRUMENTS hummed beautiful, upbeat melodies through the village square. Creatures from every part of the wood were happily participating in the festivities, enjoying themselves with sweets, dancing, and simply spending carefree time together. But there was still no sign of Bratan, causing my stomach to coil in distress. Wrapping my arms around myself, I remembered Ani's words, hoping they weren't true.

*No, Theodora is right. He wants me. Why would he need an heir? He lives forever, doesn't he? He's immortal.*

But I didn't really know anything about him or his kind—about what his duties were, or mine—and if we were to be Keepers of the forest forever or not. How many leshies were there in the world? If he found an heir, he would likely not need me anymore, and maybe he'd be free. Maybe he was confined to these woods until he had someone to take his place. Would it have to be someone of his blood if he did?

A loud pop from a party cracker split through the air, and the glee of children dancing beneath falling confetti pulled my lips into a smile. Their laughter was infectious, and my heart warmed at the bliss in their expressions as they closed their eyes and let the colorful pieces of paper fall onto their faces. One giddy child poked another, and an impromptu game of tag ensued.

I watched them as the sounds of the party settled in the evening air. What was first quiet, hesitant chatter at the party's start was now an orchestra of merriment, fiddles, and laughter from creatures of all ages. These were my people—these wildly dancing, beautiful villagers. And I had managed to bring them joy despite my grumpy husband's strict reign. If only that heart of his could soften just a little.

"Your Majesty!" Theodora called, skipping over to me, a mug of cider in hand. "The party is a huge success!" She clutched my hand in hers, eyes wide and bright. I'd not seen this side of her, but it was comforting to know that she could let loose a little. "Come join us!" she said before being peeled away by the hand of a handsome fae male who'd grabbed hold of her and swept her onto the makeshift dance floor.

"Why shouldn't I?" I said, more to myself than anything. Bratan didn't deserve my stewing, nor did Ani. I was just as much of a ruler of this kingdom as he was, and I'd enjoy the party I arranged. No one deserved the right to rule over my emotions. No one.

I dropped my tense shoulders, took a deep breath, gathered my skirts, and jumped into the middle of it all. Some of the villagers appeared hesitant to enjoy themselves around their dancing queen, but when they saw my awkward movements and the way I laughed with my whole body, they must have realized that I wasn't the stuck-up tyrant my husband was.

Theodora grabbed me by the hand, and I joined her in a chain of dancers. At least thirty of the villagers were a part of the skipping chain. Laughter spilled from me like a music box. The fiddles and clapping from musicians rose to the starry sky like sun-soaked mist.

It wasn't until I let go of Theodora's hand and lifted my arms above my head to dance on my own that I saw him across the square. His eyes hooked mine into an almost physical trance. His hair was a mess of dark waves around his usual stoic expression, but his attire was unlike his usual garb. Switching out from a three-piece suit and cape, he wore a thin, black tunic unlaced at the top, the material casually falling untucked over black trousers with matching boots.

His eyes briefly flickered to my legs, and then he raised an eyebrow and crossed his arms. I resisted the urge to roll my eyes. This was my night. I wouldn't let him ruin it.

I plastered on a smile and raced over to him. He staggered back in surprise, appearing unsure what to do with himself. He clearly wasn't expecting this response, and his shock only increased when I took hold of his hands.

"Dance with me!" I said.

"I don't dance," he grumbled, and I could barely hear him over the music.

"Nonsense! Come on!" I tugged harder, but it was like his feet had sunk into the ground, rooting themselves like the trees canopying the space around us. His forehead creased, and there was a hint of worry in his expression like he was afraid to dance, so I smiled brighter, my cheeks hurting at the effort. His green eyes inspected the crowd, and then he sighed and let me drag him into the square.

I jumped in glee, twirling myself under his arm with his long fingers. But then the music stopped, as if his presence had sucked every shred of merriment away from the party and villagers. My hand fell, but I didn't let go of him. I beamed at our people, then turned my attention to the musicians.

"Why did you stop? The night is young! Let's dance!" It took a moment before the lead fiddler started up again, slowly at first and then faster, the others in his accompaniment following suit.

My husband's look of annoyance was deep and searing. Ignoring it, I twirled myself under his arm until my back was pressed against his chest. I winked up at him, and the tight line of his mouth finally broke into a smile. Soft clapping erupted from a handful of villagers, and I made it my mission to loosen Bratan up.

To my immense surprise and relief, he twirled me back out until I was spinning on my toes in giddy laughter. I stumbled in a fit of dizziness, but he caught me before I fell. My breath caught in my throat. His nose brushed mine, and time stopped. We looked at each other, the music around us spilling away. Before I knew it, he was pressing a soft kiss to my lips, the taste intoxicating, dizzying me more than the cider or ale. When he released my lips, he dipped me until my head fell back. He kissed my throat, and his mouth left sparks against my skin. I was lightheaded as he lifted me upright and pulled me in close. Our fingers laced together, then our arms stretched out, and he led me in a methodical dance, pulling me in and moving in step with the music.

I tried suppressing an impressed smile, but it didn't go unnoticed. "I said I *don't* dance, not that I couldn't."

My tongue pressed coyly against my cheek as I stifled a laugh. "I see." I looked back up at him, amused, and he spun me again. The merriment was back. Everyone around us danced and hooted, and the sounds of everything were loud and beautiful and free.

My new husband and I danced and laughed all night, especially when he gracelessly spilled wine down his tunic. He didn't look amused at my hysteric laughter until he scooped me up and kissed his wine-covered lips all over my neck, which only made me laugh harder.

The energy eventually died down, and the music slowed. The fiddlers had traded spots with other musicians so they could enjoy the party too, but the melodies soon turned into unhurried sonnets of sound, graceful and smooth. Bratan held me against him as we swayed, slow and heady. He was different than I'd thought, and despite my initial hesitation, I was enchanted by everything about him. The way he smelled of rich spice and cloves, the sound of his deep voice, and the way he held me and looked at me like no one else in the world mattered. But above everything else, I loved the way he smiled tonight. It opened a curtain to who he truly was. The man behind the monster facade.

My face fell softly against his chest, and I could feel the quick beats of his heart. I breathed in deep, content, and winding down from the exhilaration of the evening. His arms wrapped around me, lifting me until his lips pressed against my ear. "You are such a magnificent creature, Leena."

"I know," I teased. When he chuckled, my heart skipped. My voice quieted. "You're not so bad yourself."

We continued swaying in slow, dazed steps. "I don't know what you've done to me," he said, "but I can't stop thinking about you." I looked up without a word, not knowing what to say and desperately wanting to hear more. "All day, all I can think about is your curious eyes and the rush you send through my blood—a sensation you can bring on at any given moment with just a touch. Just a kiss." He leaned in, cradling my jaw in his hands. "You have a good heart, Leena, and you're incredibly beautiful and a crack of thunder. My precious bolt of lightning..." He kissed the space beneath my ear so slowly it made me weak. "And I am drawn to you so much it hurts."

My blood heated, and against my better judgment, I slid my hand around the nape of his neck, closing my eyes and listening to the hum of his voice. "I haven't stopped thinking about you either," I whispered in ragged breaths. My head was still cradled in his hands, his face buried into my neck. His teeth gently grazed it, down to my shoulder and then back up to my ear.

"You've poisoned me, little dove. I crave you. I *crave* you." He growled, and my knees nearly gave out. My fingers gathered the cloth of his tunic.

"I can't escape you, can I?" I said, a deep ache thickening in my blood.

He chuckled into my hair. "Not if you desire me half as much as I starve for you." His already sultry voice was low; the bass of it thrummed in my ears. I had to silence a sound as he pressed another kiss into my neck. "Do you want to go home?"

"Yes," I whispered, breathless. He clutched the back of my dress as he brought me into a deep kiss. He tasted of wine and frosting and something only of him. "Take me home."

# CHAPTER TWENTY

LEENA

W E BURST THROUGH THE door, Bratan's hands grop-
ing my back. Lifting me by the backside, he pulled me
up, and I wrapped my legs around his waist. His fingernails
dug through the lace of my dress, tearing apart the bodice
and strings in one flawless sweep. I grabbed his face and sunk
deeper into his kiss. He staggered forward, finding his footing,
then moved with precision, eyes closed as he kissed me. He
moved around a chair and pressed my back hard against the
wall.

My head fell to one side, welcoming his lips as he kissed my
neck. I let out a sound as his tongue slid over my collarbone,
and gently, he bit it, sucking on it until thoughts of him and
his touch muddled and melted into a dizzy haze in the back
of my mind. He trailed his tongue up my throat until he was
kissing me again. His fingers tangled into my hair, ripping out
the ornaments with insatiable hunger, then cradled my head
and pulled me harder against him.

I clawed at him, just as voracious, my skin hot, my desires wildly aflame. One of his hands hooked into the neckline of my dress until it split down the middle. Immediately, as the cloth ripped, his lips found the top of my chest, and he kissed it before licking back up to my mouth. I let out a shaky breath, muttering his name as my fingernails scraped down his flesh. He let out a low growl, ripped off the bodice of my dress, and flipped me around, throwing me on the table.

I watched him prowl over me, his eyes dark and primal in the dimness of our cabin. I sucked in what little breath I had and let my eyes close as his hands roamed up my legs. First, he pulled off my stockings, then my dress, and then my under-things. He was so strong he only needed one hand to tear off every piece of clothing. He kissed my hip bone, biting it and sucking on it before pressing a kiss on the soft crease of my inner thigh. I couldn't take it anymore. I needed him. I wanted to submit to him in every way.

I clawed his back, pulling him on top of me. Leaning up, I kissed him, insatiable, and we moved together without skipping a beat. He kissed down my body until I was in a flurry of sparks.

"I want you," I breathed, and he snarled, climbing back on top of me and pulling off his clothes. I helped him rip off his shirt while he did the rest, and then, before I could think, his body weaved into mine. I let out a sound, my eyes rolling back. At first, there was a flash of pain, and then my mind danced with stars.

"Open your eyes," he purred. "I want to see you as I take you." I did as I was told. The look in his eyes was filled with overwhelming heat and yearning, and he kept me there, locked in a trance. He lifted my wrists and pinned them above my head. The aching sparks continued blazing between us with each movement. I gasped, and my eyes were about to flutter closed when he grabbed my face. "You're a flawless creature, Leena." He raked his teeth against my chin. "I want to devour you whole." I couldn't speak, and my eyes couldn't stay open anymore. The feeling was too great—the pleasure too intense. But along with the fire in my blood was a softness in my chest—a warmth that pooled through me.

A sudden burst overtook me, a force beyond mortality. A power we shared—something that bound us beyond our bodies. My mind went numb. I lived by feeling. The more heightened the sensation became, the more the power surged through my veins. His fingers and body moved in a way that made me experience something beyond comprehension. My hand gripped the edge of the table, the other clawing at the slick, wooden surface until I had no choice but to grab hold of him. My nails scraped hard into his back, maybe a little too hard. I felt a trickle of blood beneath my fingertips.

He hissed in delight. "My little lightning bolt." He bit my neck and touched every inch of me as I ebbed against him like a thrashing wave.

I wanted him more than I wanted anything, and when another burst of light bloomed through me, all I could do was gasp and open my eyes, gazing at him as he watched me, his hair lined with sweat. Then he, too, let out a sound, and together, we caught our breath as the world around us came back, and time began to tick again. Slightly panting, he trailed a finger from my forehead to my lips. "Oh, little dove."

"What?" My chest heaved as I leaned into his touch. "Are you going to say I can never escape you now?"

"No." His voice was molten honey. He lifted one hand to grip the side of my hair, then let it fall down my arm. He entwined his fingers in mine. "I'm the one who could never escape you." My chest was still quick with rapid breaths, but emotion swelled within it. His forehead fell softly against mine. "I am wholly and completely yours." He kissed the bridge of my nose. "Will you have me?"

I didn't want to fight it anymore. Something between us was too real to ignore—a power beyond anything that seemed possible.

"Yes, Bratan. I am yours."

A satisfied sound rumbled from his throat. "I'm so glad to hear those words on your lips." The sultry lilt in his voice warmed me from the stomach down, and my lungs stopped pumping. "Nothing can stop us now. Together, we will light this world on fire and make love in the flames."

\*\*\*

The fire crackled as Bratan drew circles on my bare back. The fire's gentle heat kissed my misty skin, adding to the flush that already dusted my face and chest. I was on my stomach, my cheek rested on my folded arms. My eyes were closed as I soaked in the pure contentment of this moment.

I let out a blissful, easy sigh, reveling in the happiness I was allowing myself to have.

"What are you thinking, little dove?" His voice was soothing as it reached my ears.

I couldn't help but smile. "Absolutely nothing."

He let out a low chuckle. "Then I've done my job." His hand sprawled over my back before sliding around me and tucking me into an embrace. I turned around, facing him as he held me; I listened to his heartbeat as my hands danced along his chest.

"You certainly did." I flashed him a sultry look beneath my lashes, and something lit in his eyes.

"Good." Embers snapped in the hearth behind our tangled bodies. The rug was divinely soft, especially in Bratan's embrace; I could fall asleep here and now, completely serene. But I didn't want this moment to end. I studied the lines of his face; they were usually hard and tight, all taut skin and jagged edges. But now, they were relaxed. He looked just as content as I felt.

He smiled, his eyes trailing to my neck before giving it a quick kiss. "You have a little love bite," he said, pleased with himself.

My fingers found the place that he kissed. "I do?"

He traced it, catching my fingers in his and kissing the tips. "I guess I bit a little too hard." His hot breath soaked into my palm as he slowly kissed it, dragging his bottom lip over the lines of my flesh. "You're so delicious. I can't help myself."

A hot wave fizzed through me. Even though we'd just made love, I wanted him again. Something about him made me ravenous. I raked my fingers through his hair, lifting myself up to kiss him, and he hungrily received it.

He pinned my wrists at my sides and pressed against me, pushing me into the plush rug. He always kept his weight controlled; if he placed his full weight on me, he'd probably crush my bones. Our kissing grew more feverish. He sucked on my tongue. I scratched up his back. We were lost in a flurry of each other. Pleasure and pain, heat and bliss.

He licked down my legs, biting hard on my inner thigh. The sensation was so darkly pleasant I cried out, which made him growl. "I must have you," he said, breathing against my flesh in a way that made me ache; then he wove himself in me again, and that ecstasy returned.

I could taste the feeling. How was that possible? It was like we were one in every way. Body, soul, blood. He was in my veins like roots spreading and spiraling around my bones, power pulsing and capturing me in a place that transcended reality. We were heat and sweat and feverish movement until that flurry of sparks and blinding cluster of stars shone beneath my eyelids. His body and fingers found all the right places until my hands dug hard into his back, and I was nothing but liquid heat.

Our bodies slowed, our hearts pounding against each other, desperately wanting to burst through our skin and become as one as the rest of us. His cheek pressed against mine as he rested his head beside me; I could hear his heavy breathing as we once again returned to earth.

"I'm never letting you go," he whispered.

I nipped at his lips, still buzzing from our uninhibited intimacy.

"I wouldn't let you if you tried."

# Chapter Twenty-One

## Leena

I HUMMED IN SATISFACTION, reveling in the beauty of our connection—of the bright heat and dancing sparks still skating through me. My arms stretched lazily above my head. Bare and relaxed, I delighted in his touch as he outlined my form with his fingers, tracing every curve.

"Your body is incredible," he said, leaving a slow trail of kisses from my chest to my stomach. "Delicious," he grumbled against my navel, and if I weren't so satisfied, I'd have begged for him again. His large hands grabbed hold of my hips, kissing the hollow beneath the bone. I loved that my body was his and that I could be vulnerable and completely open to someone. Especially someone I felt such a strong connection with—a strong, inexplicable bond.

"Yours isn't too bad either." I winked at him, squealing with laughter when he grabbed me, wrapping his arms around me and rolling me on top of him until my hair fell around his face. His gaze was warm, searching me in a way that made me feel even more bare than when I was sprawled out on the floor.

His hand slid up the side of my face. "Leena." His eyes still searched mine. "I'm so glad you're mine." For the briefest moment, my heart stopped.

It had been such a short period of time. Just this morning, I couldn't stand this man, but now, I couldn't deny my feelings or the overpowering bond between us. I should have thought sensibly, but instead, I whispered the truth. "I am wholly, completely yours."

His lips turned up before sinking into mine, and he held me until I fell asleep in his arms, content and on top of his strong, hard body, warm and enveloped in the heat of the crackling flames.

***

When I awoke, I was still on top of him, but he was asleep. I thought of staying there, but my back hurt, and I wanted a decent night's sleep, especially if he was intent on taking me again in the morning, which I'd gladly accept. I tip-toed upstairs, the floor cold beneath my bare feet.

I hadn't reached the top before I heard a hiss and felt a cold scrape against my shoulder blades. The sudden shock made me choke on my own breath. I spun around, searching the dark, but there was nothing. A sick chill coiled my stomach. I must have been more tired than I realized. I'd been through a lot, and I was more convinced than ever that I needed to get a good night's sleep. For over a decade, I'd been worked half to death by my uncle and often forced to sleep outside, sometimes after he'd hit me until my ears rang. But never had I hallucinated.

I shuffled to the bed, tucking myself into the sheets that were still in disarray from this morning. Surprisingly, I wasn't that tired; I was weary but wide awake. It could have been from adrenaline, but I at least needed to try to sleep. Resting even without falling asleep was better than nothing, so I wrapped the soft duvet around me and closed my eyes. I let out a long sigh, my head growing heavy as if to remind me that I *was* tired.

And then I heard it again. Louder this time. A whispered creak from the corner of the room. Fear skated up my back. I tucked myself deeper in the blankets but couldn't resist looking toward the sound, especially as it returned louder. And louder.

There was nothing but darkness. But for a flicker of a second, there was movement, like a black snake sticking its tail from its hiding place before slithering back into its hole. I wished I was braver—that I could call out and ask who was there—but the fear that it was nothing was almost worse than anything answering back.

Swallowing, I turned around and squeezed my eyes shut. *It's nothing. It's just exhaustion. Nothing's there.*

Before I could so much as turn, a cold, searing pain clawed down my back. I tried to scream, but my voice was gone. The pain intensified, the weapon sinking in deeper, but still,

I couldn't cry. When the blade, or whatever it was, retracted, I looked back. But nothing was there.

My body shook. The agony was unbearable, and I wailed silent tears as the room went black.

\*\*\*

"Leena?" Bratan's deep voice roused me from my sleep. I blinked up, clearing my vision to see my husband's worried face hovering above me. It relaxed slightly. "Leena. I thought you were hurt."

My head was throbbing. Had I been dreaming? I looked at the corner of the room, but nothing was there. Not even a shadow. Bratan said something, but I couldn't process it, and when I sat up, I let out a cry. The pain was there.

It was real.

"What's wrong? What is it?" His hand quickly found my back, but at the sight of the slick, ruddy blood that painted his palm, his eyes widened. "What happened?" Fury flashed across his face, pupils dilating, his eyes going black. "Who did this to you?"

"I-I don't know." The words came out cracked, and I burst into tears. He quickly gathered me in his arms, and I let myself cry against his chest. "I heard a hiss, and then it got louder...there was something black in the corner, and then I felt pain, and then nothing. And then I woke up." I burst into harder sobs, and he stroked my back, avoiding the gash.

"It's okay," he whispered. "It'll be okay."

I was trembling; I couldn't stop feeling the claw ripping through my flesh or seeing a slithering black tail from the corner of my eye. Bratan's arms squeezed around me, and it was oddly soothing. My heart rate slowed, and my body gradually stopped shaking. When I looked into his eyes, where once was worry was now a darkness—a determination rimmed with anger. But there was something strange about the way he was staring off like he was figuring out his next move.

I thought about asking him, but the thought of a deep conversation left me exhausted. I didn't want to talk, and I'd already decided to trust him. He'd take care of this. I laid my head back down, burying my face in his chest.

"I'm scared," I said.

His large palm glided down my back, dodging the scrape until he placed his hand softly on the gash. That healing power he'd sent through me the day we got married pushed through me. This time, it was a steady pulse beneath my skin until the gouge closed up. "Don't worry, little dove. I'll get to the bottom of this." Wrapping me in his arms, he kissed my temple and whispered low. "Stay by my side, and you'll be safe."

"Okay." The word was barely audible, but my throat was too dry to repeat it. But by the gentle squeeze he gave me, I knew he'd heard me. Smiling against his chest, I leaned into his embrace. Being in his arms made me safe. Protected. I never wanted to leave his side. It was strange. Less than a day had gone by since I'd been bent on hating him, but the pull to him was strong. And now that I'd given in to the feeling, everything had clicked into place.

It was like I'd been resisting fate, and now that I'd embraced it, all was right and how it should be.

I was so sick of living my life in fear, and in this new realm with threats lurking in the shadows, I was okay asking for help. I'd basically been on my own since my parents died, but I didn't have to be anymore. That in itself was worth it.

As if knowing exactly what I was thinking, he held me tighter.

"Distract me," I said.

"What would you like to talk about?" The question opened a door with no walls. There was so much I wanted to know. "Actually," he said, "there's something I want to clarify." I looked up at him. His fingers stroked down my newly healed back. He paused, then sighed. "I didn't know you were forced into our marriage."

I pushed back to look up at him, my eyebrows practically shooting into my hairline. "What?"

He looked away, scratching the back of his head with a pained expression. "I was told you wanted to wed me to bring our two worlds together. To offer peace through our union."

My raised brows turned quizzical. "You told me there was no escape for me. That I belonged to you."

His eyes squinted with his deepening wince. "I know this sounds ridiculous, but I was also told that human women liked to be treated that way by their romantic partners as part of sexual foreplay."

"Foreplay?" I couldn't help the laugh that burst from my lips. "You didn't get the hint when I slapped you?"

"I thought it was part of the foreplay."

I laughed even harder, and soon he joined me. Maybe it was due to the quick shift from the fear that had just racked my bones, but I was now laughing so hard my sides hurt. "I now realize how absurd it was that you'd be interested in that."

"Who says I wouldn't?" I said, still smiling as I looked up at him from beneath my lashes.

"But...you didn't like it..." The look of confusion on his face was adorable.

"I didn't then, but I think that in the right context, in the right time and place, I just might. For example," I lifted myself up, stretching my back to look up at him, my nightdress conveniently pulling down in the front, "if I knew it was a game... and we were together like this...I might entertain the idea."

Understanding flashed in his eyes. He leaned forward, pressing his forehead against mine and pushing against it until I fell on my back. "Like this?" He wrapped his fingers around me, and I felt claws form as they pinned me to the mattress. The ripping sound of the cloth beneath me sent a thrill shivering up my spine.

"Yes," I said, the air leaving my lungs., "but I think we should save this for another day. I'm tired, and I'm still a little shaken up." As much as I hated putting a halt to this before it began, I knew that if we engaged in this right now, I wouldn't be able to fully enjoy it. His lower lip almost formed a pout as he released me. "I'm sorry."

He vehemently shook his head as he gathered me in his arms again. "You have nothing to be sorry for, little dove. Would you like to sleep, or did you want to talk?"

I had so many questions for him, but I probably wouldn't retain the information if we did that, either. "I need to rest, and I think I'll be okay as long as you're with me." He squeezed me as I kissed his chin, and then I let myself drift away in the comfort of his arms, not knowing what the future would bring.

# Chapter Twenty-Two

Leena

When I awoke, Bratan was trailing a map along my back, his fingers dancing down my spine. "Good morning, little dove," he said when my dewy eyes found his.

"Good morning," I said sleepily.

"Even in the morning, you're perfect." He stroked my hair, and my head fell back in bliss. When he then kissed the tip of my nose, I smiled and sat up, scootching against him and pulling up the duvet to cover myself from the morning chill.

And then the memory of last night came back. Of what he'd said about our wedding. Our arrangement. "Bratan?"

"Hm?" His hand paused on my shoulder blade.

"I believe you that you didn't know I was forced into this. I felt something when we were wed, something in the power that flooded through me... When I came to this realm, and you told me I belonged to you, I thought you simply needed a bride and that you would take me because I filled that need. I hated you for it."

"I'm so sorry, Leena, I was an ass and had no idea I was being one."

I laughed. "I know that now, but that isn't the point." Still nestled under his arm, I threaded my hand in his and looked up at him. "After we wed, I felt a bond with you beyond explanation or understanding. There was something both supernatural and spiritual about it. I thought maybe it was fate and that we were somehow meant to be, but I quickly dismissed it because of everything that led me there. But now, I'm wondering if I'd been right."

"You were," he said, and I was surprised at how quickly he'd said it. "I believe that anyway." Gently, his fingers found my chin, and he lifted it, gazing deeply into my eyes. "I believe we were supposed to meet, Leena," he said, but his eyes turned somber as he continued. "But I was told you'd come willingly, and I am so sorry that wasn't the case. If you'd like to leave, you're free to go."

Warmth soothed the last tangled edge of my feelings for him, convincing me he was telling the truth. The last thing I wanted was to leave. "It's okay. Oddly enough, I'm glad I'm here."

"Really?" He leaned closer.

"Really," I said, and my mouth opened for him.

After one unhurried kiss, he leaned back. "Is there anything you'd like to know about me? I want you to be comfortable and to know you can trust me."

Maybe I was a fool, but I did trust him. And I wanted to know everything there was to know about him. "Tell me about your family." The words tumbled out before I could think, but I wanted to know. I wanted to understand him—to learn how his world worked and what secrets he'd locked away.

"They were very special," he said. Again, I was surprised at how quickly he'd responded, but I didn't want him to stop. Closing my eyes and nestling against his chest, I listened to the hum of his voice as he continued. "I haven't seen them in years and unfortunately never will."

"Why not?" I asked.

His hand had been lazily stroking my arm, but now it stopped.

"My mother was killed in this very forest. Turned to ash like she was nothing but a pile of wood." The silence that fell between us was suffocating. He buried me deeper into his chest, and I wondered if it was so I couldn't see his face.

"I'm so sorry." It was such a flimsy response, but I didn't have the words to express my true sorrow for him.

"It's okay."

"It's not," I replied, but if he'd heard me, he didn't acknowledge it.

"It's a long story for another day, and I want you to get some rest. For now, I'll say that I was young. I was raised mostly by my mother. My father..." His body tensed. "He was never here to begin with. It was just my mother and me, and a friend of hers, and we were the Keepers of the Woods. Technically, my father had been the official Keeper, but since he'd been gone for many years, my mother took over. She should have been the

Keeper from the beginning anyway, but she didn't have Leshy blood. When I was born, I had the powers and form of my father, so I was next in line." There was a beat of silence. "She was the official Keeper until I took over. Even then, I wasn't ready."

His hand swept over my back, softly playing with the loose hair falling over my shoulder. I felt his throat bob, but still, he stroked me in a loving way I'd never felt from anyone else. I never knew someone's touch could be both exciting and soothing.

"And then the humans came." His tone was sharp. "They burned down half the forest before I could do anything. I was still young, but technically, I was a man at that point. I felt every flame, every sharp, splintered snap of wood. And then almost everyone I'd ever known was either killed or captured. And my mother...she was just as part of the forest as I was, but since she was the Keeper, losing half the forest like that burned her alive from the inside out. And then there was only me and a handful of my people."

"Bratan..." My arms slid over his shoulders, wrapping around his neck. He held onto me like I was his lifeline. "I'm so, *so* sorry." I stroked his hair until I felt his arms loosen. "What happened to those humans?"

There was an uncomfortable silence before he pulled away. A dark flare lit in his eyes. "I killed them. Every man responsible. I killed them all."

My eyes widened. "What?"

He looked at me heatedly. "They deserved to die, Leena. They killed my people and nearly burned down the forest. It's my job to protect it. I had no choice."

"But what about the children? The innocents?"

"Of course, I didn't kill them! Do you think I'm a monster?" The question hung in the air, and his jaw clenched when he clearly remembered that I'd accused him of that very thing not long ago. His voice lowered. "Do you *still* think I'm a monster?"

I couldn't answer. I didn't know the first thing about being a Leshy, and I still didn't know him very well, but I couldn't bring myself to accept what he'd done.

"I-I don't, but—"

Hurt flashed in his eyes. He bit his lip, nodding swiftly in pained understanding. "I see. You'll always think I'm a monster." He whipped off the blanket and strode to the wardrobe.

"I didn't say that—"

He slammed it shut, putting on his clothes and throwing a cloak around his neck. "You didn't have to."

"Bratan, wait!" I reached for him, covering myself with the blanket as I scampered over. I let it fall as I took his face in my hands, but he wouldn't look at me. "I don't think you're a monster. I just...I don't understand."

He took my hands and returned them to my sides. Still avoiding my gaze, he said, "I have business to tend to today. You need rest. Sleep here until you're ready to leave. I'll fetch

Theodora to bring you breakfast and to watch over you so that you don't get hurt again."

"Bratan..."

He took one step down the stairs before turning enough for me to see the side of his face. "We're both part of this forest now, Leena. If it dies, so do we, and our people would follow soon after." My chest cramped with guilt, but I didn't know what to say. He waited a moment, probably waiting for a response, but when I didn't give one, he was gone.

My heart was heavy when the front door closed much more quietly than usual. I knew I wasn't getting any rest today. And I had no idea what to do or where to go from here.

# Chapter Twenty-Three

Leena

With Theodora close behind, I wandered through the village searching for Bratan, but he was nowhere to be found. Theodora was at the house soon after he'd left, but I didn't want anything to eat, and the last thing I wanted to do was talk. So, after some convincing, she relented to my leaving the cottage so long as she was with me. We'd been wandering for some time, but I still couldn't find my husband anywhere. And I couldn't stop thinking of what he'd said and of the hurt on his face when he'd left.

I felt sick. The truth was that I didn't know the full story of what he'd done or the pain he'd gone through, both physically and mentally. And I was holding him to human standards instead of the guardian spirit he was and who he had to be. I needed to apologize and ask him more questions. To me, killing was never an option. But his job was to protect the forest, and now it was my job, too.

I nervously twisted the dark green fabric of my dress. I chose a simple piece today because I didn't want the help of lacing a corset or getting anyone to assist me. I was drained. All I wanted to do was find Bratan, apologize, and hear him out. And I had so many questions about what my place was here.

I made it into the part of the woods I'd found him in the day before, but venturing deeper through the trees brought up a newfound anxiety. What happened last night still didn't make sense, and if I could get hurt in my own house, what would stop me from getting hurt out here?

Having Theodora trail behind me was a small comfort; if Bratan trusted her, I must be safe with her. But still, even with him in the house himself, I was attacked by whatever faceless monster had lurked in the shadows.

With no questions asked, Theodora helped me look for my husband, but the longer we searched, the more my heart sank. He was nowhere to be found, and I hated that we'd left things on such a sour note. I was still figuring things out, and he probably was, too.

The fresh air helped to calm my nerves a bit. It may have been from my new position as the wife to the Leshy, but the aroma and feel of the trees, shrubs, moss, and everything else around me filled me with peace and energy. The woods were a part of me now, and I felt it. A purity that surpassed mortality in the form of leaves and vines.

The smell of fresh pine and evergreens made me think of Christmas. It used to be my favorite time of year. As a child, my parents always made an effort to make Christmas special. We never had much money, but each year, they managed to save enough for fruitcake and materials for a gift. One year, I got a doll made from scraps of material my mother got from women in the village. When I opened the wrapping and saw its hair of different colored cloth, I was elated. I played with it for years, up until it fell apart and grew too soiled to recover. But the memory of how I felt that day will never leave me. It was one of the happiest moments of my life.

Christmas had lost its spirit when my parents were killed. It wasn't uncommon, but they'd died on a hunting trip. I never knew for certain what happened that day, but I was told a wolf had gotten to them before they could hide or escape. The people of the village used to take turns hunting, but after that day, only a handful of trained archers went out. Until recently, when food became scarce.

I wondered what Christmas or Winter Solstice would be like here and if it was celebrated at all. The thought of Bratan holding me by the fire, a thick blanket wrapped around us, cider and plum cake sticky on our fingers, was a thought I could get used to. Winter would indeed spread through these woods, and so would the holidays. I would make sure of it.

Something snapped behind me. I turned on my heels so fast that I stumbled back, about to catch myself, until a cold ache filled my insides like seawater, and a great mass of darkness shrouded my vision. A cloud of thick, black fog spread above me, engulfing the space around me like a storm cloud brought to life.

It let out a deep croak that sounded like it came from two separate voices as it got closer. Then it pounced.

Gasping, I stumbled, falling hard onto the ground. I thought I heard Theodora's voice when the dark smoke slithered around me, making clicking sounds as it slid down my throat and clogged my lungs. Clasping my neck, I scratched at it, desperate to breathe. Pain took over, pushing me back to the ground as I writhed for relief.

Then, a cold gust of wind rushed over me, giving back my breath and causing my braid to whip over my head.

"Get out!" Bratan roared. The shadow fled in a flash, a giant storm cloud racing into the distance. I lay stunned on the ground, staring at where the black mist had just been. Bratan scooped me into his arms. "Are you okay?"

"What was that?" I rasped. "Was that what hurt me last night?"

Bratan's usually green eyes were black. Even after what I'd said, he came to protect me in an instant. Despite the pain I'd caused him, he leapt to my rescue without a second thought. My vision blurred, and I hated that I was starting to cry. "I'm so sorry," I whispered, grabbing the neck of his cape. "I'm so sorry for earlier. I know you must protect your people. I'm sorry."

He held me against him as I cried. "You have nothing to be sorry for. You'll learn our duties soon enough." He paused. "I just hope you can accept me for who I am and that I will always protect you at all costs."

I blinked up at him. "What do you mean?"

His eyes returned to normal, but they had a curious glint. His face was still rigid. "I will do what needs to be done to protect you," he answered, but he didn't look at me as he said it, then continued. "I'm glad Theodora called for me and that she was here to watch over you while I was away, but we need to be more careful, at least until I find out what's going on. When I find out who did this, I won't let it go unpunished. They'll wish they never laid a grisly finger on your perfect skin."

"Why?" I couldn't help but ask. "Why would you do that for me?" I still couldn't wrap my head around his feelings for me, but I supposed my feelings were just as intense. I'd never wanted to apologize to someone so badly in my life, and I'd never been so inexplicably drawn to someone before.

His hand combed through my hair. "You mean so much to me, Leena. You're the blood in my veins and part of my very soul. I am now, and have always been, completely yours. If anyone tries to take you from this earth or burn you by harming our forest, I won't let anything stand in my way from ripping them to shreds."

It was suddenly hard to breathe again. Excitement sizzled from his words. "Nothing?"

His breath was on my lips. "Nothing," he growled, and I opened my mouth. The tears instantly dried, and the skin around my neck warmed. "Maybe I *am* a monster," he said against my teeth, "But only to protect those I love." We looked into each other's eyes. His voice lowered. "I will always be a monster if it means keeping you safe."

My legs were liquid, and my body was weak. His lips grazed mine. Slowly, my head tilted back, and he found the space beneath my ear. He kissed it so tenderly, so sensually, I let out a sound of shaky desire. He kissed a trail to my mouth, and slowly, my hands slid up his chest and wound around his neck as I kissed him back. He grabbed me by the back of my thin dress, sliding his tongue against mine. And then we were at it again, voracious and mad. Completely insane. He ripped off my clothes and made love to me on the forest floor, pressing me into the soil, entertaining my every request and desire.

I couldn't help my longing for him, and he obviously couldn't help his. We were crazy about each other and so filled with wild, primal passion and a sudden surge of love and affection. Something changed—intensified—when we tied our souls together on our wedding day. And I loved it. I loved that we were wholly and completely each other's and had this fierce connection.

My fingernails were caked in dirt by the end when we reveled in messy bliss. We allowed a long moment of sweet afterglow with loving embraces and flurried kisses before we got dressed.

We were so consumed by each other that we failed to notice the darkness that never truly left.

\*\*\*

After our escapade, I accompanied Bratan to the village, giggling when he took the occasional leaf out of my tousled hair.

"You're insatiable," he teased, to which I smacked him hard on the shoulder.

"*I'm* insatiable?" I tried playfully hitting him again, but he caught my knuckles and kissed them. I bit back a smile and leapt on him, wrapping my legs around his middle and, to my delight, knocking him into a tree. "Do you surrender?"

His grin was wide; I loved how bright it made his eyes.

"Never." He spun around and pinned me to the tree. It was easy to feel the rough bark through today's ensemble. Usually, I had a corset and at least two layers of underthings beneath a thick dress and bodice. Today, I only had my underthings, a slip, and a thin dress with a fitted bodice and cream-colored shirt underneath. The olive-green lace that looped up the front of my bodice held it all together to accentuate my figure. It wasn't stunning or regal, but it did the job well enough. It was a nicer version of the clothes I'd worn back home. Not home—where I used to live. This was my home now.

It was still hard to believe.

"Do you want to greet the villagers?" Bratan asked.

I looked at him in surprise. "*You* want social interaction?"

"No, but I know you do, so I'll deal with it." He was still smiling, and I realized how much he truly must have fallen for me to subject himself to idle chatter.

"All right, Your Majesty, lead the way." I drew out his title in a flirtatious drawl, which made his eyes light up in the way I'd hoped it would.

"I like the sound of you calling me that," he said, playing with my hair and tucking a messy lock behind my ear. "Maybe next, you can try 'master.'"

"In your dreams," I said with a playful glare.

He smiled wickedly. "All right. I'll start there, and then I'll hear it as you mutter in your sleep."

"You're devilish."

"Only for you, my love." He grabbed my chin and tilted my face up with a kiss. "Now, should we go to the village?"

"We probably should. I need to introduce myself to anyone I haven't met yet, or at least start."

"You didn't meet anyone at the party?" he asked as we walked hand-in-hand to the village.

"Not many, at least not through anything but my manic dancing."

His head fell back with a laugh. "I love your manic dancing. I could watch it all day."

"I'm sure you would," I teased, but inside, I was warm. He accepted me in all my strange, uninhibited glory. I'd always had trouble making friends, but it seemed that nothing I did deterred Bratan from looking at me in any way other than awe, adoration, or of course, voracious desire, though I wasn't sure if my dancing could incite that last feeling. If it could, he was more insatiable than I thought.

"I mean it." His voice was gentle. He cradled my face, looking deep into my eyes. "Everything you do is a dance to me, and I will never stop watching." He kissed me again, and I rested my arms on his shoulders.

Kissing me once more, he led me to the first house down the path from the trees. "Be a good girl," he said after he knocked on the hut's thin oak door. "You're flushed and giddy. Don't get me wrong, I love it, but if you want to make a regal impression, you need to be a good girl." He winked and pinched my backside.

Suppressing a smile, I smacked him on the shoulder. "You're terrible."

"I never said I was good." He winked. "That's why you need to be good for both of us."

"No. I won't accept that. Be a good boy, or you don't get the naughty side of me."

"I highly doubt that, you little minx."

"Oh, Your Majesties!" A waif-like, middle-aged elf with orange freckles and pointed ears stood in the doorway, her face crimson. How long had she been there? If the woman was crimson, I was molten. "I deeply apologize," she said with a bow. "I didn't mean to interrupt—"

"No, no, we came to your door," Bratan said, waving his hand. "My wife would like to meet her people. Please introduce yourself."

The elf nodded feverishly, messy red curls bouncing atop her head. "My name is Mila, My Lady."

I bowed my head slightly, trying my best to move on from the awkward situation. "It's wonderful to meet you, Mila."

"Please come in," The redhead said with a smile that indicated she'd pretend she hadn't heard anything. I breathed a sigh of relief and followed her into the hut. The home was small but cozy—a cylindrical living space with everything one would need: sitting room furniture, a table, cooking space, and a fireplace. Little paintings also decorated the walls, and the air smelled of citrus. My eyes landed on the bowl of fruit in the middle of the dining table—an orange mountain that made my mouth water. I adored clementines, and they were most delicious this time of year.

When the woman noticed my staring, she cupped a fruit and held it out to me. "Please, take it, Your Majesty."

"O-oh...thank you." I awkwardly grabbed the fruit, and Mila continued, asking me questions about where I was from and apologizing that they didn't have better furniture. "Please don't worry. We are happy to be here."

We enjoyed the rest of our stay in her cabin and meeting her husband, who soon joined us as he came home from collecting food for their supper. I happily peeled my first clementine, but when I started on the second one, Bratan took over, peeling it quickly so I never had to lift a finger.

"I'm perfectly capable of doing that, you know," I whispered to him.

"I know, but I want to do it." He handed me the plump fruit, and it tasted even sweeter than the one I'd peeled myself.

We stayed at the house for about an hour and then made our rounds through the village until the sky was ruddy with the melting rays of sundown.

Bratan and I walked home hand in hand when a brawny man with pointed ears and short black hair bowed quickly and whispered something in Bratan's ear. The light in my husband's eyes dimmed.

"Is everything okay?" I asked when the man stepped away.

"Yes, of course," he said smoothly, kissing my knuckles, "but I apparently have some urgent business to take care of. I'll likely be gone for the rest of the night, so I'll bring you home and have Theodora stay. I'll check the house before I leave, and I gave your maid something that allows her to more easily call for me. You'll be safe, and I'll check on you periodically throughout the night. Is that okay?"

My shoulders dropped, and my spirits fell with them. I wasn't sure if I was more upset at him leaving or at the anxiety that something might happen if he wasn't home. "Well, if you have to, and if you check the house first and everything is okay, I'm sure it's fine."

"I wouldn't do this if it wasn't important. Dire."

"Dire?" I asked, and he looked to the man who'd given him whatever message initiated this. "What is it?"

"I can't talk about it now, but let's get you home. As soon as things are settled, we can discuss it, okay?" His eyes searched mine, and I could tell he truly did care. Something I hadn't experienced from anyone but my grandmother in years.

*Grandmother...*

"Okay," I said, "but can I ask you a favor?"

"Of course, anything. What is it?" He held my hands in his and kissed them, waiting for me to speak.

"Can you find out how my grandmother is doing? I want to know she's all right."

"Of course, little dove. I'll see to that." He leaned in and kissed me on the cheek and mouth. He was still close when he whispered, "I'll try to be back before you go to bed. If not, please go to sleep without me. Just make sure you have supper."

I nodded, feeling the soft brush of his wavy hair against my temple.

"Let's get you home," he said. "Try to rest. I'll make sure everything is okay." He kissed my forehead and then the tip of my nose, and my thoughts and suspicions grew.

# CHAPTER TWENTY-FOUR

## BRATAN

IT WAS HARDER THAN I thought it'd be leaving Leena at the house. Even after checking it for anything suspicious and recruiting Theodora, I couldn't help feeling uneasy. I wanted to be there—to be the one watching over her—but I couldn't. I was the only one who could put an end to what was happening and to stop another looming threat giving me grief. I'd have to trust she'd be okay with Theodora and come back as soon as I could.

When she waved goodbye, my chest ached. Protecting her was my top priority, a feeling so intense I couldn't think of anything else. It was incomprehensible how she'd already captured my heart so completely, but she had, and I couldn't deny that I was falling deeply in love with her. It had to be because we were mates and that we were always meant to be one, and with that came the intense desire to protect her and an overwhelming passion that made me blind to anything else. It drove me half-insane, especially when I thought of anyone hurting her, like that bastard from the other day.

It was a good thing I'd rid the world of the disgusting vermin. That blasted man could never hurt anyone again. He could never touch Leena.

I had to protect her at all costs, which was why I had to take care of this.

I strode into the woods near the entrance to the human world. The sky was darkening, now a deep shade of lavender. The birds were fast asleep, and the insects were starting to sing. I had to get to my friend. Fast.

It was as if he'd heard me coming because Damir soon appeared with my other two right-hand men. The three couldn't be more different, but they all shared the same hardened face of those who'd seen war. They'd been with me for years and had proved their loyalty many times over. Though Damir was fae, the other two were elves—two of only a few in these woods. The first of the other two was Andre, a half-elf warrior who'd been born about a hundred years after my mother's death. He was almost as tall as I was in my human form but about half the size in muscle and weight. His skin was a shade of evergreen, and his hair was a thin black strip on the middle of his otherwise bald head. His eyes were just as dark and sharp as his teeth and complemented his pointed ears.

The second was Bialas, an elf with pale skin and ice-colored hair that fell down his back in one slick sheet. His irises were gray, and he never smiled, whether wicked or pleasant; his expression hardly changed, even in the thick of battle. He was a little brawnier than Andre, but he was twice as strong.

"I spoke with the village matron," Damir said. "She wouldn't tell me anything other than that she'd already spoken with you and settled things."

My jaw tightened. "We spoke, but we certainly didn't settle anything." My fists tightened just thinking of the conversation with the wretched bat. The matron of Leena's old village cared nothing for my wife, refusing to refer to her by anything other than 'that girl' and the occasional 'your new bride' when we'd spoken. "They refuse to cooperate."

A beat of silence passed.

"What did she say?" Bialas asked.

My fists clenched tighter at the memory.

*"I don't care what happened to that girl or what happens to her next," the old wretch had said. "She's your problem now." My teeth grated, and my form grew, casting a shadow over the woman and bleeding darkness through the room. But she didn't so much as flinch; she remained the same, staring up at me, unfazed. "A deal was struck. I gave you a bride, and now the forest should be balanced, hm?"*

*My eyes still blazed. "I never asked for you to pluck someone against her will. Whatever Melora told you was a lie."*

*"You've had no complaints thus far, and look at you. You're all twisted up in knots for the girl." She said 'the girl' like it was a curse. My blood boiled. "You have your wife, so we deserve our peace. Now," she laced her fingers behind her back, "I'll let this incident slide so long as another deal is struck. I expect more food*

and gold, and you are not to step foot in Woodsmeadow again. I'll contact Melora if you do, and all deals will be off."

"It's not that simple," I growled, the bass of the sound shaking the matron's glass trinkets adorning her tables and shelves. "If you let your filthy vermin into my woods and harm my bride, even if we're halfway across the world, I will kill them. That human garbage you called Casimir ventured into my woods and hurt my wife. You cannot retaliate."

Slowly, I forced myself back to my regular size, which was still large enough to be intimidating for most, but not this woman.

"You killed one of my people, so our deal of peace has been broken. However, if you choose to strike another deal, I'll turn a blind eye this once."

"He tried raping my wife! I won't let a filthy sack of shit like that stay breathing!"

The woman stepped closer, baring her teeth. "There were no conditions on our bargain. We offered you a bride for peace. You got your bride and have been doing who knows what with her. How do I know you aren't just mad that someone else tried to play with your toy?"

My vision went white. My body no longer remained human. Roaring in rage, I tore myself from my human form and grew into my true self, destroying the matron's disgustingly curated home. I wished I could watch her die the way Casimir had, but I knew that would only make things worse for Leena.

*Instead, I grabbed the heap of wood that had been the ma-*
*tron's house and threw it into the forest with a war cry that shook*
*the village and surrounding trees.*

*The woman coughed up at me, stumbling out from the rubble.*
*"You'll regret this, Leshy."*

*"You have no power in my forest," I bellowed. "Leave these*
*woods. NOW. Next time, I won't spare you."*

"Your Majesty?" Damir tore me from my thoughts, noticing when the worry turned to fear. "What happened?"

I knew what he really wanted to ask was *what did you do?* But my right-hand man would never speak like that to his king. Although he was the closest thing I had to family, there was a line no one seemed to cross. I wasn't sure why it had never bothered me before, but I'd never wanted anyone too close to me. After what happened to my mother, I didn't want to ever care so deeply again. Until Leena.

The thought of her twinged something in my chest.

The matron's home was destroyed just before Leena's party. I'd left that damned village, changed into the proper attire, and then saw her dancing in a way that made nothing else matter. I'd never known anyone who was starlight incarnate, but I was sure it was her. She was too good to be human and too good to be mine. But I couldn't let her go. As long as she desired to be here, I would keep her. I wasn't sure if I could breathe if I lost her.

But now, I may have inadvertently put her in danger while trying to keep the danger away. Guilt built into a lump in my throat.

"They wouldn't cooperate, so I'm not sure what she thinks we've settled. The only thing I wish is for them to leave my forest at once. If they don't, we'll have to take matters into our own hands."

"What should we do now then?" Damir asked.

"We'll give them a week. If they're not out by then, we'll infiltrate, or at least regroup, find out what's going on, and act accordingly." The darkness thickened around us—too dark even for the night. Cold panic settled on our small group. "Go home. Only come to me with pertinent information." I started to turn when I remembered Leena's words. "Oh, and find out how Leena's grandmother is doing. Make sure she's being cared for and fed well. Then report to me." I awaited no reply before striding home, desperate to evade my men's suspicions.

"You've done well," a voice hissed through the trees.

"You're not welcome here. Not after what you pulled. You better leave, or there'll be hell to pay."

"But I've only just started having fun with her," the woman croaked. I froze, whipping around to face her, but all I saw was a mist of darkness fading away with the echo of her laugh. Blood pounded in my ears. Did she just admit to what I thought she did?

I chased where the mist had been, scanning the trees for any sign of her, but there was nothing. My heart pounded hard against my chest, and my mind was frenzied. I would find out exactly what happened between Melora and the matron of Woodsmeadow. And I would find out why and how she was hurting Leena.

Things were already coming together, but my mother's old friend was getting harder to deal with. It was difficult reconciling that she was the same person who'd once been like family to me. Ever since my mother's death, Melora had slowly changed, but she hadn't been malicious until now. Odd and unpredictable, yes. But this?

The lights were off in the house; Leena must have gone to sleep early. Slowly, I made it up the stairs, heart still pounding, but stopped when I saw her sleeping soundly in our bed. She was innocent in all of this. She'd never asked to be wed. That wench in the village essentially sold her off, with Melora's aid. If I had known...

Guilt twisted my insides. Melora had told me she'd arranged a potential bride for me to keep peace with the humans and for me to have a suitable companion. I'd needed one for some time, so I agreed to meet Leena and make a choice. If I'd known how far gone Melora was, I never would have entrusted her with such a task. It was reckless for me to believe her, and it was naïve to think she was the same person I'd known all those years ago. I think a part of me had known something was off about Melora for a while; I just didn't want to see it.

But now Leena was suffering because of it—all because of my bad judgment and skewed sentimentality.

My wife made a noise as she nestled into her pillow, and my heart sank. How did I ever think she'd come willingly? I was the monster of the woods. No maiden would willingly come to me. Much less someone like Leena.

I often tried reminding myself that she'd been starving in the human part of the forest back in her old village, but nothing shook the guilt. I was also starting to realize just how much I didn't deserve her, and when I destroyed the matron's house, I only further proved that fact.

Sitting on the bed beside her, I gently stroked her hair. She looked even more innocent when she slept. My love for her was once again overpowering but accompanied by guilt. I could still hear the splintering wood as the matron's house came crashing down, the gasps of the villagers, and the bark of the old woman herself.

*You'll regret this, Leshy.*

As always, I'd made a mess of everything, and the future was murkier now than it had ever been before.

# CHAPTER TWENTY-FIVE

LEENA

I WOKE TO THE soothing motion of Bratan's fingers combing through my hair. I looked up, still bleary-eyed from sleep, and his eyes instantly flicked to mine.

He smiled. "Good morning, beautiful."

I stretched my arms above my head. "Did you get everything taken care of last night?"

His smile dropped. "What do you mean?"

"What you had to do last night; did you get it done?"

His hand stilled for a moment, and then it continued running through my hair. His eyes followed the movement of his fingers.

"You could say that." Silence thickened between us. I tried searching for something to say—maybe something to ask—but he smiled at me and said, "I want to take you somewhere special today."

"Oh?"

"We haven't had much time to ourselves since our wedding. I'd like to connect with you and get you the scone you like so much."

"How did you know about that?" I said, acutely aware of my warming cheeks.

"I could smell it on your fingers when you confronted me so adorably in the woods the other day." I threw him a faux glare, and he laughed. "Come on, *Your Majesty*. Let's get going." He kissed a lock of my hair and looked at me in a way that made my mind go foggy.

"I like it when you call me that, too." I leaned forward and kissed him, opening my mouth to welcome his tongue.

He pulled away, placing his hand on my face. "As much as I want this, and it kills me not to take you right here and now, but I have somewhere special to take you. Can we wait?"

I could hardly believe my ears. "I didn't think it was possible for you to say those words."

"Neither did I." He kissed me on the forehead and pulled me out of bed. "Come on," he said, patting my bottom. "Let's get going." I squealed as he pinched it, skipping playfully away while covering the spots he touched.

"What should I wear?" I gave him a coy look over my shoulder.

"Something casual. Maybe Theodora can help you. If you're willing to wait for that scone." He winked, which warranted a playful shove to his arm.

"I'm not that obsessed with food."

"I wouldn't mind if you were." He kissed my cheek and gave me one last spank. I let out a small yelp. "That was a very satisfying sound." I tried leaping on him, but he evaded me, and we did that, laughing and chasing each other around the room until he finally caught me in an embrace and then a kiss. I loved the way he kissed me like he wanted to eat me up. He pulled away and stroked my cheeks with his thumbs, gazing down at me. "Wait here. I'll be back when Theodora fetches me." He kissed me one last time and let me slide from his grasp.

"All right," I grumbled. "I'll see you soon then."

"It will be worth the wait. Trust me."

"If you say so."

***

Theodora and Ani came over in impressive time. The former had brought a trunk full of trinkets and casual, yet extremely fine outdoor wear, as well as a vanity set. She sorted through it, searching for the perfect piece. When she pulled out a sheet of teal fabric, she cast me a smile. "I've never seen His Majesty so happy. I don't think I've ever seen him smile like he did when he was in the village with you, let alone for an entire day."

"I'm happy, too," I said, biting back a smile of my own. She pulled out another piece of fabric—this one was teal and consisted of matching trousers, which I'd never worn before. It was beyond scandalous in Woodsmeadow to wear anything other than a dress, so the thought of wearing trousers was liberating. Like I was slowly gaining more freedom than losing it, rather than what I'd thought would happen upon my arrival here. I was finally free of my old life.

The thought left a slight twinge in my side. All I was missing now was my grandmother. I'd always wished I could whisk her away and give her a new life. To show her that love didn't need to be sharp and broken. She deserved so much more than the life she'd lived. She was being fed now and was hopefully safe since Vasska was being fed too, but life should be about more than surviving.

I'd have to follow up with Bratan about how she was doing, and maybe I could ask if there was a way to bring her here. The thought of my husband left butterflies springing in my chest. He'd infected me in the best possible way with the smile that reached his eyes, the smooth, darkly rich cadence of his voice, and the way he touched me. Just thinking about it made me weak.

"You're blushing, Your Majesty," Theodora teased. I absently ran my fingers over my collarbone in giddy bliss, making my way to the newly set up vanity the two maids had brought upon their arrival. But when I sat down and glanced in the mirror, I caught Ani's disapproving glare. I chose to ignore her; she wasn't worth souring the mood.

"Bratan said to wear something comfortable," I said to Theodora, "so I think the teal frock with matching pants is the perfect choice."

"I agree," she said, laying the silk ensemble across my lap. "It's beautiful and will bring out the pins I'll put in your hair.

"I actually think I want my hair down today if that's all right. I want to feel as free as possible."

"Of course, Your Majesty." She turned to get something out of her chest of jewels, and my eyes once again found the blue-green outfit on my lap. It truly was a lovely ensemble. The color was like a still lake on a clear day. Small, clear gems—possibly diamonds—encrusted the low neckline. The top flared out and had wide, mesh sleeves that would barely cover my shoulders. The bottoms were the same color and appeared to have a waistband meant to land low on my hips, and the legs puffed out until they cinched at the ankles.

I'd never seen anything like it.

It was perfect.

***

I awaited Bratan's return in a cloud of excitement, swinging my legs over the bed in eager anticipation. But when time stretched on since the maids left to fetch him, I decided to pass the time through distraction.

I went to the window and watched crows and multi-colored birds flit from branch to branch on a sun-bathed path along the treetops. The lush green canopies were perfect—not a leaf out of place—and the sky embracing them was a protective coating of perfect blue. Inspecting the branches yielded the detection of bright wildlife that couldn't be in the human realm, such as the shockingly pink and green bird with a puff of a body and a third wing upon its back. As if knowing I was watching it, it flew away, deep into the woods where I could no longer spot it.

More wildlife in similar shades continued to pass, only bringing more awe to this new world I called home. It was amazing that such a place existed. Things had been a whirl-wind since I arrived here; I hadn't been able to appreciate the beauty of the forest's creatures. It was a sight unlike any I could have imagined.

My hands sprawled out on the glass; it was surprisingly warm from the afternoon sun instead of cold like the wind on the other side. I wondered when winter would come and if time passed the same way here as back in Woodsmeadow. Here, the weather had been inconsistent and erratic; on the human side, it grew more frigid by the day. Had Bratan caused the sudden change in seasons on the other side, or did humans' presence affect the woods? I would assume the former; perhaps it'd been one of Bratan's tactics to drive the humans out of the woods. I wondered what Woodsmeadow was like these days.

The front door creaked open, and my stomach flipped. Grateful I didn't have to grab thick skirts to avoid tripping, I sped down the stairs. My hair fell around me when I made an abrupt stop. Bratan was raking his hand through his thick black-brown hair, his bicep flexing beneath the thin white tunic that was unlaced at the front. My heart leapt up my throat at the sight of him. The contrast of the white tunic with his form-fitted black pants stirred something in me that I couldn't wait to satiate.

He halted, his eyes wide. They went straight to my body and the new clothes I proudly wore, dragging slowly from my neck to my feet and then back up to my face. In a sudden rush, he grabbed me, pulling me in by the hips. His thumbs grazed the tops of my hipbones, which were visible from the low-fitting trousers. He grabbed hold of them as he kissed me, and I melted at the feel of his hands on my bare skin, especially as they slid beneath the back of my shirt. I felt near-nude without a slip and underthings, which added extra heat to his touch.

"You look incredible," he murmured against my lips.

"Thank you."

He kissed me again, took my hand, and led me to the open doorway. "Are you ready for some fun?"

"No Leshy duties today? Don't I have a lot to learn?"

"Eternity is a long time. I want to make sure you enjoy yourself, too." The way he said it wasn't coy or flirtatious. It was warm and caring.

"Okay," I said with a soft smile.

"Now, let's get you that scone. Then I have somewhere special to take you." He leaned down and kissed me again. The rush of blood was starting to intensify when he pulled back with a chuckle. "We'll never get anything done if we let our passions take us away all the time."

"We're immortal. We have the rest of time to get things done." We kissed again, but when I started pulling him toward the stairs, he stopped.

"I want to take you somewhere, little dove. We should go before the sun sets."

I grumbled in mild disappointment. "All right. But it better be good."

He grabbed my hand again, drawing circles on the back of it with his thumb.

"Believe me, it is."

\*\*\*

Bratan covered my eyes for the last half of the journey to wherever it was he was taking me, though we did, of course, stop to eat scones before the adventure began. It wasn't until the cool wind of the wood shifted with a strange sensation and a change of sound that we stopped. Suddenly, the sun was warm on my face.

"Are you ready for your surprise?"

I laughed giddily. "I am."

When his hands moved from my eyes, my jaw dropped. We were at the edge of a clifftop overlooking a clearing that stretched to the horizon. Infinite blades of grass danced in perfect disarray at the foot of everything. Stretched in a c-shape, with us in the middle, tall walls of rock and trees protected the grassy plains below—like they were holding up the rest of the world to keep it at bay. And in the middle of everything was a glittering lake, a perfect oval in a field of green.

"Wow. I'd have never guessed that a place like this existed so close to the woods, or at all for that matter." I turned to him. "*Are* we still in the woods?"

"We're in a special pocket of it, and there's so much more. You haven't seen the beginning." He slid his arm around my waist and offered me his other hand. "Would you like to get a closer look?"

"Definitely." I slid my hand in his, and before I could prepare myself, his body stretched, his features shifting, and he was as enormous as the trees behind us and looked like a part of the woods himself. I was still gaping at him when he leapt off the edge of the cliff. My stomach jumped to my throat, but I still managed to scream all the way down. I was still screaming when we landed on the cushioned earth. Bratan roared with laughter as he returned to his typical form. "That wasn't funny! I thought I was going to die!"

"Oh, little dove," he said, brushing his knuckles down the side of my face. "It would take much more than that to kill the wife of the Leshy." My face heated as he set me down. He took my hand again and led me to the water. The breeze was warm and sweet—the whisper of an imagined summer.

Bratan crouched by the lake, dipping his fingers in the shimmering water. A glitter of fish glided by, their colors an enigmatic rainbow brought to life. But as Bratan moved his hand, the creatures swam away, making the lake look like a glass canvas of moving paint.

"This place is amazing." The water was warm as it ran through my fingers. I dipped my hand deeper until a curious fish stared up at me in an almost human way.

"Would you like to see more?" he asked softly. I nodded.

He looked to our side, crouched, and swept his fingers along the grass. Wherever he touched bloomed flowers of a deep cobalt blue. His gaze shifted as he swiveled, and without touching the grass, flowers flourished all around us.

The plants reflected exactly how I felt: unbelievably free. I followed the trail of blue, spinning until I fell on the grass. I swore they hugged me on my way down. I breathed it all in, intermittently laughing and catching my breath. Bratan lay beside me with his face propped on his knuckles.

"I can't believe this. It's so fantastical." I turned to see him studying me, the trace of a smile on his lips. A gentleness in his eyes matched the way this place felt.

"I'd do anything for you. You know that, right?"

He was so close I could feel each of his words against my bare shoulder. I didn't notice that my shirt had shifted until then, but it added to the heat that sprouted in my belly. I nodded, and that familiar spark ignited between us.

"I do." I couldn't tear my eyes from his or stop the boiling heat in my blood. "Kiss me slowly," I whispered.

For a moment, he studied me, desire kindling in his gaze, and then he leaned down and softly kissed me—a good, deep kiss.

My body burned in longing with every swipe of his tongue. He didn't do it in a feverish rush. It was slow. Sensual. His breath was warm in my mouth as he licked my tongue, slow and deliberate. My body shivered, and a great yearning gnawed at every nerve with every touch. His teeth carefully scraped down to the tip of my tongue before he sucked on it.

I was ready for him to take me, but he slowed, teasing me with those careful kisses. His hands made their way to my face, sliding into my hair, fingers curling into my mess of blonde waves. My mouth stayed open as he leaned back. I opened my eyes to him staring down at me, the muscles of his arms still tight as he held himself above me.

"Like that?"

The heat was thunderous as it pulsed through my blood and pooled down my legs. My arms were splayed out, leaving my body vulnerably open to his touch. Desperate to be taken over and driven mad.

All I had to do was lean forward, my eyes falling to his mouth, for him to grab me by the back of the neck and kiss me again. But this time, he was unleashed.

He kissed me deeply. First on my lips, then my neck and shoulders. He grasped onto one of my hips and pressed me against him.

He made love to my mouth, kissing me feverishly in that field of flowers, among the sweet aroma of fresh earth and dewy grass. The air was warm, but the breeze that swept over us was cool enough to create the perfect temperature. It enhanced the feel of his body and hands, of his kisses, and of his taste. I loved the way he moved with me like he knew my body more than I knew it myself.

He tore off his shirt, then pulled mine over my head, continuing to kiss every inch of me. We shed off every inch of clothing—anything that stood in the way of us being one. I needed nothing there. To feel nothing but him. I ached at the forceful firmness of his grip, the masculine way he pressed his thumbs into the hollows of my hips and the meat of my thighs. He growled low into my neck, and it sucked the air from my lungs. He pulled me lower by the hips until he could take full advantage of his position above me—of the tangle of our bodies and the bareness of our flesh. Licking up my neck, he wove his body with mine, moving with me and touching me as I cried—*begged*—for him.

He knew all the right places to touch and kiss. Involuntary noises spilled from my lips as he claimed me. He squeezed my legs, moving deeper, and I ached for him to possess every part of me, body and soul. My legs wrapped around his waist, and I drowned in him. He did everything I could ever want until a crescendo of pleasure shot through me, and I shivered in blind ecstasy.

We were thunder and lightning, trembling beneath the gentle heat of the sun.

He gathered me in his arms and held me. We lay there together in perfect bliss, our chests ebbing and flowing with the rise and fall accompanied by that now-familiar afterglow I found myself longing for.

"Do you want to take a dip with me?" He bit at my earlobe as he said it. My arm fell on my forehead as I caught my breath.

"I'd love that." Scooping me up, he carried me to the lake and, without hesitation, jumped inside. I squealed in surprised delight as we fell beneath the surface. I rolled from his arms but quickly found my bearings in the water. Just like the breeze outside the lake, it felt perfect—like bath water—and it was so clear I could see every feature of his face. He glided to me and gripping me and kissing me deeply before swimming away. I chased after him, gliding until he caught hold of me and kissed me again.

I wrapped all my limbs around him, diving into his mouth as we surfaced. Our bodies were slick, our hair soaked, but we kept kissing. He tasted of salt and life and a sweetness unique only to him.

"You won't catch me this time," I teased, then sank back into the water, swimming away as fast as I could. Of course, he had centuries of practice building up his strength and muscles, while I had very few opportunities to steal a swim in small ponds and hidden lakes, so he caught hold of me from behind and brought me back to the surface.

My head fell back in laughter, and he joined me. We swam for what must have been hours before he dragged me to the ring of sand surrounding the lake, fell on his back, and pulled me on top of him. My hair fell in wet tendrils around him, and we smiled together in incandescent bliss.

He kissed me, then looked into my eyes. "I love you, Leena. I think I've always loved you."

The breath snagged in my throat. "I love you too. So much that it doesn't make sense."

"It doesn't have to." He grabbed the back of my neck and sunk into my lips. We lay like that until the sun set in our perfect corner of the world, and the cool air beckoned us home.

After we dressed, we walked back to the cliff and the wall of trees that led us home.

"Let's warm up by the fire," I said.

He wrapped me into another embrace and kissed the top of my head.

"I like the sound of that." We pulled away slowly, and his thumbs stroked either side of my face. That sweet smile looked good on him. It brightened his eyes and chased away the shadows. He pulled me in, holding me tight, one hand running up my back. "I'll always protect you, Leena." His grip on me tightened. "I want you to know that."

My lips tugged into a smile. "I know. I trust you."

# Chapter Twenty-Six

Two weeks went by in a haze of happiness. Bratan finally started showing me around the woods and taught me about our relationship with it. We spoke of our lives, and I vaguely told him about mine back in Woodsmeadow, though I didn't want to spoil my bliss by getting into the details. One day, I would, but for now, the basics were enough. He'd ask me questions, and I'd answer. Mostly questions about Vasska.

"And no one did anything to stand up for you?" he'd asked one day when we were strolling through a section of the woods. "You were hurt by that brute, and no one did anything?"

I sighed. "Unfortunately, no. The only person who cared enough to do anything was too frail, but you know that part. It's what led me here in the first place."

His jaw set in cold fury. I put my hand on his shoulder in hopes that it would ease him a bit, but the anger blazed in his eyes. "I'd give anything to get that man over here and—"

"It's not worth it. It was a hard part of my life, but it's over now."

His eyes were still hard stones as I got on my toes to reach my hands to his face. "Let's not think about him anymore, okay? Let's just think about us." It took some more convincing, but I managed to bring him back to our moment together and moved forward.

We enjoyed doing a lot of things together, but my favorite part of each day was when we spent time in our secret world. Today, we were relaxing on the grass, eating blueberries and basking in the sun. The fruit was sweet and plump, and I let out a satisfied sound as I rolled one into my mouth, savoring what once was a delicacy and feeling it pop on my tongue until it was sweet nectar sliding down my throat.

"You have to try this," I said, offering Bratan an especially large berry.

He opened his mouth, and I couldn't help but smile at the sight of the big bad monster of the woods adorably leaning in for a piece of fruit. The juices spilled onto my fingers as I tucked it into his mouth. His lips closed around my fingertips, then parted. I watched his tongue slowly lick the dark juices off my skin, and the blood buzzed in my veins. He dragged his bottom lip up my fingers, then grabbed them and kissed my palm. His teeth trailed to my wrist before kissing it and biting it until I couldn't take it anymore.

I leapt on him, knocking him into the grass. Blueberries spilled from the wicker basket at my side, now completely forgotten. I was addicted to his taste—to his touch, his body, the way he felt when we moved together. I'd loved every second of the last two weeks, hiding away, stealing kisses and moments between trees and in this little slice of the woods that was all our own. I'd never known such happiness, and with each passing day, I became more convinced that I was always meant to be the bride of the Leshy.

His hands gripped the back of my thighs, and I hissed in pleasure, a sound both feminine and feral. "You have the most sumptuous legs, little dove," he said, flicking his tongue along mine and pinning me down. I watched him move down to my hips in ravenous anticipation. He breathed on them, trailing his teeth along my inner thigh. "They're so delicious." His grip tightened on the thickest part of my legs. He gently bit my thigh, then guided his tongue in a teasing trail along the inner creases. "I just want to eat them," he said. My teeth buzzed, desire consuming me. "I want—"

A loud crack tore through trees on the clifftop. It was ferocious and unsettling, accompanied by a low, melancholy groan. The echo that followed was so vicious that it sent ripples shuddering across the lake's surface "Did you hear that?" My heart raced while I waited for an explanation, but he didn't respond. A sudden eerie chill swept through the clearing. Bratan's grip loosened, his gaze frantic as it scanned the clifftop. I rose to my feet, frantically searching for any sign of life—maybe even a spirit or something undead—that could have made such a noise.

The strong desire that bubbled up inside me vanished in an instant, replaced by an overwhelming sense of dread. And crippling fear.

Bratan stood and took a step forward, narrowing his eyes in concentration. I followed his line of sight, my heart still pounding.

"What was that?"

"I don't know." His voice was tight. "Nothing can enter this portion of the woods without my explicit permission." That sense of unease amplified. If even Bratan was surprised and didn't know what was going on, then whatever that was could have been anything.

Images of the darkness sweeping across our bedroom slithered through my mind like a viper. That feeling of the claw returned; I could still feel it ripping down my back.

"I think it's been haunting me..." My eyes trailed off with my voice, but I felt Bratan's stare tear from the trees.

"What's been haunting you?"

I grabbed my elbows to stave off the chill and discomfort, but my skin only grew colder.

"I keep seeing things from the corners of my eyes. And remember that day? That wound? I think I've been seeing it—*feeling* it. I-I don't know. It's probably nothing." I winced. Why did I always do that—dismiss myself in fear of doing anything that could end up being wrong?

His hands found my face, and he slowly turned me to look at him. "Your feelings are valid. Now tell me what you've seen. Tell me what's been haunting you."

I held myself tighter. "I've told you all I know, and you saw me that morning I'd been hurt."

His brows furrowed; his eyes almost turned black. "We should go."

The abrupt shift only made things worse. "Do you think it's the same thing?"

He chewed on his cheek and looked back into the woods. "I don't know, but I want to get you home. I want you safe. And I'll get to the bottom of this. I promise you." He pressed his lips on my forehead and held me close. "I'll keep you safe at all costs."

I wasn't sure if I should find comfort in his words or feel uneasy, but I chose to let them comfort me.

"Okay. Let's go home."

***

Theodora accompanied me when Bratan left, busying herself with needlework by the fire. It was jarring to see her hands work; before I saw her face, I swore it was Karina. My stomach sank as I thought about them. I'd avoided following up with Bratan about my grandmother or Woodsmeadow, and I hated myself for it. But I wasn't ready, in part because I was afraid to know, but mostly because I wanted to wait for the right time. I was finally happy after all these years, and I knew that if something was wrong, Bratan would have taken care of it. He wouldn't let Grandmother suffer. He'd made a deal and was proactive in his duties. I was sure she was safe.

But I needed to know, and I needed to ask if there was a way for her to be here with me.

I'd ask him when he returned, as long as whatever he was investigating didn't cause more trouble first.

The chill of his absence was suffocating. He wouldn't leave until Theodora was at my side, but I still felt safer when he was with me. He'd grumbled something to her before leaving, something about contacting him if anything went awry. Whatever was out there must have been a bigger threat than I realized. It had to be. But I was still in the dark about it, and I was growing extremely tired of being in the dark.

The unease creeping through the house was palpable. I tried ignoring it, but that was like asking the sun not to set. I stayed by the upstairs window, wringing my nightdress and focusing on the yellow eyes of owls poking through dark branches. In the quiet night, the trees looked like blots of ink spilling upwards into the sky. The moon wasn't out tonight, which made things all the more eerie.

I was scared. I hated to admit it, but I was.

"Your Majesty?" The floorboards squeaked as the maid ascended the stairs. I focused on the trees. "Would you like something to eat? Or maybe some tea?"

"No, I'm all right. Thank you." My hands were cold. Everything was too much. It was caving in on me. Would Bratan be all right? Would I be okay? What about Grandmother? What was going on?

My chest tightened, cranking like the turn of a key.

"Are you sure?"

"Yes." The word was curt, but I didn't have the energy to be polite. I could barely stand. My hands were shaking.

"Maybe you should rest. I could get you—"

"I said I'm all right." My eyes stung, and my body trembled. Suddenly, I was crying, sobbing uncontrollably in a haze of confused fright. I used to be good at suppressing my tears. Maybe being happy lately had allowed me to actually feel again. "I'm sorry," I whispered. "Really, I am." My throat constricted, the sobs forming a knot in the middle.

The floorboards squeaked as Theodora placed her hands on my shoulders. "No need to apologize, but please let me help you."

The Leena from a month ago would have walked away, pretending to be fine, but today, I surprised myself by sinking my face into the maid's shoulder and letting her wrap an arm around me. She patted my back as I cried and quietly led me to the bed.

"Try to get some rest, Your Majesty. I'm sure it will help you."

I couldn't bring myself to speak. I was cold, my stomach was sick, and there was such an obvious sense that something was wrong that it made everything unbearable. I felt it in every bone, every joint, every nerve.

"Good night, Your Majesty. Please don't hesitate to beckon me if you need anything." Theodora waited for a moment after covering me with the duvet. I was still shaking when she went downstairs.

My eyes fixed on the windowsill as I slowly went numb. It felt like something was sucking the life out of me, draining my insides until I was completely hollow. The night sky went from a scattered black sheet freckled with stars to a faded purple. Soon, it was dawn, and Bratan still wasn't home. I hadn't slept all night, and I had no idea where he could be or if he was safe.

A new fear suddenly poured into me, filling me with dread. Perhaps this was the end of it all.

Happiness hadn't been my companion for years, and it had never felt like this. Maybe I had used up all my days and years of happiness, and I wasn't meant for it anymore. Maybe happiness didn't come to poor orphan girls playing dress-up in a make-believe world.

Ani was right. This life wasn't truly mine. It couldn't be. I wasn't a queen or some deity. The joy I'd felt so briefly had to come to an end eventually. It was never meant to last.

Not for someone like me.

# Chapter Twenty-Seven

## Bratan

M Y HEART POUNDED AS I ran at a near-uncontrollable speed. I couldn't risk changing into my true form. I had to remain discreet. The air was sharp in my throat, cold and stale. Every direction only yielded more trees and no results. No one was here.

But I couldn't rest until I found that wretched devil.

Something stung my eyes, and to my immense disbelief, something wet fell from one of them. I swiped it with one finger and inspected it, my stride momentarily hitching to a stop. The small tear glimmered, mocking me. I rubbed it away, trying to ignore the fact that tears had been foreign to me until the events of late. Other than when it concerned Leena, the only moment I could remember crying was the horrific night when the forest went up in flames and my mother along with it.

Even then, the fear didn't compare to how it consumed me now. I was Leena's sole protector and the only one who could fight back. She didn't have the strength yet; I hadn't seen any inkling of her powers. Even if I had, it would take time for her to learn how to wield them.

I would end this—whatever it was—before it really began.

Brushing my hand against my thigh, I smeared the tear away. There was no time for this, this fear, this emotion. I had to find Melora and put an end to this once and for all.

Lunging forward, I managed to run even faster, weaving through more of the forest until a familiar chill coated my skin. Accompanied by a whistle.

The air was void of sound, and I knew she had come. I whipped around, rage spiking. The old woman smiled. Wispy, tangled hair fell to her hips. Each time I saw her, she looked a bit different, more aged and disheveled but thick with power. Why she always appeared as an old woman, I would never know. She was a shapeshifting deity that controlled the wild demons of the world below. She could appear as youthful and strong as she pleased.

Perhaps it really was to taunt me whenever she was one step ahead.

"Fancy a chat?"

I gritted my teeth. *Speak of the devil.* "It's you, isn't it? You're doing this to her." I was ready to pounce at the creature, but she clucked her tongue in recognition of my gathering strength.

"Oh, Bratan." She shook her head with a sigh. "You can't be talking about that human, can you? That pathetic little thing?"

I felt my eyes go hot, turning black, the immortal blood seeping into them the way only a monster like me could do. I couldn't hold back anymore. My true form tore through my human exterior and shook the earth like the weapon I was.

"How dare you speak of her like that. As if *you* are someone significant. You're nothing more than a shadow skittering around corners and hiding with the others."

Melora inspected her hand as if a ring hugged her finger. "Bratan, you fool. How could you fall for the girl?"

I was too angry to go back to my less lethal form, but I couldn't talk to her as enormous as I was, so I shrunk to just a few feet above her head and grabbed her by the cloak.

"If you speak ill of my wife again, I'll have no choice but to punish you." My voice was unearthly and cruel, but the woman didn't budge. "And you were the one to initiate the deal and to push for me to find a bride. What are you plotting?"

A smile splintered across her face. "You know you only need an heir. If she produces one, you won't need her anymore. Why don't you—"

"Watch what you say next, Melora," I hissed.

Her eyes widened, emphasizing the malice in her smile. "Or what?"

"I've told you before. I don't think I need to repeat myself."

A rickety laugh tumbled from her throat. "You think you can harm me? Oh, child, if you could harm me, you would have already."

Her words struck me, hitting a raw nerve, but I couldn't let her know it. "You lied to me about your arrangement with the village. You worked with that hag to force Leena to come here."

The woman's mouth snapped shut. "And?"

"*And?* What do you mean *And?* You tricked me! You tricked her! You told me she'd come willingly—"

"I said no such thing. I told you the humans would leave your people alone if you made them a deal. You've told me before that you've needed help to guard the woods, and we both knew you needed a companion. But you've also expressed to me that you wanted a *Leshy* to help you. This was the perfect solution. You needed peace and an heir, so I got you a bride."

"I only specified that I wanted a Leshy to help me because I didn't want you to squirm your way into anything, Melora. Your sense has been disintegrating for years. I just didn't realize how much."

"You took that human girl to wed, and her village hasn't bothered you, and you haven't bothered them," she said, ignoring me. "You got what you wanted, and since you bed that girl, you will soon get an heir."

My claws twisted in her cloak, tearing at the fabric, but when I didn't respond, a look of understanding flashed across her face. She let out a steady stream of laughter. "You didn't follow the simple rules of the arrangement, did you? What did you do?"

"It doesn't concern you," I growled.

She cackled. "You can't help yourself, can you? Well. It's not my fault what happens from here. I'll stop helping—"

"I never needed your help! Especially if this is what you consider helping!"

"Then why did you ask for it?"

"Fine. You're right. I did ask for help, but I merely wanted guidance because of the humans in that village. I now realize how foolish I'd been in thinking you were sane enough to do anything resembling aid. I didn't ask for you to kidnap Leena and force her to marry me. You've been unreliable, and now cruel, ever since Mother died!"

"Yet you can't stay away from me, can you?" she snapped. "And I got you that girl—Leena, is it? I don't know why you're so angry. You've taken to her so well, like a little puppy. I thought you'd be thanking me."

"Stay away from her," I snarled, shaking her by the shoulders, "or you'll regret it with your dying breath."

The old crone laughed. "You can't kill me, you fool."

"Believe me. I'll find a way."

"Is she really worth—"

"How did you do it?" I asked in a rushed breath.

"Do what?"

"You know damn well what!" My form started to shift again, but hers did too. Her true form was not reminiscent of a woodland monster. She was evil incarnate. Darkness. A demon—a dark spirit with no body. Just ashy smoke. She had nothing to hide behind but nothing to tie her back, either. Her form slid from my elongating fingers.

In that form of nothingness—just dark mist and glowing eyes—something like a mouth split open to rattle out another vicious laugh. "Once you get your fill of that human girl, you'll come crawling back to me."

"I've never once crawled to you or anyone."

"That's not what I meant." She wasn't hostile in speech, but in aura, she was abhorrent. "You'll need me like you always have. As a mother, since your own died, and as an aide to save you from the mistakes you constantly leave in your wake."

"I don't need your help, Melora. Leave my woods before I do something you won't like."

"As if you could hurt me."

"As if I wouldn't try," I barked. "You should know better than anyone that if I set my mind to something, I see it through." The threat hung in the air, finally sending her back into her human form.

"Try all you like, Bratan, but you can't do anything to me, and if you so wish for me to leave you alone—to no longer offer any protection to your woods—then so be it."

"I don't need anything from you," I growled. Once again craning my neck to look into her milky eyes, I continued. "And if you, or any of your followers, so much as frighten my bride again, I'll summon every creature in this world and every other to rip you apart. Over and over. Until there is nothing left of you but dirt that will forever crumble beneath my feet."

For a moment, fear flickered in her hollow gaze, but it was quickly replaced with fury.

"And what about whatever you did to that village?"

"What of it?" I snapped.

"You think they'll sit idly by and do nothing to your precious wife?"

"What are you getting at?"

"You've created quite a mess for yourself, Bratan. Your little world is quickly falling apart. Soon, it'll topple completely, and I won't have to lift a finger to watch you burn. Or her. And you no longer have my aid." She laughed again, a drawn-out, creaky sound that grew mad as her head fell back. "I think I'll enjoy watching that particular show."

I was done taking this. My claws lengthened twice the span of the woman's body, forming where my hands once were. But before I could use them, power encircled her, and she blasted me against a tree. I undulated in and out of my true form until I found my bearings and let myself ignite. Letting out a soul-splitting roar that shook the trees, I reached out to slash her—to shred her to pieces. Before I could make contact, she whisked into mist and fled the woods.

Panic swelled in my chest, and I couldn't help the unruly wail that rattled out my throat. My branch-like arms cut the trees behind me until I plunged them into the dirt to get a hold of myself. I thought of Leena and her smile, her sweet countenance, and carefree dancing. Slowly, I returned to my human form. Melora was right about one thing—I'd once again made things harder for myself. And harder for Leena.

I had to find a way to destroy Melora, no matter the cost. As long as that cost wasn't Leena.

I closed my eyes and steadied my breath. I couldn't allow myself to become a beast—an uncontrolled monster. I needed to keep my head. Each time I didn't, I made things worse.

There was no way Melora would give up, but I couldn't allow her any sort of home in, near, or around my kingdom. I may have officially made her my enemy today, but she'd sparked that rivalry when she laid her knotted finger upon Leena's back.

I would make enemies with every creature in the world and beyond if I had to. As long as it kept Leena safe, I'd gladly burn everything to ash.

***

*Leena*

The front door creaked, jolting me upright. My eyes were dry from staring off all night; I wasn't sure how long Bratan had been gone, but the sun gleaming through the window indicated it was early afternoon. I got out of bed so quickly I was dizzy, but I pushed through, ran down the stairs, and jumped into Bratan's arms before he could so much as take off his cloak.

"I was so worried." I buried my face in his shirt, grabbing hold of the ends of his cloak's collar. His hand found the nape of my neck, and he curled my hair into his fingers and pressed a kiss atop my head. I thought I might sob. "Did you find out what it was?"

"I believe so." Something held him back from saying more. I wanted to press it, but the darkness that shadowed his far-off gaze told me it wasn't the time.

"We should rest. I have a feeling you slept about as much as I did, if you slept at all." I lifted a hand to his face, but his expression was the same. He didn't even blink. "Bratan?"

He blinked, suddenly out of his trance but still not entirely there. He looked to Theodora. "Thank you for being here. You may leave now."

The maid dipped her head. "Of course, Your Majesty." Then she turned to me. "I'll see you in the morning, Your Majesty."

"That won't be necessary," Bratan said. "I'll be with her. You should find Damir. He'll have instructions for you." A curious look passed between them. I knew that that should have been the most unsettling part of the exchange, but all I could focus on was the panic in Bratan's eyes and how his irises were no longer green but completely black.

Theodora glanced at me. It was so quick I wondered if it'd actually happened. And then she was gone. "What was that about?" I asked.

"What?" He unbuckled his boots, illuminated by the glint of the crackling flames.

"I'm talking about the cryptic instructions you gave Theodora." I walked closer, only stilling when he sat upright and I saw his face. The fear etched there was so potent it made me want to cry. "What happened?" I whispered.

"I think something is coming." The words came out in a clipped rush—a punch to the gut.

My blood went cold. "What?"

"There are two parts at play here. I'm not sure how to stop them, but I think they're connected." He took my hand, pulling me closer and looking into my eyes. "But I *will* get to the bottom of it, and I'll squash it all before it gets worse. I'll protect you. No matter what. Remember?"

I stayed locked in his fierce, uneasy gaze until, finally, I nodded. But he didn't smile like I thought he would. That was typically how we worked. I would smile, and he would smile back. He would promise me something, I would nod, and he'd be gleeful. But not now.

He pulled me into his lap and wrapped me up in his arms. I buried myself in him, nuzzling into his shirt and curling up in his lap. "So don't be afraid, my love. I'll take care of it." His fingers gripped my hair as he added, "And anyone who stands in my way or so much as touches you won't live to speak of it."

"Don't talk like that," I said, pulling away.

He frowned. "Don't you want protection?"

"I don't want you to kill someone for looking at me wrong."

"Come now, Leena, you know that's not what I meant."

"Isn't it?"

I hated the sick feeling that mixed with the intense pounding in my chest—this stressful, anxiety-ridden tension between us. It was nothing like the usual tension that typically accompanied our union, the kind that set fire to my blood. I didn't want to fight with him. We were in danger. We had to stick together.

"No, it isn't. I'll protect you, but I'm no animal."

"Good." I tried sounding tough, but I still felt like crying. I clutched his shirt until my knuckles were near-white. "I'm so scared. I—" I choked on a sob as he held me, and I let him soothe me and wrap me up in him.

He shushed softly, stroking my hair and back before rising to his feet and cradling me as he took me upstairs. I let my composure completely fall; any self-consciousness or shield broke down as I curled myself deeper in his arms.

I knew I was safe with him, but this new, chaotic world was completely beyond my comprehension. I didn't know the rules or the Leshy or what lay in this realm. I didn't know what creatures lived here and what was possible or impossible. All I knew was how strongly he felt for me and of our deep connection that seemed to have sprouted long before we met. Like the seed was always there, ready to be watered and brought to life—to fill the woods that belonged to us. The world we were sworn to protect.

He laid me in the bed, my hands still desperately clutched onto his tunic. He rounded his body around mine, and I cried against him. The sun poured into the room, only slightly warming my chilled skin. And I kept on crying. He didn't say a word. He only held me, occasionally shushing me as the sun warmed my chilled skin. It was exactly what I needed. I had fourteen years of built-up sorrow that I'd pushed down since my parents died, and it was all coming out. I'd reached my tipping point. Every bad day and horrible night, every lashing and beating, and every time I wanted to mourn my parents but couldn't because I'd be punished by an uncle who didn't accept any action or thought he considered a weakness.

All I ever wanted was to feel safe and have the freedom to feel without fear. Now that I could, it was all coming out.

When my eyes were dry and my eyelids grew heavy, he spoke. "I need you to understand something, little dove. I am the protector of this forest and all in it, including and especially you. I am no animal, but I am a monster. If someone tries to kill my people or my love, I will not stand idly by."

My stomach sank. "What does that entail?" I held my breath, not sure if I really wanted to know the answer.

"That I'll do what is necessary to protect you."

"Why does that make me nervous?" I sniffed and wiped my face with the back of my hand. It was warm in his embrace and with the thin rays of sun peeking in on us, but an uneasy hollowness left the room devoid of comfort. "I desperately want to believe you, Bratan. That you'll..." *Do the right thing.* I wanted to finish, but I couldn't say it.

Unfortunately, he could already read my face like a picture book.

"Like I said, I'll do what is necessary. Nothing less, nothing more." His voice was calm and low, a soothing melody rocking me to sleep. "Sleep, little dove. We can talk more when you wake." I laid against his chest, letting him hold me again, letting him convince me that I could trust him.

It was odd, but I wasn't nervous anymore. I trusted him. I understood where he was coming from and what needed to be done, but my life before this one had been about strict to-dos and don'ts. And in the years since my parents' death, I'd learned that no one could be trusted and that it was safer to be still and fade into the background. To never speak up. Truthfully, I had no idea what was right when it came to fighting back or protecting people. My entire adolescence and adult life had been spent keeping my head down and trying to survive, but now I was in charge of critical actions as a protector of this forest.

I didn't like the idea of retaliation, but I also didn't like the idea of innocent people dying and us standing by. These villagers and this forest were mine to protect, too, and it already felt more like home to me than Woodsmeadow ever had, even without Grandmother here. Finding Bratan was like finding a part of myself. He sealed the safety and love into my chest that I thought was forever gone.

My eyelids couldn't stay open anymore. His arms were too warm, and my tears had drained me. I hadn't realized I'd been shivering until it stopped—until I was so comfortably tucked against him, and he placed me against his chest, securing me under his protective wing. Part of me still hated that I welcomed the protection, but I was scared and had decided to jump wholeheartedly into these feelings, riding the wave and accepting it all as it came, no matter how irrational. I really ought to fight—to do something—but I didn't want to deal with the details right now.

I wanted everything to fizzle to a stop, so I let him hold me until I was whisked into a dreamless sleep. A welcome, warm slumber.

# CHAPTER TWENTY-EIGHT

LEENA

B EFORE I KNEW IT, I was awake, and the sun was rising. I'd slept the rest of the day and through the night. Bratan was still holding me, peacefully asleep. I leaned back just enough to comb my fingers through his dark hair. He was almost childlike when he slept. No one would ever know he was capable of turning into a monster larger than the forest itself, with strength as deadly as it was ferocious.

My fingers fell to his lips. Warmth filled my blood, and almost like he'd sensed it, Bratan's eyes fluttered open in a tired daze. "Good morning, little dove."

My cheeks burned. "Hello."

He leaned forward with a kiss, not holding back despite it being so early in the morning. I soaked it up—every taste, sensation, and movement—basking in this tiny moment of tranquility before my mind wandered back to unpleasant things.

He moved on top of me, kissing more deeply by the second. My hands slid beneath his shirt, scratching up his back until he hissed with pleasure. His eyes were wild, his teeth gritting, somehow both pleasantly and like a stalking beast. Sparks danced in his eyes, along with something else.

"I'm going to devour you," he growled, diving into my neck with a sensual bite. There was a pleasant flash of pain, and I moaned as he scraped his teeth down my throat. "But don't worry little dove. You'll enjoy every second of it." I uttered a sound as he made his way to my ear. "I won't stop until you're completely satisfied, from the basest of your primal desires to each fantasy that pops in your head." He bit my earlobe. My toes curled, my chin tipping up with the arch of my back.

"If you're trying to distract me from what happened last night—"

"It's working," he finished, smiling against my neck. I felt the pleasant threat of his teeth against my flesh.

I giggled, throwing my arms above my head. "Yes. I hate to say it, but it is."

"Good." He pushed his thumbs into my hips, pulling me up against him like he always did. And every time, I crumpled in submission. He licked the top curves of my chest and up my throat until he made it to my mouth. He sucked on my bottom lip, biting it before sliding his tongue along mine and sucking on that too. My arms fell limply against his shoulders, but I still managed to kiss him back with a passion that almost equaled his. With every fiery pulse of desire, we moved.

I writhed with him, moaned with him, tore off his clothes, and helped him tear off mine. I kissed him and thrashed against him and cried out until—as he'd promised—no desire was left unfulfilled. We didn't stop until every burst of light had left my body—every spark of pleasure and heady release.

My head was still spinning when I let out a long, satisfied sigh. The back of my hand fell on my forehead. "You're wicked. Do you know that?" My face was warm, as was my entire body, every inch of flesh and bone. I couldn't get myself to open my eyes. I was goo. Completely useless, happy goo.

"Of course I do," he said. "What a silly question."

I stuck my tongue out at him, but he didn't even let me do that without it being tended to. He sucked on it for a fraction of a second, just long enough to let it slide between his teeth and leave me pleasantly shocked and laughing.

"Leena." His voice was low, and he stroked my cheek with the back of his hand. "Do you know how much I adore you?"

The warmth along my face deepened. "I think so. If it's as much as I adore you."

He leaned in, forehead almost on mine, our noses near touching. "It's so much more than that." I hummed in response as he kissed me. This time it was soft, sweet, and just for a moment. He leaned back, winking at me before getting out of bed. I watched his bare form move to the wardrobe. He peered at his clothing options as if he were examining a wide range of clothing that didn't look uniform and identical.

"Is it really hard to choose your day's attire? You wear the same thing every day."

"I do not," he said, still sifting through the wardrobe. "I'm offended that you'd even think such a thing, my queen."

"I know you have at least a handful of the same pairs of trousers and at least a dozen of the same tunics. I thought you used the same cloak each day, too, but I now realize you probably mix it up. I'm sure that they're all similar enough that I wouldn't know the difference, though." He grabbed the garments he needed and closed the wooden doors.

He looked at me impishly as he made his way to the side of the bed. "You have me all figured out, don't you?"

"Of course I do." I tried to be coy as I rose from the bed, not expecting the swift spank he gave me on my way up. I let out a high-pitched yelp.

"You naughty thing." He nipped at my chin before throwing his tunic over his head. I enjoyed watching his muscles move, with or without his tunic on. It was almost as nice as the peace that came with our time together. It was hard to believe anything could go awry.

But it could, and I was worried there was no way around it.

Suddenly, I couldn't ignore it anymore. The warmth of my flesh quickly cooled with the drop of my stomach.

"Bratan?"

"Hmm?" He was focused on fastening his trousers. I tried gathering what I wanted to say next, but my mouth was dry.

"Have you received any word on my grandmother and how she's doing?"

His hands stilled. "Yes, I have."

My chest went cold; I rubbed it as I nervously asked, "Well?"

"I had one of my men look into it. She's being fed, and she isn't hurt..."

"But?"

He closed his eyes and took a deep breath. "She's struggling. I'm sure she's worried about you."

"What?" The word was a squeak, and I tripped stumbling to him and grabbing hold of his arm. "How do you know?"

His brows were heavy as our eyes met. "He observed her for a while. I'm sorry, Leena. I wish there was something I could do."

"Is there?" I quickly asked, and he frowned. "Is there something you can do?" I clarified. My heart was wild as I awaited his response.

"I don't know what you mean."

"Can you do something to help her?" My voice was loud and shaky, and I finally blurted the question that'd been burning in my mind for weeks. "Is there any way she can live here with us?"

The silence that fell between us was thick and stifling. Finally, his jaw set, and he said, "I'm not sure. I've had...difficulties with your old village's matriarch. I don't think she'd allow it."

"Can we at least try?" I squeaked, and he offered me a gentle smile.

"Of course, little dove. Just not right now. I have to clean up some messes and ensure you're protected. After that, we can try."

It wasn't what I'd hoped for, but it was a start, and it wasn't a definitive 'no.' "Can I at least see her?"

Again, there was stifling silence.

"I'll look into that too, but Leena, I don't think you realize how precarious things are right now."

"Then tell me! I'm so sick of being in the dark! Why won't you tell me anything?"

His head drew back. "I had no idea you were so upset. I'm just trying to keep you safe."

"By not telling me anything?" I was aware how loud my voice was and that my arms were wagging in the air, and that I was still bare. I must have looked like a maniac. But I didn't care.

"I'll explain things when the information is less murky," he grumbled, and I could tell he was trying to keep his voice steady.

"At least let me come with you. If you want to protect me, you can do so while I'm out with you, and maybe you can teach me to fight in case something ever goes wrong."

"Absolutely not," he snapped.

A shot of rage flashed through me. "Why? Aren't I a Keeper of these woods, too?"

"You're the bride of the Leshy," he said firmly. "I'll protect you. You don't need to fight."

"I *want* to fight. Don't treat me like a delicate flower."

"Why are you so stubborn?"

"Why are *you* so stubborn?"

His eyes narrowed, but I didn't break eye contact. Finally, he sighed. "I'll think about it."

I crossed my arms, anger swelling in my breast. "You can't tell me what to do."

"Are you done being childish?"

"No. You're frustrating, and if you don't teach me to fight, I'll find another way to learn."

"Good luck finding someone who will help you with that," he said flatly, and I glowered.

When he sat on the bed with a groan, I decided to switch tactics.

I walked to the other side of the bed and crawled to him slowly. I didn't stop until my lips were a whisper away from his.

"It's a good thing I don't have to follow the rules then, isn't it?"

I felt the quickening of his breaths, the flustered movements of his chest. "What are you thinking, you little minx?"

My lips parted. His eyes closed, and his mouth opened. "You'll teach me to fight, or I'll be very naughty."

I felt the flicker of his smile. "I like it when you're naughty."

"If you want *this* naughty side of me, then you'll teach me to fight."

A low chuckle rumbled from his chest. "You aggravating creature." He gripped the hair at the base of my skull, and my head fell back in quiet euphoria. His breath was hot on my throat. "How could I ever say no to you?"

"You can't," I said, but I was flustered. The words barely made it out.

He snarled and dove into my lips, knocking me over until we rolled in a flurry of kisses. When I pinned him below me, I cocked my head and gave him a triumphant grin.

"You'll always do what I say. Right?" I asked, making sure my voice was husky as I trailed a finger along his jawline.

He growled, lightly biting it. "I'll give you all that you desire." He dragged his bottom lip up my fingers and bit my wrist. His eyes found mine as he licked it. It was a good thing I was fully satisfied.

"Good." I kissed him one more time and rolled off him. "Then let's get to it."

# Chapter Twenty-Nine

LEENA

B RATAN WAS REALLY STARTING to get on my nerves. "I
can tell you're stalling," I said.

He gave me a sidelong glance. "I'm not."

"Then take me somewhere to train." I stepped in front of
him, glaring into his evasive stare. "What's going on, Bratan?
You told me you'd take me to train."

His tongue pressed into his cheek as he thought, then he
looked at me. "Fine, but I don't know where we're going to
go. Our place at the edge of the woods isn't safe anymore, and
there are eyes everywhere, and who knows where she could be
slithering around—"

"She?" I asked. His lips sewed together. "Bratan, what are
you not telling me?"

He looked around, grabbing me by the arm and slinking
behind a tree at the edge of the village, away from prying eyes
and listening ears. His back pressed against a wide trunk, my
chest against him.

"I promise I'll tell you," he said, "but not now and not here."

"Tonight, then." My voice was clipped. I wasn't taking no for an answer.

"Tonight," he agreed, and my shoulders relaxed a little.

He hooked his forefinger on my chin and lifted my gaze to his. "I love you, Leena. I want to protect you."

"Then show me how I can protect myself." A beat of silence passed, then I added, "Show me more of the woods. Please take me everywhere you can. If I know my surroundings and my way around, it could be valuable if anything goes wrong."

His finger stroked my chin as he thought. I had no idea what answer danced on his lips. He was aggravatingly evasive. I had to keep telling myself that he was used to ruling this place alone and was new to love and letting someone in. But I could only be patient about something like this for so long.

In the meantime, I would fight for him to see my logic—the logic that was right before his eyes that he refused to see or couldn't through his blind fear and vengeful rage of whatever lay out there.

"Okay," he said, his voice quiet. "Come." He threaded his fingers in mine and led me deep into the woods.

I wasn't sure if it was Bratan's anxiety soaking through his fingers and into mine, spreading through my belly like bad ale, or if the woods themselves were afraid, but there was a thick blanket of unease around us the deeper we ventured through the forest. It left chills dimpling my skin and a taste like despair on the tip of my tongue. Bratan's face was devoid of color, and his jaw was set, his features rigid, even more than usual.

His grip on my hand tightened by the minute. Something was terribly wrong, but I could tell this wasn't the time to push. Besides, he'd promised to tell me later tonight. I'd try again when we returned home. For now, I feigned ignorance.

"Tell me about this place." My voice was soft and melodic and fortunately did what I'd hoped for by slightly relaxing his shoulders. But only for a moment.

As swiftly as they'd relaxed, his muscles tightened again, but at least he spoke. "It's been here since the beginning of time. It's a sacred place, often the destination for creeping souls and demonic beings because of it. They want a part of it—to touch its power and sanctity. To defile it with their presence." He blew out a breath. "Vile creatures. I can feel them."

"So that's what it is," I said mostly to myself, but he lifted a quizzical brow.

"You feel them?"

"I think so...it feels like death. Cold, hollow, in between places and forgotten things. *Terrible* things. It's hard to explain, but it's palpable. It makes my insides itch."

"That's the feeling. It appears you truly are a Keeper of these woods now. Only we can sense such things." He jerked to a sudden stop.

"What is it?" He didn't move, and that creeping feeling intensified. "Bratan, what is it?"

His Adam's apple bobbed. "I think that's why you can see her. Melora. You've felt her presence. Heard her. Seen her shadows." Fear permeated his eyes. "She won't stop now she knows we're one. How could I have missed something so important?" His free hand coiled into a tight fist, and I felt his heartbeat quicken through the bond between us.

"Bratan, it's okay." I let go of his hand to cup his face. "Breathe. We'll get through this."

"I still don't know how to stop this. Melora has been hot and cold for centuries, but she's gotten worse, and I think it's because of you. She wants you."

"What are you talking about?" *Melora.* The name rang a hideous bell in the back of my head. I'd heard that name before but didn't understand then. My life here had been a whirlwind, so I'd let it fall by the wayside.

"She's a demon—one of the strongest out there. Creatures like her are the complete opposite to us—they protect nothing but themselves, slowly going mad in the process. She once cared for my family and me, but she's been erratic for a long time. I know she wants to be one of us and join the forest and claim a corner of it. Maybe now that I have a weakness, she's grown drunk with power." His eyes fell. "She was like family to me for so long. I think it was hard to see what was right in front of me. But after she hurt you the other day....after she..."

He swallowed, and I swore I saw tears form, but he turned away.

"She'll try slithering her way between our bond until she succeeds," he said. "She knows more about us than she's let on, and if she *does* succeed...I don't know what will happen to us." Emotion swelled in his voice. The tears were obvious now; one slid down his face.

I tucked myself into his arms and rested my face against his chest. "It's okay. We can get through anything. I believe..." I couldn't say it. Even though we'd talked about it before, it sounded silly to say out loud—to even think it. But I was more convinced of it now than ever.

"You believe what, little dove?" His voice was a soothing balm to the aches in my chest. He stroked his hand down my back.

"I believe we were always destined to be one." I didn't think—I just spoke.

"Of course we were. That's why we were able to bond so seamlessly. It's why she wants you. I think it's why you've been in danger."

"What?" I staggered back, but he caught me by the hands.

"As I mentioned to you a few weeks ago, we are mated souls, Leena. We were always meant to be one, and there is a strength that will come from us being together. A power I could have shared with no one else but you."

I shook my head. "But we're from different worlds..."

He combed his hand through my hair before cupping my cheek and planting a kiss on the other. "At the beginning of everything, we're all the same, and every day, I'm more convinced that before we breathed our first breaths, our souls were one. We were simply torn in two, and then we waited, wandering, completely unaware we had another part of ourselves somewhere out there until we wove back together." His words warmed a part of me I hadn't known was cold, and it gave me a sense of peace that sealed every shattered piece of me, fixing every bruise and break. "I never knew of such love until you."

I sucked in a shaky breath, emotion rushing through me like the wind. I studied the deep sincerity in his face, the matchless adoration.

"Have you ever been in love before?" I asked.

He absently tucked a lock of hair behind my ear. "Maybe once or twice, but not like this. Nothing could ever be like this—nothing but us."

"What was it like?" I asked, though an unjustified jealousy soaked the words.

"Before you, I lived many lives but loved only a few. Romantically, I had two loves before you over the centuries. The first was the typical first love—I was merely a boy back then and loved the way many adolescents do. So fiercely but not fully. The second love was when I was a little older and had firmer edges but with you..." His hand found my chin. "With you, Leena, I have found myself. The love I have for you is incomprehensible. I don't think I could have believed such a thing existed until it did. I can barely utter your name without falling deeper in love with you, and every breath I breathe is steeped in my desire to forever hold you in my very being. With you, Leena, I'm whole, and I'm yours. Completely, fully, and everything in between."

The power of his words overwhelmed me until my knees were weak. "Kiss me," I breathed, gathering his tunic, and he did. His lips sent beautiful shudders through every nerve, and I fell into him. We wrapped ourselves in each other's embrace until I couldn't think, until my fears were dulled, and all I felt was lightness and hope. How could I continue through the woods after such a declaration?

I had to. Despite the fierceness of our sudden love, danger was still imminent, and preparations had to be made. It took immense self-control, but I peeled myself from him and gained my bearings, looking at him with a resoluteness even he couldn't fight.

"Show me what I need to know. Teach me what I need to learn. Let me carry this burden with you. You're not alone anymore. We'll do this together. Together, we'll take down this Melora person and any threat that crosses our paths."

He twisted my hair in his fingers and tugged me in close "Of course, my queen. We'll take her down together, and I'll do anything you wish."

***

To my relief, Bratan showed me around the woods, even bringing me across the threshold to the human realm to explain the ins and outs of our duties and what to look out for. "They're tricky, the mortals, and there are always adolescents who think they want to fight me or trick me in some way. They usually regret it."

"Please don't tell me you hurt them," I said as I followed him through a thick wall of vines.

"Of course not," he grumbled, "but I do teach them lessons. Maybe give them a slap or two with a root for good measure." He gave me a sly grin, and I couldn't help but laugh.

When we got back to our world, it was long past suppertime. Before we went into the human realm earlier, we'd made a quick stop in town for food. I didn't realize how much better food would be in this new, fanciful world until it consistently left me filled with a sense of sheer delight. I found myself greatly anticipating dinner, though that wasn't entirely new. I loved a good meal. It was just seldom back in Woodsmeadow. Here, it was every few hours.

"Are we going to the market?" I asked, practically skipping ahead of him, pulling on his hand. "Hurry up! Do you have lead in your boots?"

"I'm tired, and I'm not hungry." His brows were sharp, but he wore the trace of a smile, which showed me how he really felt. I was starting to understand his silent language—the different quirks that told me what his words didn't.

"Well, *I* am." I stuck out my tongue and let go of his hand, swiveling around to skip faster. "We should go to the deli stall. Those sandwiches were to die for."

"The market isn't open in the evenings. We'll have to go to the tavern."

"How's their food?" I threw a glance over my shoulder, and he sped up to catch me by the waist.

"Not as delicious as you." He snarled into the crook of my neck; I giggled as he kissed it, surrendering to his touch. "After dinner, why don't we—"

His hands stilled, his body rigid, freezing until he bolted upright.

"Bratan, what—" I tried pulling away to face him, but his grip tightened. He was looking somewhere far away, as alert as a Rottweiler at a prison cell.

"Did you hear that?"

My stomach sank the moment a chill passed over my body. That same feeling of death accompanied it.

"No, but I feel it."

"We have to go. Now." He nearly crushed my fingers as he led me along faster than I could keep up with.

"Stop! I'm tripping!"

He swept me up in his arms and kept running. I was pretty sure the sweat pilling at his hairline was from distress and not from the strain of holding me while running faster than mortally possible.

The trees were a blur of green and black, only illuminated by the full moon glinting above us. My arms wrapped tightly around him, my chin buried in the groove of his collarbone as I watched the woods speed behind us. The space between my brows puckered when a shape emerged from the distance. I couldn't make it out. Not at first. But when it came fully into view, horror plucked at my nerves like a broken harp.

"Bratan!"

I didn't need to explain before he changed. The smoothness of his skin quickly turned to coarse, jagged bark, and the trees fell below us as we rose beyond the woods' ceiling. The ghastly shape chased us, crawling up Bratan's tree-bark legs at a disturbingly quick pace.

"What is that!" I squealed. "What's happening?"

The creature's face was nearly human, but its body was that of a monstrous-sized spider. With ten long, crooked legs and a gray pallor, the creature buried its tiny rows of black eyes into me with a hungry gaze that made my stomach lurch. The closer it skittered, the more haunting features I could make out. Its skin was so thin I could see every black vein beneath its white casing. Oddly shaped bones snapped and popped as it moved. Even its neck bent as it crawled, and it was nearly the size of Bratan in his human form. And almost as fast.

"Bratan!" I cried. The creature's hands were like a human's, but the fingers were unnaturally long and crooked, with the tips forming black points at the ends. Its mouth formed a circle, which spread across its oblong face and exposed two sharp fangs steeped in black liquid that could only be the blood of something immortal.

It reached one long, crooked limb above my face, its claw opening and about to sink into my skull when Bratan flung me onto his back and crushed the creature with his massive hands. I blinked in shock. Such a terrifying creature was taken out like a common housefly.

My heart raced. "Thank goodness."

"Stay on guard." His voice came in every direction. I dug my fingers into his rough skin. "There are more."

The blood drained from my face, and I was dangerously close to vomiting. Tears stung my eyes, but I needed to be strong.

"Show me how to fight," I pleaded, but my face remained buried in his protective skin.

"Now is not the time, Leena." His voice boomed with frustration.

I didn't care.

"Help me so I don't die out here!"

"You're not ready!" he bellowed. Any further argument was cut short by three ghostly hounds pouncing at us from all sides. They were greater than any wolf and the color of night. Their eyes were red as fresh blood, which matched whatever liquid was still caked on their yellow teeth. Bratan swept them off like they were nothing, but I recoiled in fear.

"I'm protecting you. If I show you anything now, you'll only suffer."

"You can't order me around and do what you want!"

"I'm not ordering you around, Leena! I'm protecting you! We're being attacked!"

I scowled, finally gathering the courage to pull away. I looked down at the long drop. If I tried scaling down from here, I'd be dead unless he caught me. If death was possible. At best, it would crush my bones. But I couldn't rely on him or anyone. My life had taught me that I may end up alone one day, so I had to learn to fight for myself. I truly did believe Bratan and I were one soul—a true, mated match with an unbreakable bond—but what if something happened to him, or he was fighting one creature and hounds pounced on me? I couldn't be useless.

"Let me go! I can take care of myself!"

"No, Leena, you *can't*!"

"I need to protect myself! I can protect you, too."

"I don't need protection," he hissed. "I'm supposed to protect *you*."

"Is there a rule book I don't know about? Because I feel like I'm just as much in the dark now as I was when I came here."

"Leena, I—"

A sound like a warped bell chimed from the distance, shattering every angry thought in my mind. Something was out there.

"What was that?" Another chime sounded. I could have sworn Bratan replied, but I couldn't make it out. It was like he was underwater. I tried calling out to him but couldn't hear my own voice. Before I tried again, something sucked me from his back.

All I processed was the drop.

And then darkness.

# CHAPTER THIRTY

## WOODSMEADOW

"THE MONSTER IS STILL out there, and he always will be unless we do something about it!" Cheering erupted from the crowd, thundering beneath the villagers' feet. The only people in town who weren't roaring with enthusiasm were the gray-and-ginger-haired old man next to Ms. Tomlin and the matriarch herself, though the latter had a small smile resting on her otherwise stoic face. "We shouldn't have to follow his rules and make sacrifices or offerings to simply live on his land!"

The man leading the crowd was a gruff fellow with a dark dollop of hair, a stout body, and the voice of an ancient beast, perfect for riling up a mob. He turned to the man beside Ms. Tomlin. "Do you have something to add, Boris? The bastard killed your son!"

"Of course I do!" he barked. The prim, older man turned to the crowd. His wiry hair was askew for the first time in decades. "People have gone missing for weeks! Children! And you saw with your own eyes what he did to my son! Do you want that to continue? Don't you want to avenge my son's death? The death of one of us!" He continued scanning the now quiet crowd. Unease was in the air like a puck of curdled milk. His eyes stopped on a wasp-like woman with mousy hair. "Will your son be next?" The woman gasped, instinctively grabbing the small boy at her side.

Boris met the eyes of one of the village's elders. "And what of you, sir? What if you are next? Or Ms. Tomlin? What if he picks us off one by one, starting with our leaders?" Murmurs broke out among the crowd; it only took moments before some of them shouted in angry agreement. Fists rose in the air, and the thundering below their feet resumed.

The dark-haired man stepped forward. "We won't take this anymore, will we?" A chorus of "No's" rose to the sky, and the man took a step back, looking at Boris. "We'll make a plan. We won't take this." The older man nodded, his face a stony canvas in contrast to the stout man's animated fury. "We will rid the forest of that beast once and for all!"

The crowd roared into chaos, and cheers rang to the tops of the trees.

The leaves shuddered in reply.

*** 

*Leena*

When I woke up, my head was throbbing. My body was screaming. It took me a few minutes to gather myself and clear my vision enough to look at where I was. Disoriented already, being somewhere completely foreign only made me more confused. I had no idea where I was. I was in a white bed with a starchy sheet tucked beneath my legs. It was one step up from sandpaper. There was an odd smell in the air, and a curtain separated my place in the small bed with the rest of what looked like a small wooden cabin. To my right was my husband, his face in his hands and fingers threaded in his hair. His shoulders were slumped.

"Bratan?" My voice was hoarse. I tried sitting up, but he immediately leapt to my side, catching my shoulders with large, gentle hands.

"Don't move, Leena. You fell a long way. If you were still mortal, you'd be dead right now."

The pang of his words struck something deep. I nodded and did what I was told. He eased me onto my back and called for someone behind the curtain. A few seconds later, a fae woman with pink skin and a tight, brunette bun pinned to the back of her skull emerged with a basin of water and what looked like medicine.

"I'm relieved to see you're all right, Your Majesty. You took quite the spill." She placed the basin on a table at the other end of the bed, unscrewed the medicine bottle, and poured the thick red liquid into a small cup. "Take this. It's a potion that will help with the pain."

"Ella is a healer," Bratan explained as I threw back the vile liquid. "She's the realm's best potion master, too. She's already fixed your shattered bones."

"You shouldn't stand, though," Ella added, dipping a cloth in the basin and placing it on my forehead. "Rest as long as you need."

"I'll be sure she does," Bratan said. His tone was soft, not controlling at all. My shoulders relaxed. He gently placed a hand on my head and pressed a kiss to my cheek.

"I'll leave you be, Your Majesties," Ella said with a bow and disappeared behind the curtain.

"She seems nice," I said, voice still hoarse. Bratan handed me a goblet of water, which both helped quench my thirst and rid my tongue of the potion's nasty taste.

"She is. She's been the healer here for centuries."

"She looks so young."

"Yes, she's nearly immortal. She's fae. They live longer than any other mortal being."

"I didn't realize they weren't immortal."

"Only gods are immortal, and there are still limitations." He gently placed his face against mine. Steady warmth spread through my chest. "I'm so glad you're okay, little dove," he breathed.

"Me too," I whispered.

"Don't ever scare me like that again. You were so stubborn. I'll teach you what I can when you're better, but that wasn't the time or place."

"I know," I sighed. "I panicked and wasn't thinking straight."

He sat back and raked a hand through his tousled hair. "Please be more careful, Leena."

I nodded, ashamed of my childish antics and timing, though I still had that anger in the back of my mind that wanted to spit insults at him for not teaching me sooner. I tried granting him grace, though. He was just as new to this union as I was, and he had centuries to be stuck in his ways as the only leader. Still, I couldn't help being angry.

I at least deserved answers. "Can you finally tell me what's going on?"

He paused, then with a solemn nod, he carefully took my hands in his and began. "Those sinister spirits are some of Melora's demons. She has many throughout this realm and likely some I don't know about."

"Did she send them?" I asked. He nodded. "Has she always tormented you like this?"

"Not like this. I was actually pretty surprised when I saw them coming. It seems she's bent on our destruction now." He tucked a loose strand of hair behind my ear and kissed it. "I'd do anything to protect you, and she knows it. She's spotted a soft spot in my defenses and is leaping on the opportunity."

"Why does she want you dead? Just to rule this place?"

"I think so; she's become more erratic and malicious. From things she's said and done, I'm assuming she either wants to have a place at my side because she was so close to my mother or because she's going mad from not having as much say as she did back then. She could also be jealous that I have you and snapped when she realized she no longer had any hold on what's left of my family. I don't really know. I'm still trying to figure it out myself."

"Is she trying to destroy you or convince you to let her be a part of things here?"

He shrugged. "I don't know. Maybe she thinks I'd bend to her will out of sheer despondency if something were to happen to you." He let out a bitter laugh. "She doesn't know me at all if that's the case."

His hands were still tight on me like something could snatch me from him at any moment. Maybe that was possible if what he was saying and what had just transpired was only a taste of things to come.

"What do you think she'll do?"

He released a shaky breath. "She was once a friend of my mother's, but from her ease of making malicious deals with the villagers, I'm starting to wonder if she contributed to the riots of the humans centuries ago. She could have thought Mother would want her to be more involved if things got out of hand. As I mentioned, she had a lot of say when Mother was alive, and I used to go to her for help after that. That slowed over the years and has now ceased altogether. This may be her last-ditch effort to sink her claws into my forest and this realm."

I wondered if I should ask the next question, but it seemed pertinent for me to understand this demon. "With the death of your mother, how did she manage not to take over?"

"I was strong, and I had a commitment to my mother and every ounce of fury I'd have if anyone were to do anything to you. But if I were to lose you now, I'd go mad. She's probably hoping for that. I don't think I could ever be more devastated than if half my soul was ripped from me like it almost was tonight."

Guilt pulled in my chest. If I hadn't been so stubborn, then I may not have almost died. I must have scared him senseless. "I'm sorry," I whispered.

"It's all right, little dove. You were right. I should have trained you. I'm sorry it came down to this."

I shook my head. "It's fine. What matters now is moving forward." I paused. "Please continue. I want to understand and hear you out about Melora."

His features tightened. "I think the day my mother died, something in Melora snapped, though I always got a strange feeling when she was around."

Voices whispered behind the curtain as another patient was brought into the cabin.

"What do we do then?"

"We fight."

My eyebrows shot up at his abrupt response and the response itself. "Really?"

"Really. But first, you need rest. And healing." He lightly stroked the top of my head. "Sleep, and we'll work on getting you ready when your body is stronger. I'll show you defense techniques in the meantime, but just so you know, I'll be watching over you. Please don't be offended."

I leaned into his touch. "Your protection is welcome. Thank you." The sensation of being cared for, although new and sometimes frustrating, healed a part of me I couldn't explain. And with the peace that accompanied it, I drifted back to sleep.

***

The next few days were spent recuperating, and it felt like the eye of the inevitable storm ahead. Melora was at our heels with her creatures, but Bratan and I stayed in the village and our home as I recovered. The only thing we did other than rest, stroll, and eat was socialize with the townspeople and have the occasional self-defense lesson. I was in no shape to fight or even practice the defense moves myself, so I watched Bratan, which got distracting. My eyes often levitated toward the tautness of his muscles and the way his arms tightened and released as he showed me different positions. It was a good thing I was in no shape to do anything other than watch. No matter how disappointed it made me. We'd spent enough time tangled up in bed for now; we had to keep our heads screwed on straight if we wanted to stay alive and keep our people safe.

We still had no idea what Melora wanted. Bratan wasn't even completely sure what she was planning, and he was getting more on edge by the day. He tried hiding it, but it was easy to tell, at least to me.

"Are you even watching?" He folded his arms. A thin layer of sweat glistened on his biceps.

"I assure you I am." I resisted the urge to wink and had to bite my tongue so I wouldn't continue flirting. *Keep your head on, Leena. Cool yourself down.*

"I know what you're thinking, you wicked thing."

"I'm not thinking anything! Besides, I'm in no shape to—"

He rushed forward, grabbing my jaw and smiling against my lips. "No shape to do what? Because I don't think you were about to say, practice."

An aching stretched from my hips, but I managed to shake his hand away and glower at him. "You're not as tempting as you think you are."

He chortled at my obvious lie. "Is that so?" He leaned in closer, trailing his warm breath against my throat and down to the top of my chest.

I grabbed him by the tunic. "Now, who's the wicked thing?"

His mouth was tempting. I wanted so badly to sink into it, but I couldn't succumb. Before I could resist, though, he kissed me, and I hummed in pleased relief. I grabbed hold of his back at the same moment he gripped the sides of my thighs.

"I didn't think your body could get more sumptuous, but this forest suits you."

My face flushed. "I like to eat, okay?"

"It was a compliment, little dove. I absolutely love it." He let out a low, sensual growl; the sound rolled into my throat, causing my head to fall back with desire. "Every time I see you, I want to lick you. Bite you. Suck on those curves that grow more delicious by the day. I wish I could eat you whole."

The blood in my legs blazed.

"Will you stop?" I breathed. "You know I'm in no condition to do anything."

"Who says you have to do anything? What if I want to do things to you?"

My breath hitched in my throat. "I couldn't resist going further than that."

He chuckled, giving me one last kiss before leaning back and taking my hands in his. "Then I guess you'll just have to keep studying until you're fit to be taken completely. But I warn you," he grabbed the back of my neck. An involuntary sound escaped me; he leaned forward, "After so much time without your body on mine, I won't stop until the whole world quakes and crumbles beneath us and I've satisfied you beyond comprehension."

My toes curled against the wooden floorboards.

I couldn't open my eyes as I begged, "Please, just do this blasted defense training, or we won't stand a chance."

"You're one strong woman," he teased, pulling away.

I let out a shaky breath. "I'm counting on it." Opening my eyes, I gave him an unimpressed side-eye. "But don't get cocky. You want me just as bad."

"Oh, I assure you I want you so much more."

# Chapter Thirty-One

S EVERAL UNEVENTFUL DAYS WENT by without that disconcerting chill or seeing shadows in corners and cracks. The fear that something could happen at any moment had lessened but was still there, and I made sure I was alert.

Bratan had brief moments of being at ease—as much as he could be. In addition to him being a tightly wound individual already, he possessed a newfound fear that amplified whenever I wanted to do something alone. I could tell he did his best to give me space when I needed it, but he was eager to return to my side when I called for him, though I'd bet money that he never really left and simply hid from view.

I tried not to think about how worried he was because that reminded me that something dangerous was on the horizon. It helped to keep busy, and we often ventured around the village. I was starting to enjoy the initial steps of being queen of this realm and getting to know our people. Things were calm for now, which truly delighted me, and I was able to spend time getting to know my husband properly. We had regular eating spots, he continued teaching me self-defense, and I was finally grasping what I could do as a Keeper and leader of the woods.

Venturing out into the human realm and deeper into our forest was my favorite pastime, though it made Bratan deeply on edge. Everything put him on edge, though, so I stopped paying much mind to it. But venturing into that familiar part of the woods also reminded me of Grandmother, and it took an immense amount of strength for me not to wander into Woodsmeadow. I had to trust Bratan that he would see to it once things with Melora were dealt with.

I still felt like he wasn't telling me something, but I figured he would tell me when things were calmer. I was doing the same thing. In the last day or so, I began feeling the stirrings of a dormant power deep in my core. I wasn't sure how to wield it, what would happen if I could, or if it was anything I could wield at all. There was no point thinking about it with everything going on, though. Even if I could use it, there was no way I could refine it before whatever Melora was planning came to fruition.

Whatever it was hadn't revealed itself anyway, so I'd deal with it when the time came. For now, whenever that unease left gooseflesh skittering across my arms, I quickly brushed it aside, hiding it in a place I hoped stayed sealed until things were better. Bratan said something was coming soon, and although he didn't know of this feeling, it was best to focus on the little training he gave me, especially considering I wasn't fully healed yet.

"Is something on your mind?" he asked when that odd sense of power flickered in my fingertips. I quickly curled them into my palms.

"No, just thinking."

"About what?" He shifted his weight, looking at me with concern, but my faux smile remained.

"I've been enjoying our time together and with the villagers." I wasn't sure if he noticed the quick change of subject to evade more questioning or if he thought I was offering a piece of what was on my mind. Either way, it steered the conversation in a relieving direction.

A smile warmed his face. "I have as well. I've never spent this much time with my people. I should have thought of it, but I had a one-track mind until I met you. My sole focus was on protection and dealing with those blasted humans. From the time I woke up to when I went to sleep, I was only ever angry or frustrated. Until you." He caressed the side of my face with his long fingers, and I leaned into his touch, though it was hard not to snicker at the notion that he did anything but worry now. But I let him have this. He was branching out and learning to live, and he was happy.

"It's not a bad thing to worry about your people," I said.

His fingers danced along my jawline. It took great strength to resist the temptation to close my eyes and be swept away by his touch.

"No, I suppose not." His hand continued to roam, but he withdrew it when it fell beneath my collarbone. "I now have someone precious to protect as well—someone who has loved these people like her own family." The gravity of his obvious adoration sent a pool of warmth through my chest.

I caught his face in my hands. "We make a good team."

"We do." His voice was a deep rumble. He kissed my fingers and curled them in his own. "Now let me continue in those efforts. Show me what you remember from yesterday."

I silenced the protest threatening to leap from my throat. It'd been far too long since we'd made love. I knew we needed to focus and that I wasn't in top physical form yet, but surely he was aching for me, too.

"Okay," I murmured.

"That's my girl." His fingers fell down my lips, grabbing my chin. I sucked in a breath.

"You're cruel, you know that?"

He barked out a laugh. "Do you think it's easy for me to contain myself?"

"Isn't it? You could have fooled me."

"I've been dying to take you and make you mine over and over, little dove, but I care more about your safety than satiating my desires. However," He leaned in and gently bit my bottom lip, "if you're ready enough, maybe we can take a little break."

Heat darted through my blood. "We'll see who caves first." Stepping back, I cast him a seductive look, which made him bare his teeth with a primal growl. To my dismay, he composed himself, leaned against the kitchen wall, and awaited me to display my skills. I hated how he was right. I needed to learn everything I could so I wouldn't be killed or be a liability. It wasn't just him—I wanted to protect my people too and not be someone whose safety would distract Bratan from protecting all of us from whatever threat Melora sent next. But it was hard to focus when he crossed his arms like that in his thin, short-sleeved training tunic.

Blowing out the gathering tension in my lungs, I got into position and showed him what I remembered. When he was satisfied with my posture, I did it again and again until he deemed me ready for a few simple techniques where I could fight.

My spirits soared. *Maybe I can do this after all. Melora won't stand a chance against us if I keep this up.* We'd be two steps ahead.

Unfortunately, though, that fear tightening his features was back as he trained me, and I knew he was too preoccupied with my safety to think about anything else. I'd have to let go of my desires for now.

I really hated Melora.

\*\*\*

*Bratan*

For the first time in decades, my body was sore, and it wasn't from fighting or any other activity that required dexterous movement but from sheer fear. If I hadn't been so used to walking around rigid and furious for centuries, I might have noticed the slight difference that took such a toll on my muscles over the last few weeks. The mind-numbing anxiety that something would go wrong was strong, and seeing Leena fall to what I thought was her death showed up in my nightmares, as well as in the quiet moments of my waking hours when she was still asleep.

We were immortal through nature but not indestructible. Though it was difficult, we could be killed, and there were some things we still needed, just not as much as mortals did: food and sleep. We wouldn't die from the lack of those things, but we'd be living in a death-like state until we could obtain them again. We were impervious to nature's course of aging—the one that claimed healthy humans' lives—but we were not invincible.

I'd explained this to Leena in the days following her accident. Seeing her so close to her demise made me realize how fragile a state she was in right now and how little she knew about this realm. She was new to her form and perhaps not fully grasping everything about her new self. I tried explaining as much as I could and informed her of anything that could be important for her to know, but I often worried that I'd forgotten something, second-guessing every action and decision I made as the days drudged on.

There was also the obvious threat looming above us. The fact that Melora hadn't made another appearance was beyond concerning. She was plotting something, and I feared the worst was coming, though I wasn't sure what it was. Not knowing was the worst part.

Today, Leena's movements were more fluid as she displayed her various stances. Admiring her concentration and the way her skin was lined with sweat, the sunlight trickling gold along her braided hair, brought tension to my chest. I'd need a warm soak in the hot spring tonight. It was the only thing that could soothe the pain. The spring was a little far away on foot, but it would do both of us good, especially since whatever Melora was planning could happen at any moment.

"We should go," I called out, startling a squirrel up a tree.

She nearly tripped as she stopped. "What? Why? It isn't even sundown." I shifted against the tree I was leaning on, arms still crossed in an attempt to hide the fear cranking my insides to knots.

"We need to rest our muscles. There's a hot spring at the far end of the woods. It will do us some good to rejuvenate there. You'll wake up in the morning without so much as a sore finger."

"Don't you have healing powers?" she asked, wiping sweat from her forehead.

"I do, but it takes a lot of energy, and I can't use it on myself. It also doesn't work on a lot of physical injuries or ailments, such as torn muscles or broken bones, as you know. Besides,"

I pushed off the tree and slid my hand around her neck until I caught hold of her braid, "wouldn't it be more fun to bathe together?"

Pink dusted the bridge of her nose and spread to her cheeks. "All right," she said, "if you think my body can handle it."

My lip curled. "I don't know about that, but the waters will help soothe any soreness."

She slid her fingers up my chest and played with the cord at the top of my tunic. "Does that mean we can finally make love again?"

My grip tightened on her hips. "Yes, little dove. I can't take it anymore. I've wanted you so badly I can't stand it." I nipped her earlobe and, gasping, she stumbled over a gnarled root jutting from the cracked earth. Catching her by the waist, I pulled her into a kiss. "I'll have Theodora bring you what you need for the journey. I'll escort you to her hut, and then I'll get what we need from home."

She looked up with those doe-like, ocean-blue eyes, and somehow, my chest muscles pulled tighter. At some point they had to snap.

"Are you all right?"

"Of course. Why wouldn't I be?" I forced a smile, but she saw right through it.

"Are you still worried about me?"

I tried avoiding her gaze, but she stepped in front of me and slid her slender hands up my shoulders. She awaited my response.

"Of course I'm worried. You're everything to me. Leena, you know we're not invincible, right?"

She stared at me for a long moment and then pulled away.

"I've been wondering about that...I know you said I could die, but you'd also said I was immortal."

"I'm sorry, I explained it better." *Bratan, you moron,* I wanted to scream.

"No, no, you did explain it! It probably got lost in all the information I've received, but I do remember you telling me that I can be killed and that there are limitations on our immortality."

This eased my fears a bit, loosening some of the tightness in my chest and shoulders. I brushed a loose wave of hair behind her ear and pressed my hand against the small of her back. "I can't stand the thought of something happening to you." A lump formed in my throat. If I looked into her eyes now, my own would gush with tears. "I'd go completely mad if you died."

Her fingers slipped down to my chest. "I won't die. Not until it's time for us to go together."

"I won't let that happen."

"If it does, I'm sure we'll go together. You and I are one, remember?"

I lifted her braid and kissed it. "I love you, Leena. I adore everything you are, and I'll protect every hair on your head and freckle on your body, even if it means sacrificing and the life I once knew. You're my present and future, and I'm convinced you were my past."

"Don't worry about me. Please. We have to stay strong and fight whatever comes next together. And whatever comes after that, and after that, forever. We're a team. Okay?" She touched my cheek. The scent of her skin was sweet. Honeysuckle and pear. I kissed her palm and then her wrist. My heart nearly melted when she giggled, and when our eyes met again, all I felt was guilt.

She didn't know who I truly was. She didn't know that I went back and killed that bastard who tried to assault her or how many beings I'd killed over the centuries. Every act was justified, but she'd begged me not to kill that vile man. Would she forgive me for going behind her back if she ever found out? I only wanted to protect her.

My life consisted of partial truths and acts of whatever I deemed necessary for my kingdom's safety and survival. I now did the same for her, and I was afraid of who I might become the next time danger flirted with my queen. Could I hold back, or would the monster inside me consume me completely? If it got bad enough, I might be unable to turn back, and I wasn't sure she could love the part of me that was nothing but a monster.

Regardless of the form I took, that's what I was—a monster. And I knew, to a certain extent, that a part of me would always be one. To my people, I was some sort of angel—or at least a demon that kept them safe. I supposed that part was true, in

a way, but I wasn't sure she'd accept it if she found out everything I was and all I'd done. If she grasped my role and how
I must protect our people—and, above all, protect *her*—she
may not accept it. I'd told her vague memories and things I had
to do, but she didn't know the scope of it or that I'd betrayed
her trust by killing that disgusting creature who tried to harm
her.

*I have to tell her.*

As soon as whatever threats Melora sent our way returned to
the pits of hell she'd conjure them from, I'd tell Leena everything, including what I did to that heinous beast she'd asked
me to spare.

As I looked at her now, prancing into the village with her
braid falling down her back, I wondered if she could love the
soul she was mated to or if she'd turn away from fate. It felt
like I'd always known her—that our souls had always been
one—and I believed that. I believed that we were one being
woven from a cloth of stars at the beginning of time. We still
didn't know each other in the way we one day would, though.
If she decided I was a monster and wanted nothing to do with
me, then what?

Her hips swayed as she walked to the carved-out tree where
she was often dressed. With one last wave, she dipped through
the doorway.

She was everything I wasn't. Sweet, kind, pure.

Even if she didn't choose me, I would choose her. Nothing
could change that. Even if I had to do it at a distance, I would

protect her and love her until my inevitable dying day. And even after that.

If every tree in these woods were to fall upon me and ripped apart my very soul, I would suffer it gladly if it meant she'd be safe. If it kept her happy and free.

I just hoped I was worthy to be happy by her side.

# Chapter Thirty-Two

T HE DRESSING ROOM TUCKED into the familiar tree was quiet as I paced and waited for Theodora to arrive with my things. The sweet smell of pine was comforting these days; it had been such an unwelcome sensation when my former people relocated to the woods. Those days were difficult, full of pain and hardship and fear. There was so much work, so many blisters, screaming commands, and thrashes to my back. *Work harder,* Vasska screamed. *Work faster. This hut won't build itself.*

I worked tirelessly, as did the other villagers, though most did so with less abuse.

I hated the smell of the trees back then. Who knew that in such a short time, I would grow to love it? That I would welcome the scent as it reminded me of Bratan and my new home.

Toying with a loose strand of hair, I thought of how he'd tucked it behind my ear and of his breath warm against my lips. My cheeks hurt from grinning at the thought of him.

*A hot spring. He's taking me to a hot spring.* I couldn't help but hope we'd finally get a good amount of time to be together—to make love in the true eye to the storm that lay before and behind us. I wondered what the water would be like; I'd only ever heard of the heavenly gift of a healing pool. I thought of my arms around him, sitting on his lap, kissing him deeply as we sunk deeper into the steaming water.

His hands would grab my hips with that hungry eagerness I so often craved. His fingers would grip beneath the meat of my thighs, pulling me closer until I was so tight against him it would be impossible not to be one. His tongue would taste of fruit and fire. My wet hair would fall freely in tangles over my bare shoulders as he grasped my neck. He'd whisper in my ear until I begged for him, and then he'd grip me and bite me as I fell and let him command me. I wanted him to take control of my body. To dominate my senses. To—

"My lady?" A voice made me jump. I quickly turned around, fidgeting and shifting my weight in a desperate attempt to hide the obvious heat coloring my face and neck.

"O-oh, I-I'm sorry, I didn't..." My voice trailed off when I saw it was Ani standing there instead of Theodora. I tried not to grimace at the unwelcome substitute. "Where's Theodora?"

"She's gathering some towels and clothing or something. She told me to fetch you." She narrowed her eyes at my flustered state. "Was I interrupting something?"

"No! What would you be interrupting?" I laughed awkwardly, hating myself for the odd answer and hoping it wouldn't garner a response.

Fortunately, she merely let out an irritated sigh and said, "Come. I'll take you to her." Then walked back through the doorway. I rushed to follow, fanning myself whenever she wasn't looking incredulously over her shoulder. The tiny maiden didn't look back much, to my immense relief, but I couldn't stop thinking of the hot spring and of finally seducing my husband after too long of a wait.

Ani stepped into the forest, away from the village or paths leading to my house. We passed tree after tree for what had to have been fifteen minutes. The route didn't make sense.

"I thought Theodora was getting supplies and wanted to meet me. Are you taking me to the spring?"

"Of course," she spat. "Theodora told me to bring you to the human realm. It would take hours to take you directly to the spring. I'm not sure how His Majesty will take you." She looked me up and down in a way that made me feel bare and humiliated.

"What is it?" I demanded, unconsciously covering myself with folded arms.

She strode closer to the portal to the human world. "Nothing."

The farther we ventured, the more discomfort became my companion, especially when Ani instructed me to open the door to my former world. "Why do we have to go through? Why isn't Theodora meeting me in our village?"

"Because she was sent on an errand to the human realm. His Majesty is eager to leave, and Theodora was running behind. So, are you going to keep wasting time, or are you going to do this?"

I wanted to scream at the little wretch, but I wouldn't let her ruin my day, and I didn't want to waste time doing it, so I faced the portal and tried to remember how Bratan had done it. Waving my hand over the vines, I felt that dormant power bubble in my veins. It stopped as soon as the portal opened, and I didn't have time to process what was triggering it before Ani stepped through. I quickly followed behind, instantly shrouded in darkness.

After too many moments without sound or sight, I opened my mouth to cry out to the maid. Only a squeak escaped before she grabbed my wrist. "You're a queen!" she hissed. "Why do you act like a defenseless child?"

I wished I had a good response, but the truth made me feel pathetic. Because I felt like one, despite my training, I felt just as defenseless as I had from the start. Whether it was from Vasska or Melora's creatures, I'd never been able to do more than hold my own enough to survive, and the scars from those moments of survival still haunted me with wounds both invisible and etched deep below the surface of my skin. Scars and bruises had battered my bones and soul too many times to heal within a matter of weeks, if they'd ever heal at all.

When I didn't respond, she irritably dragged me along until we entered the lit edge of the human realm. The trees on this side of the forest seemed different than they had before I married Bratan. I hadn't realized the way they shivered, so unlike the trees of the realm I now lived in. These stoic trees were a distant memory from a past life, their branches barely moving, their leaves only shivering with the passing of the wind. They weren't alive like the ones around my new home. Maybe Bratan had something to do with that.

"We're almost there," Ani grumbled, throwing my wrist aside and wiping her palm on her apron. The pain of how she felt about me never got easier.

We walked in silence until figures appeared in the distance. I couldn't make them out, but they were headed right toward us. They got closer at an alarming rate.

"Are those villagers from Woodsmeadow?" I turned to Ani, but the small maiden didn't answer. The group grew larger, more people coming into view, and it wasn't until they were too close that I realized they were holding torches and tools. I staggered back, once again turning to Ani. "What's going on?"

Still, the maid didn't answer. And the mob closed in.

***

*Bratan*

I slung the bag over my shoulder, excited for the respite Leena and I would take after these torturous days of training, healing, and avoiding impending threats. So far, things had been quiet, and if Leena was safely tucked into the hot spring far from the village, Melora and her demons would be too far away to find her. I could shift into my true form and attack while Leena peacefully rested in the spring's healing waters. I could fight them off before they searched for her. In my true form, I could get there in seconds.

Walking the path to the maidens' hut, I was beaming. Leena would soon be safe, and we could find solace in each other's arms in the spring and on the warm stones around it. We could bathe in its waters and finally make love. After far too long, I could smell her skin, wet and sweet, and taste it as she writhed. I'd graze every inch of her hot flesh, drinking it in as she surrendered to me, her shoulders rolling back as she screamed my name.

When we were together, something primal took over; we lived by feeling, free from the bonds of this world. I ached to search her with my fingers and taste her, bite her, grab her.

My mouth watered, but I had to quickly redirect my thoughts when her maid came into view from the large tree. I practically skipped to meet my wife so we could start on our journey, but then I noticed Theodora closing the door behind her with Leena nowhere in sight.

My heart sank as I walked faster.

"Where's Leena?" I was barely able to hear my own voice over the quickening thumps in my chest. Theodora turned with a curtsy. "Where's Leena?" I repeated louder this time.

When Theodora straightened, she looked up, confused. "I was told she'd be meeting you."

"I told you to give her what she needed and to wait here for me. Where is she?"

"I-I don't understand. Ani told me you wanted her to take Leena to the woods so you could go to the spring together. I thought there was a change of plans."

My stomach twisted. "I never ordered such a thing. I haven't talked to anyone but you. Who's Ani? Where are they?"

Theodora's head jerked back, but she quickly composed herself as if her confusion were disrespectful. "My junior maid, Your Majesty. Surely you know of her."

"I've never heard that name before. I only appointed you as Leena's maid. Who and where is this Ani? Where is she taking her?"

Theodora's head shook. "But—you don't know Ani? She's Leena's other maid. I—"

"Where are they?" I pressed. Sweat formed on my palms. Fear fogged my senses, making it hard to hear or see straight.

"A-all I know is that they're in the woods somewhere. I'm so sorry, Your Majesty. Ani has served Leena alongside me since Her Majesty was appointed queen. I had no idea you hadn't appointed her."

I bolted into the woods. I wasn't sure if Theodora said anything else or of what was going on around me. I couldn't hear a thing. I couldn't breathe. As I turned into my bestial form, all I could feel was the fear in my gut and the tightness in my chest. Panic rippled through me in violent waves, ticking with every lost second.

I was going to lose her. I never should have left her side.

# Chapter Thirty-Three

## Leena

I couldn't move. I was taught to defend myself and was even starting to learn the basics of attacks, but it had been for nothing. In the face of danger, I froze. All I could manage to do was look at Ani while two gruff men grabbed me roughly by the wrists and tied them behind my back. I wouldn't have stood a chance anyway. There were too many of them, and I'd only just recovered.

"You knew about this," I hissed to Ani, who merely looked at me coolly, that familiar glint of disgust in her sneer. "Why?" The maid watched me in what looked to be disinterest until a villager I recognized as Casimir's father walked forward and muttered something in the maid's ear.

"Tell Tomlin I've done my part," she replied. "You better do yours." When her eyes shifted back to mine, she grinned. "Why what, Your Majesty?" Those last two words oozed with hatred. One of the men grabbed me by the forearm and threw me onto a cart while another man tied my ankles together.

I was mortified. Humiliated. Ani wanted to see me like this; she knew what I was asking. She just wanted to see me crack. I begged to know the answer despite any pride that may have stopped me. "Why are you doing this to me?"

The small maiden laughed, clapping her hands as she jumped to where I lay.

"You're not worthy of the throne." She hopped nimbly into the cart, moving on hands and feet like a crooked beast until her face hovered above me, eyes wild as she pressed her nose against mine. "You aren't worthy to lick his boots, let alone carry his child, and that's all you'd be good for. A half-breed royal to take his place one day?" She scoffed. "The thought makes me sick. Besides, you don't belong there. You understand, don't you? That you'll only ever get in his way and that you'd be subjecting any child you have with him to a life worse than death?"

I tried to speak, but my mouth felt like cotton, my throat like sand. Before I could try, Ani sent a claw across my face. The sting of the cut was fierce against the cool evening air. She hopped out of the cart and signaled to one of the men. "Take her to Tomlin and do what we discussed. There'll be hell to pay if I see her pretty little face ever again."

***

*Bratan*

The world was shaking, seizing, as I tore through the woods like a hound from hell. I had to transform soon, or I wouldn't be able to go through the portal, and I needed some sort of stealth to find Leena before anything happened to her. Who knew what kind of torment she could be going through at this very moment?

My eyes blazed, my massive teeth grinding together before I let out a fierce, blaring cry that sent a blanket of crows soaring in every direction. As I shrunk to my other typical form, my vision was off, tremoring and jittery. Rage like I'd never felt was taking over me, which made shifting and staying in my human form all the more difficult. I limped to the portal, half-man, half-beast, my body undulating in protest between my two forms as I struck the gate between worlds. Snarling, I slashed at it, over and over, before finally summoning the magic to move it aside.

As soon as I could, I thundered through like a rabid beast, racing down the path. Nothing but the small chirps and skitters of wildlife could be heard, and there was nothing out of the ordinary in sight, but I could smell her. My instincts had been right. Leena was here, and she was close. I couldn't stay in this form. It was too hard to maintain in this state. It wasn't practical for finding her in time, but I couldn't morph into my true form either; I had to be discreet.

Slowly, I shifted into something else.

Falling on hands and knees, my fingers grew claws, and thick, dark hair spread over my limbs. My human-like breathing turned to the huffs of a wolf. Thick cords of muscle ran along four legs, and that same burning stung my eyes as it did when I was in my monstrous form. I was more creature than animal—part canine, part wolf, and something not from this world.

It was just what I needed to race forward and follow her scent. I sprung forward, speeding down a dirt path formed from years of trespassers looking for our realm. I weaved through trees, dodging shrubbery, logs, deer, and the like while trying to keep the trail of scent that teased the rims of my nostrils. My chest ached from it.

The scent was close but not close enough. I raced faster, my legs snapping as they grew joints, pushing me along the path. My senses heightened, and I caught hold of her scent with a firm grip. Her delicious aroma sent a mixture of hunger, sorrow, and fear crashing through me in a dizzying rush. From what I could tell and from what I'd learned from my mother long ago, I'd have sensed my mated soul passing if she'd been killed. Fortunately, she felt very much alive. I still had time.

I was so caught up in thoughts of her and what I'd do to punish whoever touched her that I didn't notice the person walking at a leisurely pace on the opposite side of the path. I couldn't stop in time, and before I knew it, we were rolling in a clumsy heap until we cracked apart against the base of a tree. Blurred flashes of color passed by as I rolled down a hill until my back hit a fractured log. I groaned at the sharp pain; changing from form to form was putting more strain on my muscles. Agitated, I peered up at the young fae female laughing at the top of the hill.

My eyes widened at the sight of her staring down at me, unscathed. No creature of my woods could have left that encounter unharmed or be in the human realm without my explicit permission. I slowly rose, stalking closer. She was smiling—the insolent imp was smiling. I couldn't take this. With a lunge, I grabbed her by the sleeves.

"You're Ani, aren't you?"

The girl still giggled. "You could say that." Another laugh peeled from her lips. "Oh, Your Majesty. You're too easy to fool." My claw uncurled, dropping the maiden to her heels.

My fingers trembled as I watched her transform, involuntarily shifting back into my human self along with her. The girl's laugh turned to a throaty cackle. Her face morphed in grotesque waves, pulling apart and rippling until she was the very creature I'd been trying to shield Leena from.

"You didn't think I'd be so easy to fight, did you?" Melora grinned; the lines around her mouth cracked, splintering her face like an old dinner plate.

"What did you do to her?" I growled, snatching her by the peasant dress she wore as part of her façade. "I'll rip you limb from limb and shred your flesh from your brittle bones unless you tell me exactly where I can find Leena."

Her smile lengthened. "What did I tell you? She isn't worthy of you. That little whore had no place with you there."

"Shut the hell up!" I tossed Melora like the wicked ragdoll she was, watching her skate across the ground like a rock skimming the surface of a pond. She was a devil, an immortal demon, and could only be killed by being completely torn apart, so I wasn't worried about losing the information I sought. But I did worry about losing control as my body tore through my human flesh, and I grew past the treetops.

"Tell me where she is!" My voice came from all directions, and the sky turned black. Thick clouds of gray gathered around us, following my colossal hand as I snatched the demonic woman and brought her to my eyes.

There were scrapes along the side of her face, but she had no blood to spill. She sighed, clicking her tongue in disapproval.

"What would your mother think of you behaving this way? You know better than to throw tantrums." Even in this state, I felt my body heat with rage. She was trying to get in my head. "Besides, I thought you were smarter than this. Wasting your time with me when you could be finding your beloved. What an unwise Leshy you've become. Maybe you should've impregnated the little gnat while you had the chance. Then—"

Melora flew across the woods, again by my hand. She would survive, and it would likely not cause much damage, but I couldn't help the satisfaction I felt at the sight of her clumsily flying through the air. Pride was Melora's greatest possession, and I just stripped her of it for a second time tonight. She was right about one thing, though: I was smarter than to waste time with her. And I was starting to realize where Leena might be.

If Melora wasn't with her demons or controlling them from afar, she needed help.

I shifted back into my canine form, in more control than before, and followed the scent that would bring me to my wife. Bounding through trees, I followed the internal map of the human side of my forest I held in my head.

I knew exactly where to go.

# CHAPTER THIRTY-FOUR

## LEENA

IF I WERE STILL human, my wrists would be on fire. The
two men who'd thrown me into the cart were tying me to
a stake in the town square, doing their best to be as rough as
possible. The crude wooden object must have been recently
built and in a rush because I'd never seen it before, despite
my only being gone a few weeks. Only a pace away from the
platform where I was now strapped was a celebratory table and
a roasting pig rolling over a fire. They were going to celebrate.
After whatever they did to me next, they would celebrate with
a feast they hadn't had the privilege of partaking in until my
sacrifice.

A fitting end to my cruel life. Just as happiness became more
than a dream, my people ripped it away and took everything
from me. And they'd dance upon my grave.

I cringed at the familiar scent of charred pork. Even after
all these years, the smell of roasting pig still haunted me. The
night my parents died, I waited for hours in the cold. It was the
dead of winter, and all I had on was a thin nightdress and the

cloak my mother had made me—the one that meant so much more than any piece of clothing ever would.

Staring into the woods, I stayed there all night, away from where our old village had once been settled. My fingers were frozen against my bony kneecaps by the time one of the village's elders appeared with two others, and dragging behind them, on a sled, were two forms covered in a blanket made of patched scraps. I didn't need anyone to tell me who they were.

I was too numb to move at first, but when I met the brief flickering gaze of the gruff man pulling the sled behind him, I stood up with a snap and vomited.

All I really remembered after that was being forced to my grandmother's house, where the three men from the forest spoke about what happened and what would come next. All the while, my uncle stuffed himself with charred pork, listening with vague interest like he was hearing about a trip to the market.

He ate that pork for days. Its smell soaked deep into my bones, sealing its place in my memory with the first strike he dealt across my face for being "difficult." A devastated child fighting through a nightmare. *Difficult.* It was the first time of many, each with another excuse and some with no excuse or explanation at all. It got easier for him, it seemed. Most of what I remembered from my teenage years was being grabbed and hit by those dry, peeling knuckles and calloused hands.

Sometimes, I'd run away for a moment's peace, but it was like my heart couldn't handle the absence of pain because I always found myself returning to the edge of the forest. I'd return to the spot that changed my life completely and turned its course on its head. It wasn't far from these woods, but it was far enough away to be so very different.

Until recently, the matriarch of Woodsmeadow found a place where we could safely hunt while still getting plenty of game. That "good luck" only lasted a matter of weeks, though. I couldn't blame Bratan for what he'd done. These people were killing his animals and trees, and he witnessed abuse and sought to end it. These people didn't see it that way, though. Now, they saw me the same way they saw him: as a monster.

If being fiercely protective of the innocent and striving to be happy made me a monster, then I would gladly be one.

The crowd was wild, a cacophony of cheering, jeering, and spitting. These people sacrificed me to what they assumed was a monster, only to take me back and punish me for surviving. Except I did more than survive. For the first time, I'd truly lived. I loved being with the Keeper of the woods. Maybe they'd discovered that I'd fallen in love with their enemy, and now they wanted to punish me for it.

What vile, mindless people these were. I could only assume the villagers were like this centuries ago—the ones Bratan had to face the day his mother died. Even after everything, I couldn't help feeling a new level of disgust as I watched them jeer. I thought there were at least *some* good ones in Woodsmeadow, but if there were, they weren't good enough to step in and do anything. There was only one person I knew was good, but I couldn't find her anywhere. My stomach sunk to my knees as I searched the crowd. Had they done something to Grandmother?

Someone threw a rotting vegetable at me. It reeked as a piece of it stuck to my cheek while the rest slid down my body and hit the floor. I wondered if whoever had thrown it thought it was righteous justice for what the Leshy had done by poisoning their crops. But they knew that that was why I'd left—to save them. I didn't understand how they could do this; what had they been told?

Regardless of the answer, people who could stand by and kill a woman they'd known since she was a child were the actual monsters in these woods. They'd always been despicable, turning a blind eye time and time again to make things easier for themselves—to not "cause a ruckus" or "step on anyone's toes." I was starting to understand why Bratan thought humans were self-serving, but I held on to the hope that someone good would rescue me. If Grandmother was okay, I wondered if she'd have a say in my fate.

The jeering continued as one person shouted about getting ready for my live burning, to which many cheered. It was almost too horrific to be true.

I laughed bitterly at the irony. Not long ago, I was afraid to go to the feared monster of the woods when I was with the real monsters all along.

"We know what you've done!" a villager heckled. "You betrayed us!"

"You slept with the enemy!" a woman cried, followed by angry roars of agreement.

"You were supposed to save us! You only saved yourself!"

"Whore!" one man spat, which began an onslaught of misogynistic slurs. Tears stung my eyes and rolled down my cheeks as the insults continued.

*You're wrong*, I wanted to yell. *You're the monsters. You're all wrong.*

A stocky man I barely knew leapt onto the platform, a torch in his meaty hand. His face was ruddy and covered in mud, and his yellowed mustache was crusted with something I didn't want to investigate. His balding patches of matching hair flickered in the light wind starting to blow colder with the setting sun.

The platform's boards creaked beneath his heavy frame as he loomed closer. He didn't look at my face before lowering the torch to the base of the stake. Panic shot through me, and I thrashed as the man spoke. "That beast will regret messing with us," he said, his voice hoarse and warbled. "He'll never break a deal again."

The fire hit the wood as I cried, "He never broke anything! He—" The smoke invaded my lungs as I wailed in pain. Embers licked my ankles, biting and gnawing on the flesh until tears gushed from me like blood.

Cheers erupted from the crowd, and I swore I even heard laughter. I squeezed my eyes shut, trying my best to wriggle free. The cheers and shouts continued.

This was how I'd die.

My body went slack. Even as an immortal, there was no use fighting this. Bratan had made it clear that I could be murdered, and fire was a sure way to kill me. I didn't know how to wield any powers I might or might not have, and it didn't seem to grant me anything but longevity to pain without a quick death.

I braced myself for the worst when the crowd's jeers turned to screams. The forest shook, the ground quaking so violently that it rattled my eardrums and shook my toes where they sat pointed against the wooden platform.

My eyes opened to trees snapping and thundering as they hit the ground with pillars of rising dirt. The pain seared up my shins. I'd lost hope, but right there in front of me, emerging through the cloud of dirt, was Bratan.

The villagers cried, most of them running for their houses, but without looking, Bratan raised his hands, stretching them at his sides and summoning every cottage's door closed, sealing them shut so no one could flee.

His face was fury, and his eyes were wild and black; they found me a beat before he rushed to the platform. Immediately, he extinguished the flames and snapped the ropes with one pull of his finger.

"Bratan," I squeaked. His name came out rattled. I could barely see through the smoke and dirt, but I felt his hand brush against my cheek, soft and slow. New tears welled in my eyes as the smoke cleared. I leaned into his touch, crying into his palm and letting the warmth of his fingers give me a moment of solace.

"I'm so sorry I wasn't by your side." A glint of sorrow ringed his eyes in red before he gathered me in his arms. "I will end this. I promise you that." He nuzzled his face into the crook of my neck; one hand held the side of my head in a desperate embrace, the other still tightly wrapped around my waist. "I'll take care of this." When he pulled back, that gentle gaze was gone, replaced by the rage he'd possessed upon tearing through the crowd. "You tell me exactly who did this to you." Not a question. A command. "Tell me everything."

Without thinking, my eyes fell on my former cottage, then flickered to the two men who'd tied me to the stake. Bratan didn't miss the motion and followed it, twisting to find its targets in a flash. The brawny men cowered behind two small women I could only assume were their wives.

Bratan rushed to them, scoffing as he examined the scene. "Hiding behind your wives? How pathetic." One of the men, a tall one with long, orange hair, stood up in quiet protest while the other sunk lower behind the bony woman in front of him. "You make me sick." He pushed the women away and grabbed each man by the tunic, lengthening his height until the men were crying out in panic, their legs dangling and thrashing as they tried squirming from Bratan's grip. "Do you think you can torment my wife and get away with it?" His voice split in two, his human form falling away, replaced by the monster.

The crowd wailed, some screaming and running into the woods or behind buildings, others too afraid to move.

"You don't deserve to breathe her air! Pieces of shit!" Bratan tossed them to the other side of the square; his blackened eyes, now swirling with red, like crusted blood, followed the men's tumbles until they attempted to get up and flee. They skittered away like field mice, moving at an impressive speed, but Bratan scooped them up in one long hand.

The crowd stilled. Characteristic of the villagers, they kept silent as Bratan tossed the men out of sight. No one said a word—not even Bratan—until, to my surprise, Vasska stumbled forward.

"You took our food, and now you're killing our people and any chance of survival! Take the slut and leave!"

"Vasska!" I choked on his name. "How could you?" I couldn't believe I was shocked, but hearing what he'd called me sent a blazing dagger into my gut. It sank deeper and twisted when I saw the woman staggering behind him. "Grandmother," I gasped.

Her hair was disheveled, and her dress was buttoned up wrong as she made an attempt to approach me. She cracked open her gray, dried lips to say something, but Vasska spoke first. "Even our grandmother wants you dead," he croaked. "Just look at her. She's a wreck. She's been so disgusted with you."

"That's not true, Leena!" Grandmother cried. "You know that's not true!"

Vasska stepped between us. "You've always been garbage, Leena. You've always been—" Bratan's claw struck up Vasska's back. He let out a wail as he fell back to scattered screams from a few of the female villagers, only one of which was his wife.

"If one more of you utters an ill word about my wife, your head will be on the top of that stake. Do you hear me?!" Grabbing my uncle by the shoulders, he tossed him to the side and scanned the crowd. After a moment of silence, he thundered back to my abuser.

I closed my eyes, waiting for whatever would come to be over. Seconds went by. Still, nothing happened.

Then, a choking noise.

And a thump.

I opened my eyes to see Vasska struggling on the ground. Bratan looked down at him with disgust. "Do you feel powerful taking your anger out on your niece who's done nothing to you?" He spat on Vasska as my uncle grabbed at his throat, gasping for air. "Pathetic human." Bratan looked away.

The brute continued gasping for breath.

Karina, tiny as a famished mouse, scurried over to her husband and panicked, but Vasska pushed her away. She held her hands against her chest as he stumbled to his feet, rage darkening his eyes. Vasska grunted like a wild boar. "You'll pay for that, you—" He started swinging, but the Leshy moved to the side, kicked Vasska in the back of the knees, and then, through some unseen power, tossed him over his shoulder and into the town butcher's simmering meat.

His body flopped against the spit before crashing into the celebratory table, shattering rows upon rows of fine plates and saucers ready to be used upon my demise.

Vasska's body was still. Everyone cowered as they waited for him to move. Everyone except Bratan and me. My husband transformed into his usual, human-like form and stepped onto the platform. "Stay away from my queen," he roared, staring each of them down.

Something heated in my blood.

Clinking sounded behind him as Vasska slowly sat up on the broken table. Wiping blood and soot from off his tunic, he looked at the Leshy. Then to me.

"You were supposed to take care of this problem, Leena," he barked, "not bring the damned monster back!" I couldn't believe he was still fighting. The only explanation I could think of was that he knew he was going to die and wanted to leave this world with the final word.

To my surprise, there was a moment of muttered agreement in the crowd, but they quickly quieted again when Bratan sent another claw ripping through Vasska's back. My uncle gave out a glass-shattering scream before crumpling on the quaking ground. Karina gasped and fell to his side. The ground shook harder. Screams filled the open air as villagers fell; I had to swing my arms out to keep my balance, but my foot tripped on the rock next to it and sent me falling face-first toward the splitting earth.

Before I hit it, Bratan grabbed me by the waist and placed me back on my feet. When I grabbed hold of his shoulders, I was surprised to see that his eyes were once again that striking shade of green, lit like emerald stars beneath the rising moon.

The villagers screamed as the ground continued to split. Dirt rattled against our feet as gravel pelleted into the sky. Thick, moving roots as tall as trees broke through the soil, growing until they touched the sky. "You humans make me sick," Bratan shouted. "You planned to kill the woman who gave herself up to save you. You label her a traitor because you can't think for yourselves. But what about you? Of your darkness?"

He walked to one gathered group of men who'd created a barrier in front of their families. Bratan crouched to meet the face of a man with a thick, black mustache that hung beneath a crooked nose. "Are you not selfish?" He pointed at one of the shivering children behind the man. "What if instead of my bride, your son was the one on that stake today? Would you have been so apathetic?"

"Get out, you beast," the man said, but his body tremored so violently that the words were nearly incoherent.

"As I thought. You cannot answer." He straightened. "But I know what's in your heart." He continued glowering at the man until he turned to another cowering villager—a ruddy woman I knew as one of the village's bakers, a particularly cruel woman when times were tough. "You're all disgusting cretins. You care only for yourselves and sweep those you deem inconvenient under the rug. You're eating yourselves from the inside out."

"H-how dare you..." the baker started, then floundered at the Leshy's glare.

"What about the ground you tread? What about the forest you desecrate?"

The man next to her quickly spoke for her. "We do no such thing." Bratan's eyes narrowed on the man.

"You came into my forest without permission and defiled my land. You take from my trees, and you throw your broken bottles on my soil. You harm my animals and your own people, and you pollute my streams. And you sacrificed someone you saw weaker than yourself to come to me—a beast, as you all seem to think." He scanned the crowd once more. "But I can see that you people are far more deadly and careless. Selfish and disgusting. To let your people suffer and ruin my home. To torment my precious wife."

His muscles relaxed as he approached me, gently touching my face. "You don't deserve this, my love. You never deserved this." His voice was silk. He cradled my face in his hands before pressing a kiss to my lips. Then his face fell, and he looked back at the crowd. "Do you truly believe my goal had been to kill you? If that was my intent, I'd have done it long ago and through a means far worse than starvation. And as I've done already, I'd save the children and other innocents."

"You'd do no such thing!" someone snapped. "You've kid-napped our children!"

"I've protected the children who you so viciously mistreated! I saved and fed them and brought them to freedom. And I took the wheels off carts to avoid further trespassing through my woods and toward my realm and hid bows to protect my creatures. But I never harmed any children, and though I didn't allow crops to grow, I didn't steal the food you already possessed or received through other means."

No one dared challenge him.

He continued, "I can only assume that the most well-fed and finely dressed in this village was behind much of your famine."

Stillness rolled through the village, and then slowly, the crowd parted to reveal Ms. Tomlin. "Some evil creatures take advantage of chaos when things go awry," Bratan continued, "and they can get away with it if they have someone to blame." His eyes sharpened on the matriarch. "You remind me of a certain devil I know. A woman whom you undoubtedly worked with to bring my precious Leena here." He jumped off the platform and approached the old woman, whose head was held high, especially as her neck nearly snapped from looking up at him. "What did Melora give you?"

The woman's chin stayed propped in the air. "She gave us the information we sought and what we needed. She explained your devious ploys and even what you planned to do with your so-called wife." Her eyes shifted to me. "Believe me, dear, the fate awaiting you now is far more merciful than the one he had in store for you. Everyone here knows what he's capable of. We bore witness to what he did to Boris's only son."

My blood turned cold. "What?" Cotton filled my ears, and it pained me to look at the man standing before the town matriarch.

The moment I caught his expression, I knew nothing was simple anymore. And the resolve that had kept me calm quickly cracked apart.

# CHAPTER THIRTY-FIVE

LEENA

"WHAT IS SHE TALKING about?" I asked. The longer he took to answer, the more my stomach twisted.

"Leena, I'm so sorry, but I had to do it. He tried to rape you—he could have left you for dead, and I'm sure he wouldn't have stopped that night. There was a determination in his psychotic face. His soul wasn't there, and when he fled, I could sense a vengeance that couldn't be ignored."

I shook my head over and over. This wasn't happening. He hadn't lied to me. This couldn't be real. He pointed at his chest and stared straight into me. "It's my job to protect my people—you above everyone. I was doing what I was supposed to do."

"You did what you wanted," I said between clenched teeth.

"Yes! I did! Why does that upset you? He was a waste of flesh and air—he wanted to rape you, Leena! He was worse than the hounds that escaped with Melora from hell! They have more humanity than that bastard did!"

"It *upsets* me because you lied and went behind my back! I understand that we're supposed to protect our people, and my perspective has changed since I first begged you to spare him. But you'd promised me that you'd respect my request, and not only did you go behind my back, but you lied to me and never came clean." He started saying something, but I cut him off. "You had every chance to tell me what you did! We've fallen in love. You could have talked to me." My voice broke. "Why didn't you?"

He went still, and that weight in the pit of my stomach felt like a bag of rocks. "I'd have forgiven you in a heartbeat," I whispered. "I understand our roles and what kind of monster he was—what kind of threat he was. But how can I trust you when you hid something so monumental from me? When you went behind my back?"

"I've changed too, Leena. It's not as clear-cut as you're making it out to be." His voice wobbled as his dampening eyes matched mine.

"It is! You just had to talk to me."

"Leena." He moved in a flash to cradle my face, but I backed away. "Leena, I—" A crack of thunder eclipsed his voice. It was too loud to be from the clouds; I'd never heard something like it.

Without missing a beat, Bratan transformed, and almost simultaneously, a mass of crows flocked to him, seeking refuge on his branch-like arms. My brows furrowed as I watched the human-like expression in the crows' eyes and how they knew the Leshy would protect them.

*What would make them act like that?* The answer was soon behind my fleeting thought as a ripple of black smoke left a thick film over the town.

Fear was an emotion far behind me now. I had no idea what to expect, but I'd come to terms with the reality that I would die today. Instead of cowering, I stood numb, watching the old woman I could only assume was Melora approach Bratan. The sinister woman leapt forward and sunk something into his leg. The unexpected attack tore a gasp from my throat. Bratan let out a fractured wail, bending back and staggering until the odd, sizzling object was removed from his thick skin. Black blood slithered down the strange blade, oozing with green fumes. Something pulled me toward it, not physically, but something inside. Like it was calling to me—to the subtle power simmering in my veins.

Bratan almost tripped over his own form, but he quickly recovered, lifted one hand, and blasted Melora across the square. She skated to the edge of the village but not before sinking another attack into his thick hand. It happened in half a second before the devil flew into the forest without a sound.

The Leshy shrunk back to his usual size, clutching his hand and examining it as he steadied himself on one leg. I rushed to him, carefully grabbing hold of his hand.

"Are you all right?" When our eyes met, my chest squeezed. That inexplicably strong connection we shared pumped through my blood. I truly loved him, but I was so upset. He may have done the right thing in killing Casimir, but he'd lied to me. He'd betrayed my trust.

"I'll be fine." He studied his bleeding hand, his face twisted in pain. "But if she gets me with that blade a few more times, the poison she's embedded into it might kill me."

"What's in it that could be so powerful?"

"An ancient magic that only exists in her world below. She's from a cursed realm filled with darkness, corruption, and chaos—and only those things. Even she can't be happy there. It's why she wants a place in this world so badly." He winced as something dark slithered through his veins, and the color beneath his skin turned black. He hovered his other hand over it in an attempt to heal it, but it only made him grunt in pain and did nothing to remedy the wound.

"Bratan, I..." He might die here today—we both might. Things couldn't end like this. "We need to be a team. We need to fight together. But to do that, I need to be able to trust you." I couldn't look at him. I didn't know how I should feel or think, especially since the rules of the mortal realm didn't apply to us in the same way. Humans shouldn't take each other's lives so easily, but we were deities in this forest, sentenced to protect these woods and the creatures within it.

"You may have been right in killing him, but you should've told me."

"I know," he whispered, "and I am so deeply sorry for that." Our eyes remained locked until he bent down to kiss me, and amid chaos and the unknown, I let his lips welcome mine. He held me tight, desperately clinging to me and burying himself in our kiss. He pressed his hand hard against the small of my back as if I might slide from his grip and die this very instant. He was desperate to keep me—to hold me—even though I knew the pain of his hand must have stung something fierce.

"You don't have to hold me," I said between kisses.

"Yes, I do." He took my face with the tips of his fingers, kissing me once, twice, three more times before a voice crackled through the space around us, forcing us to part.

"What a touching display," Melora croaked. The villagers hadn't moved, still as statues and either standing or crouched in their various hiding places. Some were standing near the middle of town, likely too frightened to move, or maybe they knew hiding would be pointless. If either of these powerful beings decided to decimate the entire village, they could do so without breaking a sweat. I knew Bratan wouldn't do anything to innocents, but they didn't believe that. And Melora was as unpredictable to them as she was to me.

I found myself frozen as Melora approached us, a growing scar spread across her face like a porcelain doll slowly cracking apart. Her clothes matched Bratan's usual attire with black leathers and a collar that covered her throat, but she wore no cape. Her silver hair was held tight behind her in a low braid. The old demon looked me up and down. She spoke directly to Bratan. "It didn't take long for your whore to forgive you."

He grabbed Melora by the throat, his hand snapping, fingers growing into roots as they curled around her neck. The woman didn't writhe, but she visibly struggled. Something like dust crumbled down the side of her neck as she looked at me. "You only know a small portion of it." Her voice was hoarse as it fought to reach me. "He was planning to kill you. He only needed to wed you to keep the forest alive and to ensure his bloodline stays in power long after he's inevitably destroyed. He never loved you. He felt great lust for you and satiated those desires as long as he could, but that's all. Once you produced an heir, he was going to toss you aside. And if you both survive today, that's exactly what he'll do."

"You're wrong." I was surprised at my own voice; it was braver than the rest of me. "Every word you speak is deception."

"How could you be so stupid?" Melora managed to bark out a laugh. "You just found out that Bratan killed someone he'd promised you he wouldn't touch, and you saw him kill more men before your eyes moments before. And you still deem him good?"

"He must protect us! To protect—"

"Who? *You?* You really are naïve."

"She's lying, Leena! Don't listen to her. She's trying to turn us against each other." Bratan's grasp tightened, but still, the woman spoke.

"You didn't even notice I was there all along." The moment my brows furrowed, Melora's appearance melted, and she slipped from Bratan's grasp, simmering in a puddle before rising to form the image of my junior maid. Though her neck was purple and still sported the grooves Bratan had split into it, there was no denying that what Melora claimed, at least about herself, was true. She was Ani.

"He didn't tell you anything about me, did he?" Her voice was young, her form small. She condescendingly skipped to me, her hands clasped behind her back. "If he'd told you more—if he'd valued you more—you might have recognized who I was instead of letting me fool you so effortlessly day after day. You wouldn't be here now. You—" Bratan grabbed the demon by the braid, whipping her back. She let out a wail of pain; He held her arms so tightly behind her back that they looked like they'd snap off with one more effortless pull.

"One more lie, and you'll be torn apart," he hissed, but Melora's expression didn't change.

"See? He won't even kill me. He needs me. He has the power to kill me but chooses not to. He needs me to help him—to show him how to rule once he gives you his seed and kills you without mercy."

"ENOUGH!" Bratan tugged on her arm, half-tearing it from the socket; she shrieked as he threw her aside, casting her back into the forest. "Leena," he lightly grabbed me by the arms. "Leena, she's lying. You know I'd never kill you. I love you. You know I love you."

If I'd doubted before, I'd have known the truth now. Everything Melora said was a lie; I felt it.

Bratan tried to hurt Melora just now. I saw him try to rip the devil's arm from her socket, but he couldn't. He only managed to partially remove it. I didn't doubt Bratan wanted the woman dead. He just wasn't strong enough, nor was she to kill him. If he didn't have claim to this land, I wondered if she would have usurped it long ago.

"It's all so much," I said.

"I know, little dove, but I'll protect you, and if it makes you feel more at ease, I'll make sure a contraceptive tonic is given to both of us each day. We can take it together. But please know you're everything to me."

"I know," I whispered. He let out a relieved sound like a half-sob and let his forehead rest on mine. "I love you. Nothing will change that."

"I love you, too. More than anything. I worship you, Leena." He tilted up my chin. "I'll worship you forever, little dove. From now until our corpses feed the earth."

Heat bubbled in my veins at the declaration, but I was soon cooled by the cruel reality we faced. "That day might be today," I said.

"It won't be. I won't let it. I promise you that, and I will never break any promise to you again. I never want to hurt you. You deserve so much better than that. Truly, I don't deserve you, but I'll strive to be every day."

Tears fell from my eyes, and I reached up to grab him, wrapping my arms around his neck and kissing him with every tender hope and feeling I possessed. He eagerly accepted it with a furious passion, holding me like everything was on the line—like we could breathe our last breath at any moment. Because we very well could. Wild flames sparked between us, a passion that pulsed between our bodies and souls. It rushed through me with an intensity beyond understanding. And awakened the power I'd been pushing aside.

A scream rattled from my throat—an unearthly one that ripped my voice in two. My back arched in pain as the surging power consumed me, and something rippled beneath the surface of my flesh. I heard Bratan call my name before my body snapped, pain throbbing in my joints as my form stretched and shifted. Bones cracked, pulling apart, growing, and reconnecting as the wind stung altering wounds. The calls of the crows were close, and the light from the moon kissed my eyelids just before they opened. I looked around frantically, trying to make sense of what was going on. The pain was severe, but it lessened enough that I could focus. And what I saw was incomprehensible.

My hands were slender roots, more feminine than my husband's when he was in his monstrous form, but just as long and terrifying. My skin was thick boards of bark, and I could only imagine what I must look like to the horrified villagers fleeing with screams into the thickness of the woods.

Fear stoked in me like wild flames, but Bratan grew too, his eyes planted firmly on mine until he was fully in his corresponding form. Even as I was, he still towered over me, but together, we were above the treetops. Covered in crows and shadowing the world beneath.

He lifted his branch-like fingers to my rough, newly transformed face. "My love." His body creaked as he let his hand fall, and despite his otherworldly voice, the words came out tender. "Let's go protect our home."

# CHAPTER THIRTY-SIX

LEENA

I T WAS HARDER TO walk than I would have thought, but Bratan helped me whenever I lost my balance and almost fell. At this height, falling would be tragic for the forest and anything within its reach. Bratan said it would be better to look for Melora at human height, but I had no idea how to change back. He said it would come with time, but he'd been born in this form. A part of me was afraid I'd never be able to turn back, or at least not be able to control when I did.

Bratan's grip tightened, and in my mind, I heard the words he didn't speak.

*Something's coming.*

A great gust of wind nearly knocked me over, and my husband's grip tightened even more. I had a new appreciation for his control in this form. I blinked, steadying my awkward new way of sight; I didn't see colors in the same way I had. Things were a little off—the trees and sky were various shades of gray and black, and the warm-blooded animals in my field of vision below were little drops of red and orange scurrying beneath shades of muted leaves. It was so starkly contrasted; it would surely make my job of protecting things easier in time. I could spot the forest's creatures from miles away.

"Do you see that?" Bratan's voice was both a grumble and a cry. I looked up, finding a sheet of white tumbling over the tops of distant trees. A humming accompanied the approaching mass. It looked like a field of snow drifting closer, but when it was near enough for my vision to properly focus on the individual forms clustered together, horror replaced curiosity.

The clacking of spindly legs with bony, unnatural feet joined the appearance of the creatures that were barreling toward us. It was an army of the same creatures that appeared the day I almost died.

"What—" I let go of Bratan's hand, trying my best to remember any sort of defense tactic he'd taught me, but maneuvering in this form was completely different than moving as my human-like self.

The creatures approached, snapping with those seeping rows of teeth and clattering limbs. At least five of them pounced on my legs. I lifted an arm to swat them, but that moment was when my magic faltered, changing me back to my usual self.

"No, no...no no no no!" Shrinking, I stared at my hands. I felt the demons getting knocked off my minimizing body and heard them being torn apart at my side. I landed on the ground flat on my back, the clattering demons bounding toward me at unnatural speed. I forced my eyes to stay on them as I got up and practiced a defense spell Bratan had taught me while I was still healing. It was a simple spell—one anyone whose life was not human could perform.

As a wall of skeletal arms approached, a surge of power gathered from my feet and shot into my hands. Strange words filled my mind. When I uttered them, a great burst of light ignited from my palms, obliterating each monster and turning them into piles of ash. I gaped at the settling dust, turning to Bratan with a shocked, triumphant smile. He transformed back into his human form, returning my smile, impressed.

"You're amazing," he said. The words were slow and deliberate, and the way he looked at me sent my cheeks blazing. He was so busy looking at me that he didn't see the creature's claws reaching out behind him.

"Look out!" I cried. He dove to the ground and lifted a hand to the beings, but before he could attack, I did, and it was even more successful than the last. Maybe it was the fear of losing him, but my powers shot out in every direction, save for where he lay, destroying every enemy in sight.

There were still more approaching—beasts of various demonic forms taken from nightmares, but I'd taken out at least two hundred, buying us time. Bratan got to his feet, dirt caked on his face, mud running down his neck.

"Remind me to properly thank you for that later." He looked around, and when he found that no more creatures were in sight, he stalked to me. "Actually..." He grabbed my face and kissed me deeply.

"I didn't even know they were there at first," I laughed.

"I won't tell if you don't." He kissed me deeper, sliding his tongue into my mouth and sucking on my lower lip before leaning back and sending one of the outrageously large hellhounds bounding toward us flying away with a morphing arm.

"You're so sexy." I leapt on him, sinking my fingers into his back as he grabbed hold of my thighs. Our flurried kisses were stoked with a heated passion that had been pent up for days. He pulled me up until my legs were high around his waist. We kissed passionately. Feverishly. He pushed me into the dirt, my body bare from transforming. He'd always made clothes appear when he transformed, but I suppose that came with time. He quickly helped me tear his off as we kissed and moved and moaned.

Mud caked my body; it was cool on my back as Bratan's warm body pressed hard on mine. We tasted each other more fully than ever before, senses heightened, power throbbing, only stopping every couple minutes when we sensed a threat, and one of us either swiped it away or turned it into nothing but dust in the wind.

He bit my chin and licked down my throat to my breasts. I sucked in a breath as his tongue trailed over them, and I pulled him closer, begging for him with my body.

"We have one more thing to take care of, little dove, and then I'm all yours."

I grumbled, grumpily relenting and letting him sweep me into his arms.

"Melora can't be too far from here," he said, placing me back on my feet. "Once she's gone, we won't have to worry about her nasty demons haunting your nightmares or tormenting us ever again. She won't have any strings to pull." He bit his lip as he drank in my body. "Would you like clothes while we fight?"

"That would be nice," I said with a laugh, and he swept a quick wave over my body until a dress identical to the one I'd been wearing appeared over my muddied skin. Strings cinched my waist, and the skirts fluttered to my ankles. It was a strange feeling, but I had no time to comment on it. A loud, maniacal scream pierced the air like that disconcerting crack of thunder.

Bratan recognized Melora's war cry before I knew what to think of the sound. "We need to kill the puppet master before she kills us," he said, and grabbing my hand, he rushed us to the village.

As soon as we returned to the village, we saw what she'd done. The humans were tied up in the center of the village, and at least fifteen of Melora's arachnid demons and hounds circled them. Ms. Tomlin was screaming something at the demonic woman, but I couldn't make it out through the villagers' cries and the monsters' noises scraping at my eardrums. Melora didn't pay any mind to the matriarch; her fuming expression and darkening eyes were focused solely on us as we met her.

"You're more than a nuisance now, Bratan," she cawed. Her voice was near-gone and her eyes were black, her skin peeling.

"What's happening to her?" I asked. The woman limped forward, reeking of putrid flesh and burnt hair.

"When we kill her creatures, it kills a part of her."

"And you!" she growled in my direction. "You were fun to toy with at first, but it's time for this to end!" She commanded something to her demons in a language I didn't understand. In unison, the hounds howled, and the arachnid creatures rushed in our direction.

"I won't let you ruin everything I've worked toward for centuries!" Melora's voice was melting, warping like she was falling underwater.

"What are you talking about?" Bratan dodged a demon and tore another in half. The fear grew in Melora's eyes. But still, she grinned, and the unsettling chill of it froze me in place. I couldn't look away. "Speak, Melora!" When she still didn't answer, he took her by the weak shoulders, shaking her until she answered.

"Your mother was a good friend of mine, but she didn't have what it took."

Bratan effortlessly demolished another handful of demons and hellhounds, but his passion behind it faltered. When her fractured grin widened, I saw the horror on his face. He closed in and grabbed her by the torn collar.

"What are you saying?" The words oozed poison behind clenched teeth. "What did you do?"

A chuckle rumbled from her chest and then burst into raucous laughter. "I can't believe, after all these centuries, you still think the humans managed to destroy the forest and your mother by themselves." Bratan's fingers trembled, loosening just enough for Melora to slip away. Horror stretched across his face. "She never had what it took to rule this place, and neither do you. All you do is protect and keep humans away like a servant. True greatness comes from wielding your power and influence beyond the woods—to let the humans know who to be afraid of so they never come into the woods in the first place. You've been too soft."

"You killed my mother." The words were quiet, but then he repeated them in a roar that rattled to the sky. "You killed my mother!" He grabbed her with both hands, his grip so tight his knuckles were white. "She was your friend!"

"She was weak!" she hissed. Bratan's eyes went black. He looked like he was going to kill her, and I waited, watching him, still frozen, expecting him to do it. But his rigid shoulders dropped.

"What did you set in place?" he growled through his teeth and shoved her to the ground.

She didn't answer at first, but then an impish eagerness flashed in her eyes, tugging her mouth into a crooked smile. "I suppose I might as well tell you," she croaked, getting to her feet and dusting off her demolished leathers. "It would be nice to get credit where credit is due." She bounced on her heels in excitement and then leaned in like she was telling him a secret.

"I took her out, instilled fear in the humans, and ensured no maiden came to you." Horror struck Bratan as he staggered back.

Melora's face dropped. Suddenly, she was seething. "An heir was the last thing I needed to deal with. When I knew it was inevitable that you'd one day meet your mate, or at least someone who caught your fancy, I decided to take matters into my own hands."

She rolled her shoulders back and scanned the captives, including the fuming matriarch. "When you came to me enraged about the humans in your forest, I met with this town's leader and asked for a sacrifice. I didn't think you'd actually fall for the girl, though, and by the time I learned she was your mate, it was too late to turn back." She cocked her head. "I haven't seen you care for something since your mother died. I was surprised, to say the least. You fell very hard very quickly. You must have been desperate for love."

Bratan was vibrating, furious, but I could tell he was keeping his head long enough to hear more. "If you kept maidens from me for centuries, why would you decide to let her in now?"

"She needed the control," I muttered. "She wanted to be the one pulling the strings."

"My soul may die today," Melora said, "but I won't let yours live on either." The flesh fell from her bones, and her body grew as it pounced. I gasped as a bony claw seeping with green liquid grabbed hold of me. Bratan pushed Melora out of the way, causing her to fall back in a crooked heap.

"I have an idea," he said under his breath. Taking my hand, he curled me into him. My body pressed against his so quickly, and with such force, I got momentary whiplash.

"What are you doing—" He grabbed my face and kissed me with soldering heat. Confusion melted into desire. My heart hammered in my ears as his hand moved down my spine; it was hot on my lower back. He crushed me against him, and suddenly, a surge of power ignited, flooding me and careening through my blood. Together, we transformed.

Above the town, we faced Melora in a haunting display of chaos. The devil leapt at us with a chaotic fury that grew clumsier by the second. She was getting weaker, but I knew it wouldn't end easily.

Melora raised her voice to the sky, howling until it was a screech that split into many, and a flurry of bat-like creatures as large as men ricocheted through the air. Hounds gnawed at our rough ankles, and other creatures of various forms attacked, too, but it was too dark and frenzied for me to see what they were.

Bratan's arm swung back, and despite its slow wind-up, it launched forward like a slingshot, his long fingers grabbing Melora by the bony neck. His other hand grabbed hold of her arm and successfully ripped it from its socket. She wailed, causing a violent quaking that almost sent me falling on the forest floor. Her bats stormed Bratan, clawing at his face and making him lose his grip on Melora. He staggered back. The world beneath us shook as he lost his footing, and I watched in horror as he fell onto a wide mass of trees. Branches and creatures below—some Melora's, some our own—snapped and cried at his fall.

A painful ache formed in my chest. I felt each and every animal and plant die. Every budding leaf and trotting doe.

Melora only had to dodge us long enough to get us to harm the forest like this. She could win; she had an army. We only had each other, which included me and my lack of coordination in this new state.

Bratan got to his feet, reaching out as another swarm of bats attacked. I was too distracted watching him that I didn't notice Melora move behind me until she took hold of me. I cried out that split scream as the skeletal creature of a woman threw me to the ground. Once again, I felt every living thing die beneath me as I crashed and skidded through the forest on my side.

Despair settled thick in my chest. Melora was unleashed and fully chaotic with an army of wild beasts from hell. We had each other, and that needed to be enough.

Melora's back was turned when I rose into a crouch. I thought of what Bratan had said to me before—how we couldn't surprise Melora in these hulking forms. So I closed my eyes and calmed myself, focusing until I felt my body shrink. It took longer than I would have liked to get there, especially since my excitement and anxiety throughout the process made me grow slightly every few seconds, but I finally managed to get to, and remain in, my human-like form. As soon as I knew I wouldn't shift back, I ran through the trees, knowing exactly where to find my husband.

I must have had added strength and agility through my awakened powers because it didn't take long to find them. And I couldn't believe the sight when I did.

Melora tightened her fatal grip on Bratan, who was also in his human form again. The demonic woman was still in her enormous skeletal shape as she squeezed his neck. He mouthed a silent cry just before a loud snap splintered through the air. I gasped, my heart nearly stopping, but he was still breathing, still writhing in the air. I had to do something. Anything.

My eyes burned, my body a blade of fire, and in one quick movement, I grew twice the size of Melora, grabbed her by the throat, and snapped her head clean off her bony neck. The attack had happened too suddenly for her to react before it was over. She let out one quick, piercing cry before her body collapsed, her bones breaking and turning to powder as they fell to the earth. The sound was like a city crumbling and lasted long enough to warrant the fear of it never stopping. Panic was a thorn in my chest as I reached for Bratan. He'd started to fall as soon as her body fell apart, but just before he landed in the pile of what was left of her, I caught him.

Relief hit me like a wave; I let out a breath so heavy that it blew the massive wall of dust rising from Melora's dismembered heap into the sky. Slowly, the air stilled, and the movement below us ceased, and the world was once again quiet. My body wasn't strong enough to do anything but lie down, so as safely as I could, I did. My arm rolled out to the side, and Bratan trundled out of my tree-like hand. All I could focus on was breathing as I returned to my human-like state once again.

My husband crawled to me, instantly gathering me in his arms despite his own labored breaths. My body throbbed, and I could barely lift my head to look at him, but I was so relieved to be in his arms that I didn't care. I curled myself in his lap and let out a relieved sob at the rise and fall of his chest and the stroke of his hand as it fell down my hair.

"You really are something," he said. I couldn't help but laugh, and in our state of sudden triumph and near death, it was infectious. Bratan's laugh burst through the trees, probably reaching our realm as I nestled against his chest. My stomach cramped as I giggled harder.

Today was the first real day our lives would begin, and it happened mere minutes after I thought our souls would fade into whatever awaited the death of deities. No other form of happiness could touch this moment. Right now, anything was possible. Everything was right.

The moon was falling from the sky, dipping beneath the trees and making way for the rising sun. The breeze was a welcome coolness against our scraped skin, which only added to the joy bundled between us. Everything was settling into place for the first time in centuries. And as Melora's demons either fled this world or died from their wounds, Bratan and I laughed, completely insane with relief and ready to go home.

# EPILOGUE

LEENA

B RATAN HELD ME AS the steam rose around us. His fingers slid down my bare, misty back, our bodies entangled beneath the warm water of the spring. My arms were permanently hooked around him as we kissed. We'd spent the last three nights here, celebrating the fresh start we finally had now that Melora was gone, and my former people enthusiastically decided to find a new place to settle far from our forest. There were still things to do, such as convince my grandmother that life here would be far better than she could imagine. But for now, I at least knew she was safe and that things would be okay. While my grandmother pondered my offer, she was in a cottage just outside our realm, with Theodora keeping her company and helping her with anything she may need.

"I'll never get tired of tasting you." Bratan's voice was low and masculine as he spoke against my lips. It had been too long since we'd been intimate together, but it was almost incomprehensible that we were now safe and that there were no more threats lurking around the corner. We made love as soon as we physically could the night after everything happened, and now, as he lifted me out of the water and sprawled me onto the slick stones beside the hot pool, I knew he would take me again. Each time was better than the last. At least some of that had to be from our growing adoration and our inhibitions flying further out the window.

I rolled onto my stomach, letting him kiss up my spine as I relaxed on the warm stones. That didn't last long, though, but I welcomed the change as Bratan flipped me over and crawled over me. His gaze was sultry and primal, riveting me where I lay. He bared his teeth, and my body thrummed with desire. A growl vibrated low in his throat as he slid above me. His hand found the base of my skull, and he tugged on my hair until I arched toward him.

He seized the back of my thigh, gripping hard as he pressed me tight against him. A sound escaped me as his rough hand slid down my leg, grabbing it and throwing it around his waist until my heel rested upon his back. The heat between our bodies beat like a drum. His tongue caressed my neck as the curves of my body molded into his. I moaned as his fingers zig-zagged in frenzied patterns down my body. Then he firmly gripped my neck, and my eyes rolled back. He knew how much I loved this little game we played. He twisted my hair and pulled my head to the side so he could bite near my throat.

It didn't hurt. He was masterful at the art of perfectly fulfilling my desires, being the precise amount of beastly and soft. I loved succumbing to him, and even more than that, I loved that I could trust that when he was savage, I was safe. Everything he did was what I wanted. I was his queen.

His hand slid to my throat, easing softly and lingering there, turning me liquid from the unspoken danger I could just barely taste. His arm flexed, outstretched, as he kissed down my body. His muscles tensed and released with every motion. I felt every flicker. Slowly, his fingers found their destination, and I let out a sound as I breathed his name, my toes curling. The sensation was almost unbearably wonderful. So deeply delicious.

My blood was molten, and somehow, I felt color. Crimson flashed beneath my eyelids, and a flower of gold bloomed in the center. I lifted my hands to his face, my fingers rushing to his scalp and curling into his hair. I could almost taste this dizzying feeling. My nails scraped up his back, our bodies moving like ebbing waves. His mouth caught mine, and I devoured its velvet touch as he claimed me—as we made the most passionate love we ever had. He let out growls, snapping at me as my head fell back. I moaned at the sudden bite he sunk into my wrist and the hot kisses he left all over my skin. He knew exactly how to fulfill my every desire.

Our passion rose, building and reaching for the sky; he leaned back so he could see the pleasure in my eyes, which only increased the intensity of the roaring bloom spiraling inside me once more. He fell on me as everything exploded in heat and light, thunder and stars, and it took us longer than usual to catch our breath.

"I'd have assumed immortals like us could handle such a task without becoming so breathless," I laughed. My arm fell across my forehead, and I couldn't stop smiling. He moved to my side and tucked me against him.

"I don't think any mortal could recreate what we just did." His eyes followed the trail his finger made as it slid down the bridge of my nose.

"That's true." I giggled at the sentiment, then studied the gentleness in his gaze and the unguarded softness of his countenance. "Bratan?"

"Hm?" His green eyes dreamily roamed to mine, then went back to the trail his finger was mapping down my body, from my chin to my throat and below.

"I never want to lose this."

His finger stopped. "Lose what?"

"This passion between us. We'll be together for centuries—hopefully longer. I'm afraid we'll lose it somehow...that you'll get bored of me."

"Leena." He cupped the side of my face. "Do you really see our passion waning? Do you see how much I want you? What I'd do for you? I could never get bored of you. And our souls are mated." He buried his fingers in the thickness of my hair, drawing me closer. "Nothing could make me do anything but love you, and so long as the two of us are living, nothing can tear us apart. Our fate is ours. My fate is you. I belong to you, little dove. I'll never stop loving you, and I'll never stop wanting you." He sealed the promise with a kiss, sweet and undemanding. "You are everything to me."

"I love you, Bratan." I leaned up for another desperate caress. "I'm so happy that you're the one my soul chose at the beginning of everything."

"I love you, too, little dove, and so am I." He smiled quietly against my lips. "From the beginning to the end, and every day in between, I'll always choose you."

# ABOUT THE AUTHOR

Elise Nelson is an author of romance, poetry, and more. She has a Bachelor of Arts degree from Boise State University, where she studied English literature, creative writing, and multimedia storytelling. She is also a therapeutic writing teacher and a passionate mental health advocate. When she isn't busy writing, she loves reading, laughing, and watching Korean dramas with her husband.

You can visit her website at www.elisenelsonauthor.com

Printed in Great Britain
by Amazon

60292639R00221